THE PASSION ARTIST

T0166613

OTHER WORKS BY JOHN HAWKES

NOVELS
The Cannibal
The Beetle Leg
The Owl
The Lime Twig
Second Skin
The Blood Oranges
Death, Sleep & the Traveler
Travesty
Virginie: Her Two Lives
Adventures in the Alaskan Skin Trade
Innocence in Extremis
Whistlejacket
Sweet William
The Frog
An Irish Eye

PLAYS
The Innocent Party: Four Short Plays

COLLECTIONS
Humors of Blood & Skin: A John Hawkes Reader
Lunar Landscapes: Stories and Short Novels

THE PASSION ARTIST
JOHN HAWKES

Dalkey Archive Press
Champaign and London

Library of Congress Cataloging-in-Publication Data

Hawkes, John, 1925-1998.
The passion artist / John Hawkes. -- 1st Dalkey Archive ed.
    p. cm.
ISBN 978-1-56478-560-2 (pbk. : alk. paper)
  1. Widowers--Fiction. 2. Man-woman relationships--Fiction. 3. Sex--Fiction. 4.
Europe--Fiction. 5. Psychological fiction. I. Title.
PS3558.A82P37 2010
813'.54--dc22
                        2009051282

Partially funded by the University of Illinois at Urbana-Champaign and by a grant from
the Illinois Arts Council, a state agency

www.dalkeyarchive.com

Cover: design and composition by Danielle Dutton, illustration by Nicholas Motte
Printed on permanent/durable acid-free paper and bound in the United States of America

INTRODUCTION

When John Hawkes began *The Passion Artist,* he was fresh from some of the unalloyed successes of the middle period of his oeuvre, including *The Blood Oranges* and *Travesty.* In retrospect, this period consists of some of his very finest work, representing a significant movement in the direction of narrative and storytelling, though without sacrificing the dense web of psychic entanglement that is a feature of his fine early efforts. You'd think, having just written the dark and monumental *Travesty,* that Hawkes would be operating with great confidence as he embarked on his newest composition. And yet, as the author reported himself, in the autobiographical note on *The Passion Artist* included in *Humors of Blood and Skin,* the imagining of *The Passion Artist* was anything but easy:

> Whenever I entered our house I thought that I saw my father's coffin propped in front of the cold hearth on one of those sinister contraptions that are usually found standing incongruously upright in the dark corners of small churches everywhere in Europe. I had this vision even though both my parents had died by then and were buried in a lovely little town in Maine. Each morning I sat benumbed and mindless at a small table of polished cherry wood. Each morning Sophie[1] left a fresh rose on my table, but even those talismans of love and encouragement did no good. All was hopeless, writing was out of the question.[2]

---

1 Mrs. Hawkes.
2 *Humors of Blood and Skin: A John Hawkes Reader.* New York: New Directions, 1984, p. 233.

What caused this violent episode of depression,[3] you might ask? And how was it resolved in the composition and vision of the book? To answer these questions, I suppose I first have no choice but to admit that I began studying with John Hawkes in 1981, not long after he had published *The Passion Artist*. In fact, when I went to see him about enrolling in his writing class, I had just plunged into this malevolent and darkly ironic novel, and had found it more than a little terrifying. Upon meeting him, I undertook that most painful of self-examinations, in which I attempted to describe for the writer himself the dynamic experience of reading his work. Always a bad idea. I remember, before running aground entirely, asking Hawkes how *The Passion Artist* could have such modern things in it as *automobiles and trains*. Hawkes, very patiently, said: "Well, they are very *distressed* automobiles." I'm sure that he meant that the automobiles (what few there are within these pages) were completely repurposed by the author, not imported from the dealership. But what he further meant, I'd argue, was that *The Passion Artist* is nothing if not a work of the liberated imagination. And yet there *are* a few literary historical glosses that might help the reader find his or her way in.

In this regard, Hawkes's note about *The Passion Artist* is so illuminating that it would be a shame not to quote from it a little more, for example the passage in which the author speaks to the origins of his paradoxically loathsome and sympathetic protagonist Konrad Vost:

> I recalled a Marxist critic whom I had encountered at a conference on the novel at a small college in the Middle West. When this critic scorned works of the imagination as degenerate, I commented that he really belonged at some other conference, perhaps one on problems in social science. Thereupon an irate

---

3   Hawkes's own word.

and self-righteous young faculty member leapt to his feet from the audience and demanded that I apologize to the Marxist critic. I, who could not bear rejection of any kind and had for a lifetime depended on approval bestowed on me by Sophie and two or three close friends, was forced to apologize there and then in a packed auditorium to a white-faced devil who hated fiction.[4]

Nearly forty years have elapsed since the conference in question, and Hawkes, alas, is no longer living, so I imagine it is fair to name the critic he alludes to, as Hawkes did when he once told me this story. I name the name because it self-evidently bears on the protagonist of *The Passion Artist*. The critic's name was Jost Herman, and he was a German theorist of some reputation. With his name in mind, however, "Konrad Vost" appears in all its blunt simplicity to be a barely concealed reversal of "Jost Herman," and in this ruse we begin to see Vost as, yes, an unhappy socialist realist. Which is to say that Central and Eastern Europe, the laboratories of socialist realism, are the real-world analogues for the cityscape of *The Passion Artist*. The miserable Jost Herman, in Hawkes's idea of him, the anti-fiction Herman, was shilling for the ideological system that gave us those unlucky and deprived Central and Eastern European cities, Gdansk, Petrograd, Tirana, Bratislava, et al., in which cement housing complexes vied with the crumbling remnants of the medieval. Hawkes was attempting to exorcise the "devil" of Herman by imagining Vost, and he was attempting it in the way in which he was best equipped, by reimagining the cities behind the Iron Curtain, in order to accord them the kinds of rich, complex consciousness that he believed they in fact possessed (that they also possessed, moreover, in Kafka's "Hunger Artist," an obvious antecedent of this text), despite the

---

4   *Humors of Blood and Skin*, p. 234.

nonsense of Soviet social realism. The incident with Herman stuck in Hawkes's craw, but he attempted to resolve it by finding a paradoxical richness in the beleaguered cities in which he set his story.

Another issue with which the author was wrestling, it seems to me, was feminism. In 1985, I interviewed Hawkes myself, and at that point he offered, unbidden, some ideas on this subject and its relationship to the erotic. In particular, he was preoccupied with the case of Monique Wittig, the French critic. This preoccupation seems to me more than germane to the thematic construction of *The Passion Artist*:

> There are feminists who insist that a woman writer is unlike a male writer, that a woman writer speaks to other women as no male writer could, and that it is important that we have women writers to speak to women. I heard Monique Wittig at a conference in New York. And a Columbia professor made precisely the mistake that I would have made at this conference. He started to talk about what was new with younger writers in France. He pointed out that most of the really important new works written these days by younger writers of significance are by women. And he was pleased to say that. Monique Wittig got up out of the audience of maybe eight hundred, and she was dressed in black motorcycle clothes, with zippers everywhere, and what she said, in the most remarkable and gentle way, was that a writer who is a woman, a writer who is a feminist, a writer who is a lesbian, thinks of herself only as a writer, never ever as a woman writer. And she was so gentle, so remarkably kind, when she could have been lacerating instead.[5]

5   Moody, Rick and Melora Wolff. "An Interview with John Hawkes." *Columbia: A Magazine of Poetry and Prose* 10, p. 31.

Femininity as a dominating force, the woman who has nothing but erotic hatred for the masculine, these are recurrent motifs in Hawkes, beginning with "The Universal Fears," an early story about a schoolteacher who is beset by his feminine charges. In *The Passion Artist*, the erotic qualities of this violent enmity are inflated further—into a prison uprising of the feminine. Why this historical moment? In the middle and late seventies? Because, as the preoccupation with Wittig seems to indicate, a certain kind of masculine literary permissiveness about sexuality, something we associate with the loosening of the definition of obscenity in the publishing world of the early sixties, was in the process of being eroded or reconfigured by literary writing composed by women, for whom being cast as the playthings of masculinity—that frequent trope of the literary fiction of the period—did not show up as an aspiration. Sexual liberation was the motivating theme in *The Blood Oranges*, sexual liberation and sexual decadence. But just a half decade later Hawkes could no longer rely on the topic being as simple or as explicable as all that. The sexuality in *The Passion Artist*, more than in *The Blood Oranges*, is deeply conflicted, tortured even,[6] and where Kafka's story, "The Hunger Artist," is about repenting of physiognomy through elective starvation, Hawkes's novel is about celebrating and expending the life force through the equation of erotic love with contempt and violence. Perhaps a portion of Hawkes's despond, the depression that preceded this marvelous weave of nightmares we have before us, was the depression in which he grew away from a historically outmoded view of the literature of the feminine. The women in La Violaine, in the midst of their riot, do what they do by categorically refusing to

---

6   For example Konrad's completely mercenary coupling with his daughter Mirabelle's friend, in which the girl penetrates Vost, and we get the following: "He gasped in a silent cry of joy and humiliation. How could he have been so ignorant of this experience?" (p. 40)

be women, in the stereotypical sense. They are violent, powerful, and unrepentant. And it's for these reasons that Vost both inflicts his own violence on them, and, in turn, desires them. (After *The Passion Artist,* meanwhile, it's worth mentioning that the author wrote not one but *two* novels in a sequence narrated by women.)

Yet another point Hawkes made about the genesis of *The Passion Artist,* in the years that I knew him, was that he had relied on a single sentence from his first novel, *The Cannibal,* as a leaping-off point. This is a detail he leaves out of his discussion in *Humors of Blood and Skin,* but let's assume it's true. Then *The Passion Artist,* already indebted to Kafka for its title and, in part, for its Eastern European setting, becomes intertextual with regard to the author's own efforts. Is this another way of saying that Hawkes feared he had expended all his material? Or that part of what was collapsing around him, in the seventies, was the idea of a unitary author who was the sole imaginer of an original work? (This notion of the death of the author was certainly popular at Brown, where he taught.) If so, then the result—*The Passion Artist*—is, again, a thrilling riposte. For my part, I wish I could say *which* sentence it was he borrowed from *The Cannibal,*[7] that map of the psychology of postwar Europe drawn by the very young Hawkes almost immediately after he returned from driving an ambulance there. *The Cannibal,* like the author's other early works, is singularly haunted, and yet you can see how that postwar experience and its attendant traumas, which Hawkes recalled again and again in his interviews, also helped create the environment for the very malevolent Europe of *The Passion Artist.*

---

7   Here's an example from the earlier novel, just so the similarities are apparent: "All during the day the villagers had been burning out the pits of excrement, burning the fresh trenches of latrines where wads of wet newspapers were scattered, burning the dark round holes in the back stone huts where moisture traveled upwards and stained the privy seats, where pools of water became foul with waste that was as ugly as the aged squatter." *The Cannibal.* New York: New Directions, 1962, p. 125.

In compiling these pretexts and intertexts, though, I haven't yet told you *exactly* what *The Passion Artist* is about. And in doing so I probably cannot compete with the author's own summary, and so I append it here:

> *The Passion Artist* is set in an imaginary Central European city whose life revolves around its prison for women called La Violaine. The prison lends its name to the café across the street where the relatives of inmates gather to be close to wives, daughters, sweethearts, mothers. One of the frequenters of La Violaine the café is Konrad Vost, who grieves for his dead wife, Claire, and maintains a sterile home for his schoolgirl daughter, Mirabelle. He awaits the release of his aged mother who has been incarcerated in La Violaine the prison since Konrad Vost's childhood, when she murdered his ineffectual father. Konrad Vost learns that Mirabelle is a prostitute, has sex with one of her young friends, then denounces his daughter to the police. When a riot breaks out in La Violaine, he becomes one of the force of volunteer policemen. . . . However, the valiant women drive out the police, take over the prison, and eventually capture Konrad Vost in a swampy marsh beyond the city.[8]

And yet even the writer's own description does little to suggest the propulsion system that truly drives these pages, which is emphatically *not* the story. The above sketches out the whole of the plot without compressing it, which is to say: not much story here. But when I recently reread *The Passion Artist*, what was of interest was not the story but the *language* with which the author details this grim vision of Europe. That is to say that the descriptive writing, and, above all, the figurative writing

---

8   *Humors of Blood and Skin*, p. 234.

here is the envy of anyone who has ever labored at English-language prose: "As for the stunted rainbow canaries, which were farthest from the light-filled space that had been the imperfectly shuttered window only moments before, these lost their feathers immediately and, smoking and roasting, resembled tiny brown glistening and shriveling shoes for the feet of dolls." (p. 111)

I have neglected also to talk about the third-person narration in *The Passion Artist*, but it too is part of the uniqueness of this novel. In Hawkes's writing workshops, he always affected a disdain for an American-style confessional first-person narrator, the first person as we have come to expect from Huck Finn to Holden Caulfield. The problem with the first person for Hawkes was that it amounted to a straitjacket. Within the confines of the first person, it becomes very difficult for a writer to impart much information beyond what is directly perceived by the narrator, unless one is gifted in the way that Nabokov was gifted, in making the limitations of the first person resemble a field of *implications*. Hawkes liked exploiting this difficulty, too, and had done so for four novels in a row, from *Second Skin* to *Travesty*, including such memorable and deranged narrators as Cyril in *The Blood Oranges*. After *The Passion Artist*, Hawkes would revert to the first person again for *Virginie: Her Two Lives* and *Adventures In the Alaskan Skin Trade*. But for this work he strayed back to the third person. And what the third person makes possible is the *density* of a narratorial point of view beyond and outside of a limited single consciousness. When the authorial voice is different from the protagonist's point of view, which is very much the case in *The Passion Artist*, then the author can mine the intricacies that ensue. Hawkes does so by judging the hapless Vost, even as he is sympathetic to him. The narrator in *The Passion Artist*, then, is like the third-person artificer of *The Cannibal* or *The Beetle Leg*, a nearly omniscient and grimly omnipotent authorial voice, connecting this later work with Hawkes's earliest efforts, and creating in the furnace of a third person some of the most ambitious prose in Hawkes's oeuvre.

A singular work, then, a transitional work, a work by a writer with a profound linguistic gift who was unafraid of shocking an audience with the darkness of his vision, who even took a certain delight in his nightmares, a work by a writer afflicted with paradox (and, in the end, if you asked me what depressed the John Hawkes who was trying to write this novel, I would say: *He knew too much about paradox*), a writer who recognized the uses of language in the rite of exorcism, and a writer who used this work to right the ship of his soul, to the best of his ability. For this reader, having read it now several times, in increments of ten years, *The Passion Artist* has only grown in its depth and its resistance to compromise. It's like some variety of poisonous mushroom: phallic, irresistible, deadly. Or maybe it's like a black diamond, used to abrade the skin of a sleeping lover, with intent to inflict harm. *The Passion Artist* is not for the timid, and that's what makes it lasting.

RICK MOODY, 2010

For Mary and Tom Moser

Great birds still hover darkly in the air
and dragons glow and guard with massive care
the wood of wonders and the rocky dale;
and boys grow up, and men prepare
to fight against the nightingale

Rilke, *The Book of Images*

Just try to explain to anyone the art
of fasting! Anyone who has no feeling for it
cannot be made to understand it.

Kafka, *A Hunger Artist*

THE REVOLT

Unlike most people, Konrad Vost had a personality that was clearly defined: above all he was precise in what he did and correct in what he said. But Konrad Vost was only a middle-aged man without distinction or power of any kind, so that to others these two most obtrusive qualities of his personality were all the more odious. And since Vost also possessed self-insight and understanding of the feelings of friends and family, such as they were, he too found odious the main qualities that were himself. But the joy of being always precise and always right was insurmountable, so that he detested himself fiercely yet could hardly change. At times he thought that he was like some military personage striding with feigned complacency down a broad avenue awash with urine.

The circumstances of Konrad Vost were as oddly defined as his personality. He was a man who spent his life among women, or whose every move and thought occurred only in a context of women. Even in this respect, however, Vost was different from others, since two of the three women who in a sense composed the garden in which he was cultivated existed only in the mind of Konrad Vost, while the third was a creature whom he considered still a child. That is, five years after the death of his wife Vost still grieved obsessively for the dead woman and weekly visited her graveside with hat in hand and flowers wrapped in newspaper. Once a week he deposited fresh flowers in the little containers that flanked the small black and white photograph positioned in front of the bleak stone marking the head of the grave. His grief tended to stiffen his posture and to draw down his lips into a sickly leer. The second woman for whom Vost grieved was alive but equally beyond his earthly reach; it was she who constantly reminded him of the maternal love that he, as a child, had never had and who also made him constantly aware of the stigma that illuminated both his correctness and his precision in the most brutally ironic light. This woman, so much more important to him than the other two, was his mother, who even now was an inmate in the prison for women that dominated the city of tin trolley cars and small gray three-wheeled automobiles. Vost was a long-time resident of this place only because of his mother's imprisonment. But there had been no visiting privileges, no letters of poetic gentleness or bitter complaint. Nonetheless Konrad Vost stayed on, remaining faithful to the landscape of his mother's punishment and disappearance. He had married and become a father. The blood on his mother's hands was always fresh in his mind, though he could not have said so. He wanted nothing more than to see this woman, no matter how much he would have dreaded the sight of her. He loved her and yet condemned her as fiercely as the judge who had pronounced her sentence of life imprisonment.

The third and final woman comprising the garden in which Konrad Vost was the only growth was his daughter, she whose maturity he refused to acknowledge and who, in his eyes alone, remained a child. To anyone else, and despite her plainness and the fact of her young age, his daughter's newly acquired adulthood leapt from her every feature like some kind of pathetic but also dangerous light. Another father might have attempted to understand and placate the silent voice of what could not be mistaken for anything but womanly determination and discontent. But here

2

Vost lacked the perceptions of other men: he ignored the obvious metamorphosis and continued inflexibly to demand of himself that totally self-absorbing responsibility the ordinary parent assumes for the activities and well-being of the helpless child. Vost did nothing that was not for her: working behind the counters of the pharmacy where he was clerk, joining the ranks of housewives in the shops of bare concrete, flavoring the small apartment with smells that were both sweet and medicinal. How could he know that in the object of his exacting labors he was in fact deceived, that he tended, not an agreeable and dependent child, but a female genie who had already discovered how to escape at will from her bottle? Occasionally he felt a tremor of estrangement. Every now and then he paused. Yet he persisted in his parental self-confidence until one day he was confronted, quite by accident, with his daughter's appalling womanhood.

Claire the dead wife. Eva the imprisoned mother. Mirabelle the daughter. Surrounded by the music of such names, it was inevitable that Konrad Vost should himself become one of the children menaced by the nightingales.

His small perfectly round gold-rimmed spectacles, his two ill-fitting suits of black serge, his black turtleneck shirts, his pointed shoes that were always worn at the heels and covered with a faint dusting of powdered concrete from the walls of unfinished buildings, his more than normal height, his lantern jaw, the imperious angle at which he raised his chin, the head of excessively trimmed black hair that suggested the hair painted on a manikin, the single steel canine in his mouthful of teeth, the womanly whiteness of the skin that covered the flesh of his deceptively masculine large frame, the nearly hostile tension of the ruthlessly exacting black eyes, the soft white hands bare except for the gold band em-

3

blematic of the formalities of that distant ritual in which he had discovered elation, the cheap steel pen and pencil always clipped into the breast pocket of the sinister black suit coat jacket: in all these details he himself clearly recognized the strange good looks of his youth preserved in the austerity of his middle age, recognized all the hallmarks of the born pedant wedded to those of the petty genius of the police state. Teacher, callow political functionary, why was he professionally neither the one nor the other? Or why not a priest? Sometimes he could not understand how an ordinary line of work and his more than conventional fatherhood could give him all the satisfactions he required. How was it possible for any man to so enjoy dispensing syrups and powders to old women in black shawls? How was it possible for anyone to take so much pleasure in knives, dishes, food, bed linen and the only too effective strips of flypaper he carefully hung in all four remarkably bare rooms of his apartment? How could the hands so suited to gripping the truncheon be comfortably exercised in the preparation of his daughter's meals or making her bed? And yet these reflections amounted to nothing more than an interesting fact: that for Konrad Vost even domesticity was a form of tyranny.

My dearest, Claire used to remark, the seed spit by the child into the street, the metal bottle cap pried off by the indifferent father and sent rolling across the floor, even these, my dearest, are among the true signs of life.

He would stand, thrust back his shoulders, tilt his chin aloft and lean his head slightly to one side, as if his head were invisibly but tightly bridled, and comment on the absolute accuracy of her philosophical remarks. During the last six years of her life she had regularly had naked fleshly relations with a man somewhat older than himself whom she had met in a bakery: that much he had tolerated of Claire's guiltless nature. Her casket, when he first saw it, only hours before its interment in the chalky soil of the walled and desolate cemetery, shocked him by its resemblance to a gigantic ingot of solid lead. At that moment he had been unable to spare himself the morbid thought that this formidable gray object was still warm and too heavy to lift. Then it came to him again how deeply he had loved the single natural syllable of his wife's name, and allowed the sound of it to slip from his lips: Claire, he said thinly. And again: Claire.

Across the street from the official entrance to La Violaine, an entrance consisting of a pair of high narrow rusted gates both barred and grilled, there was a café bearing the same name as the prison: La Violaine. A canvas awning, a few outdoor chairs and tables, the darkness and acidic aroma of the small interior behind the backs of those sitting with crossed knees and facing the street, the sounds of glass and china, the sounds of the small ancient machines producing coffee or alcoholic drinks, the sounds of the proprietor's voice or the sudden comic sounds of the paws of his little dog, the occasional sandwich of bread and cheese on a heavy plate, a song coming from the radio behind the bar, the rancid smell of burning cigarettes, the progress of a blinded fly, the scraping of one of the outdoor chairs: in all this was implicit the boredom and security of time passing as it was expected to pass, indifferently, without meaning, without the threat of impending unwanted change or even disaster. Yet only across the street stood the gates of the prison, bars and iron mesh and weathered sentry box separated from the drab vantage point of the café by nothing more than the traffic of rattling trucks and automobiles and the occasional clumsy motorcycle with its sidecar attached. Among the habitués of the café were always those who, regardless of how accustomed they had become to grieving for the absence of loved ones still alive, frequented the café for the single purpose of being close to the prison and watching for movement in the high awkward gates. For these particular men there was little consolation in the time that was safely passing among the bottles and tables and chairs; they were waiting, so that the sipful of muddied coffee in the mouth or the lengthening of a shadow was not the same for them as for the customers without a personal interest in La Violaine. Sometimes the gates were opened for the admission of a blue van bearing still another woman into the depths of the prison. Sometimes, and more rarely, the gates opened for the emergence of a single woman alone and on foot. But for days, months, the gates remained closed and the archaic wooden shutters remained imperfectly drawn behind the bars of the windows of the mustard-colored buildings visible over the tops of the stone and plaster wall. Each afternoon a waiter in a dirty apron carried a glass of beer across the street, between cars and motorcycles, to the sentry lounging in his box.

There was no mystery in the atmosphere of the café, nothing occult. Yet on those special occasions when across the street a woman was freed, occasions that came perhaps once in every several years but predictably at the hour of noon, there was always a quality that brought to mind a sudden wind in an ancient landscape or the feeling that once must have attended the divine acceptance of even the most modest offering at some archaic shrine. When the woman herself emerged, dressed for traveling and carrying her shabby suitcase in the noontime sun or rain, inevitably, and as if she had been instructed to do so, she crossed through the traffic, entered the café, and again by instinct seated herself with one of those regular habitués whose own life had once been unutterably changed by events long since associated with the prison. This person was never more than a stranger to the freed woman. The freed woman with whom the café customer talked was never the one for whom he waited. But always the unaccompanied woman crossed the street, and by chance or intuition sat with someone also bound to the prison, then arose and made her way alone to the railway station. To the special habitués it had become an aphorism: *La Violaine to La Violaine,* voiced with a smile.

Once, and within the recent past, Konrad Vost had himself been so singled out by a nameless young woman leaving the prison. Even he had found himself listening to the only faintly embittered voice and terrible words as if to the priestess of a little-visited temple of the ancient world. Yet throughout the conversation he had been preoccupied with the woman's hat and the perception that once she had worn a wedding band.

As for the proprietor's dog, it too, like its master or the occasional freed woman, had a predisposition for the café's special habitués. The dog was old, a mixture of two or three small precious breeds, and nearly deformed thanks to the short legs, the docked tail, the disease that was attacking the gray curly hair of its dusty coat. Generally this sheeplike creature would trot from table to table until suddenly it would fall into a kind of staggering as if about to collapse and die. Usually it carried an old spring-operated wooden clothespin sticking at a comic angle from its small toothless mouth. Something had misfired in the docking of the tail, which, curled briefly above the rump, was naked at the tip and revealed there a spot of wet pinkness very like the tiny anus that was always exposed. The customer most preferred by this shocking creature was the meticulous Konrad Vost.

The sound of traffic, the single vine managing to climb one of the rusted gates, the taste of beer, the sudden energetic presence of the little unsavory dog, the woman both known and unknown, in her cheap new clothes. And the passing days, the waiter journeying to the sentry, the customers parading to the urinal, the humming of the slack wires strung inexpertly above the street: *La Violaine to La Violaine,* as he too would say.

7

Oh, him, Claire used to say, referring to some friend or relative, he is so contented with himself that he could live happily in the bottom of the toilet bowl. And he, imagining against his will the water, the porcelain, the knuckle of excrement refusing the agitation of the flushing mechanism, would nonetheless nod and join in her laughter. According to Claire, the boy friend, as she called her lover, was also one of those who could live in the toilet bowl.

He returned immediately to the empty church. Not once did he lose possession of himself, whether standing at the graveside with the boy friend, their arms about each other's shoulders, or shaking hands with the priest, whose large black headgear made him think of superstition and long nights, or nodding when the boy friend offered to take Mirabelle for several hours, or noticing a cat that was playing with an insect behind an old headstone, or feeling a trickle of fresh earth lodging between his shoe and sock, or hearing the small toneless bell that was still tolling for Claire whose casket was in the ground. Throughout all this he was patient, he displayed no emotion, if anything he made it easier for those few faithful people of Claire's entourage to quit the cemetery, as they wished to do, and hence leave him alone. When he saw Mirabelle turning away, her hand in the hand of the weeping boy friend, who kissed him without shame on the cheek, when he shook the priest's hand, when finally he realized that he was perspiring alone beside Claire's unfamiliar grave, knowing even so that it was already a landmark for the course of his days, then he allowed himself to heed the sound of the tolling bell and return to the church.

It was empty, of course, and cool and dark. Once inside, standing just beyond the boundary of the wooden doors, it was then with a tremor that he realized that this squat church, despite its location in a small active city, was like a barn. Its vaulted ceiling was low, the pews suggested rude beams, the floor and columns were of the crudest stone, the light through the several poorly fashioned stained-glass windows might have been shining through curtains of loose hay. Where one might have been justified in expecting a tasteless excess of religious artistry, here was the opposite: a place that had to do not with richness and sentimentality or the decorative style of a childish faith, but had only to do with the brutally silvered fist of death, with finitude, with expiration. Even the wooden crucifix behind the stone altar was so bare, so simple, so roughly expressive of its message that for him it might have been only an enormous clump of garlic affixed by a rusted spike to the thick interior wall of an empty barn. He waited in the shadows of the doorway and faced the wooden replica in the front of the church. Yes, he thought to himself, it has that effect: garlic and superstition. The sign of fear. So our city is really a village, he thought, a poor imitation of the modern world.

The bell in the squat tower above his head was no longer tolling. He was alone, the stones were cold. Chin high, arms at his sides, he was aware of his black suit and the signification of his gold-rimmed spectacles. Slowly he began to walk up the darkened central aisle toward the crucifix hung like a mystical sign inside a fortification. He heard his own footsteps against the stone. His eyes were raised to the object in the front of the church.

Just then he stopped. To his left and right were the abandoned pews where had sat the handful of mourners who had assembled this day for a death not in someone else's family but in his own, not for another woman's death, but for Claire's. In the gray light he could see clearly. The pews were empty. The crucifix had been prepared as with an ax. The perspiration he had acquired in the cemetery had not dried here in this church. The ancient papery garlic that hung on the wall of the barn was a thousand years old.

He glanced down at his feet and, trembling, realized that he had stopped just in time. Directly in his path stood two metal objects which, in that first instant, he was unable to recognize so that for him they remained enigmatic, without purpose. They were positioned one before the other in the exact center of the aisle and close to the altar which they faced. Each was constructed in a shape resembling a square with legs and, he now saw, consisted only of several lengths of rectangular steel tubing welded together. Two flimsy metal objects so light in weight that if in his preoccupation he had knocked them over they would have filled the church with loud insufferable noise. But there they stood in perfect alignment, in silence, in an incongruity even more terrible than the clattering music they might have made.

Alone, cold with perspiration, suddenly he understood that he was waiting rigidly before the two small metal stands that had borne the immense and even intolerable weight of the casket throughout the brief time of the service. Yes, they were only devices upon which to rest the casket. Someone had forgotten to remove them when Claire and the priest and mourners were no longer in that cavelike church. He felt as if he were looking at the two empty metal stands with an impossible clarity of sight.

But another realization came to him: if now, at this very moment, the two stands had been in use, if the leaden casket were resting upon them, of course he would have been paying his own last respects to Claire. That would have been the sense of the situation. But now, when the stands were not functional? When there was nothing to be seen but two incongruous reminders of what had already occurred? As he stared down at the pathetic metal objects, the answer came to him: The obverse of the tomb of Christ, he told himself. The obverse.

When he was again outside, he noticed a high rusted iron stake driven into the chalky ground and becoming at its top a rusted cross. The rust was so old it was nearly black, and the arms of the cross were punctuated with cruel hooks from which were suspended small iron trinkets of obvious meaning: the circlet of thorns, the spikes, a soldier's lance, a ladder with crooked rungs. He stared at the cross with shocking concentration. But it was nothing, he knew, compared with what he had seen inside the church.

His exacting consciousness spared him nothing. He knew only too well that the city in which he lived was without trees, without national monuments, without ponds or flower gardens, without even a single building to attract visitors from other parts of the world. It was a small bleak city consisting almost entirely of cheaply built concrete dwellings and unfinished apartment houses. It was a city without interest, without pride, without efficiency. Sacks of concrete lined the streets; the low-hung electrical wires fed only the barest energy to the tin trolley cars and the precious unshaded light bulbs; in the single park the play equipment for children resembled a collection of devices for inflicting torture. As for shape or plan or boundaries: to the east was the school, to the west the railway station, to the north La Violaine, to the south a hospital that bore on its roof an enormous cross the color of blood washed in the rain. The cemetery, not far from the park for children, more or less marked the center. And always the dust, the dry air, the sound of iron against iron, the visibility of systems (for trains, traffic, school, prison, playground, cemetery), the signs and posters displayed in shopwindows or pasted to bare walls in order to fix for the eye a steam-pressing mechanism, a suit of clothes, a wrench, a bowl of food. Here was the outcome of the centuries of death and agony; the paths of the great minds ended

11

here; dreamers of palaces and holocausts had invented nothing. And what was this city, denying in its daily life the validity of recorded history, if not the very domain of the human psyche? The irony of order existing only in desolation and discomfort was a satisfaction beyond imagining.

His apartment, the apartment of father and daughter, was like the city itself: bare, inefficient, nondescript. There was no attempt to hide or disguise the squat iron bottles of compressed gas that stood in kitchen and bathing stall and were replenished monthly by full bottles dragged up from a truck in the street below. Even the hoses bolted like artificial arteries to these iron tanks were to him agreeable, as agreeable as the sight of a cleaver in a chopping block or a single hairpin on a shelf of glass.

Beyond all this, beyond the four rooms, beyond the low white walls of the cemetery, beyond the fuel pumps and the motorcycle drivers in their leather suits and enormous smoke-blackened goggles, lay an endless flat countryside that was like boot to foot or shawl to shoulder to the small city. Dust, patches of marsh, a slaughtered animal in a wooden shed, a hooded woman beside a well that would soon be dry, vast natural gardens of rock or clumps of grass that resembled hopelessly tangled coils of electrical wiring, and the dirt roads and encrusted gardens and the red dragonfly on a sunken post, and over everything the light and shadows that told of nothingness: in all this was to be seen the only terrain appropriate to the city that featured La Violaine in its racks of weathered postcards and denied the image of woman to advertising or to public artwork. Where they met—desolate countryside, desolate city—there was a constant competition of expansion, earth and water invading the porous symmetry of the outskirts of the city, incompleted pipelines and abandoned concrete telephone poles invading the harshness of the landscape that mirrored light without meaning. The days passed, the competition remained at a stalemate. But occasionally he gave himself the pleasure of a long walk or a ride on the trolley until all at once he could enjoy the shock of that confused sight: of torn earth, of muddied concrete, knowing at such moments that he himself could not have been imagined by even the most morbid of the ancient poets.

He was indeed a traveler in a small world. There were the daily visits to the café bearing the name of the prison, the daily conversation with his friend Gagnon, the weekly visits to the grave, where the small glass-enclosed photograph revealed through indistinct features the broadness of Claire's smile, the occasional trip to the edge of the city. Perhaps once a month he allowed himself the somewhat labyrinthine walk to the railway station. Several times a year he gave himself the pleasure of taking off an afternoon from his white coat and the sterile order of the pharmacy and surprising Mirabelle at the end of her day at school. In boredom he found all the exhilaration of the proof of life's boredom; everything he perceived had about it the strictness, the tension, of life's boredom. And he knew the landmarks: the iron angel on the gate to the cemetery, the faded fleur-de-lis on the awning of La Violaine, the abandoned coal-burning locomotive that dominated the sooty area of the railway station, at the edge of the city the small yellow road-working machine, abandoned with its tortured iron claw in the air.

Since his arrival so far in the past on a westbound train, he had never again set foot in a railway car. Yet he knew that at the station he was indistinguishable from someone actually arriving or setting forth. In particular the railway station produced in him sensations of recognition, exactitude, approval. He approved of the systems of iron barriers, of schedules chalked on slate and tickets printed on cheap paper; he approved the wooden benches, the broken clock, the vending machine bereft of anything to appease the waiting passenger or angry child. Unnatural sounds, the voice of the telegraph, the grass growing between the rusted tracks, the vast dark burning smells of the dragon of travel: he approved of it all. He felt significant in that sooty mausoleum. His own tattered suitcase might have been waiting on one of the baggage carts or in one of the metal bins like crypts for the dead. Approaching a ticket window, turning away, standing on the rotted passenger platform with his hat on his head and his black figure casting a long shadow, always there was the cornerstone on which the entire edifice was built: that he longed for the sight of unseen vistas from the train window, that he had already arrived amidst smoke and whistles, and that there was nowhere to go.

He was the stationary traveler, that much he knew. He had the precise phrase clearly in mind—the stationary traveler—and he was pleased that he, an ordinary widower, had become so remarkably self-defined. But the intensity of his desire to visit the railway terminal, that edifice as imposing and frightening as an opera house once gutted by fire and never restored, depended most of all on a simple event of the past. Periodically he called it to consciousness, while lighting gas in a burner or waiting for the return of Mirabelle. He could not enter the railway station, could not breathe in the first breath of that sudden harmony of public smells (of smoke, oil, liquid porcelain), could not walk the empty length of the sinister passenger shed without again enduring and yet savoring this particular living tableau, as he allowed himself to think of it, from his own past. The recollection always reminded him that the storehouse of memory was like a railway station.

There had been a crowd. It was a Sunday in summer. The sun was shining on an island of tattered luggage. Despite the heat, he was wearing his gray fedora tight on his head and carrying over his arm a cheap green raincoat in sharp contrast to the black suit, and he was feeling a crispness that came of anxiety cloaked in anticipation, and at that moment was nearly capable of imagining

14

in his breast pocket a great wad of documents for travel. He paused, a sudden steam whistle quickened his senses; he turned and passed directly into the passenger shed, where he recognized at once that the horror that inspires the elation of ordinary life was revealing itself. Abruptly he stopped and attempted to discover what was so arresting in the familiar scene.

A train stood beside the platform, its length protruding at either end from beyond the blackened wood of the platform and from beyond the protection of the shed roof that was now diffusing the light of the sun. Many of the train's windows were open; its doors were ajar; its chocolate brown color was awash with layers of fresh dust from the terrain through which it had already sped. Obviously the train had entered the station only moments before his own arrival; the passengers milling in small groups were concluding rather than commencing their journey. A conductor was fanning himself with his official peaked cap. The crowd, the fatigue and excitement of the journey's end, the pinging of a workman's hammer, the spent quality of the long silent train: in all this he was suddenly entrapped as if he were about to be exposed for what he was, the only person who had no business meeting that train or standing in the midst of those who had traveled. But again he allowed his glance to return to the three people nearest him, a mature woman and two young men in shabby but nonetheless intimidating uniforms.

It was this trio that added the tincture of distortion to an otherwise neutral scene. He perceived in slow rotation the elements that were the clues to this revelation of both poison and light. He noted that not a single other person was glancing in the direction of the woman and two young men. The trio, he realized, possessed no baggage except for one small case decorated with flowers; the men and woman stood together as if they did not know where they were or did not care; the identical black kepis lent a sinister tone to the white youthful faces of the men; the woman was attempting to joke with her two companions, one of whom, he now perceived, was staring directly at himself, the solitary spectator, with an obvious message in the youthful eyes: keep away.

Why was it that in this public place he alone had intruded into the privacy of these three people who shared not intimacy but the burden of impersonal disgrace? Surely there were others who had seen what he had seen, that the older unattractive woman was openly manacled to the two young men, and was restrained by the most explicit of all possible devices, by chains, as if the most archaic tools of justice were merely commonplace in a world of crying children, muzzled dogs, and peasants balancing fattened cardboard suitcases on the tops of their heads. Poison and light, the horror that inspired the elation of ordinary life revealing itself, and only he had been a witness, guilty accomplice, shocked participant. Only here could a woman be paraded publicly in chains.

And the woman herself? This bony older woman with her stunned expression hardly concealed behind her efforts to laugh? This woman who cared nothing for her disheveled dress because in moments she would be wearing a uniform plainer, more pathetic than the much worn aggressive garb of the young men? This woman who did not know or care where she was because here at the very crossroads of daily life she had already been removed from it? Was she too merely embarrassed to be brought so unusually into this public hour, or was she distracted in shameful awareness of the act she had committed?

There was no answer. But one fact was obvious: that the woman was unable to comprehend her crime and did not know how to carry the persona that had been thrust upon her by all those in the labyrinths of criminal procedure. She was merely a woman who had been shown no mercy because of some passion she could not distinguish from eating, dreaming, riding on trains. In the muscles of her legs her youth was still evident; her middle age expressed itself in the gauntness of the frame rather than in excessive weight;

16

the tragedy of the face lay not in its incongruity, in the thickish lips, the crooked nose, the dry skin, the eyes too bright, but rather in its need to weep. The crime, no matter what it might have been, merely helped the poor face to radiate the inner compulsion to shed tears. Until this moment he himself had never recognized or understood that radiance.

The woman moved. Behind her, dark figures were entering the train with buckets and brushes, and now, with fewer people on the platform, he, Konrad Vost, felt himself more than ever singled out by the eyes of passing strangers and more than ever entrapped in the proximity of the woman. Then came the simple climax of the fateful encounter: in her agitation, while attempting to hold the attention of her two guards and feign unawareness of everyone who milled about her, while twisting her shoulders, turning her head and imparting slight jerky motions to her body and the incongruous chains, it was then that she looked at him. In an instant he saw it all: the sudden alignment of her face with his, the quivering in the head of hair so untended as to betray the complete collapse of vanity, the eyes darting, widening, looking in the fullness of the moment into his own directly, clearly, so that he saw without any question the dark color of the irises, the latent pinkness of eyes filled with tears, the hardness of eyes that revealed, to his dismay, the woman's hopeless determination to comprehend the drab enigma of this situation and even to protect herself, if possible, from the effects of it. His eyes met hers and she returned his stare despite herself.

But even then he knew the truth. She did not see him. Looking full into his eyes, she was blind to him. This person, a woman and a prisoner as well, could not admit to consciousness the only man who, in the railway station of a city that existed only for the sake of its prison, had experienced even the slightest concern for her plight. The irony of her disregard covered all the skin of his body with a wet chill; he blushed at the realization that he, a man dressed purposefully in black, was invisible to a homely disheveled woman in chains. If this woman was unable to feel the weight of her guilt, he himself was suffused with it.

The moment passed. She looked away. The self-important sound of a teletype machine intruded itself upon them. The guard picked up the small valise pathetically feminized with the stencils of flowers, and the three moved slowly off in the direction of the concealed loading area, where, he realized, the ominous blue van from La Violaine had only now appeared.

As for himself, he turned on his heel and went directly to the terminal's small antiquated bar that catered to derelicts and hasty travelers, and without hesitation ordered a glass of cognac. He noted the wet metal surface of the bar, the tarnished and dusty mirror behind it, the flaking cherubs nestled into the corners of the mirror. The floor, the bottles, and the mirror as well began to shake with the arrival of another train. He squared his shoulders, rested one elbow on the bar, stared at his face in the glass (the golden spectacles, the grainy whiteness of the cheeks, the heavy jaw, the black hair, the black neck of the shirt rising high and tight like a hand on his throat), then toasted himself and silently admitted that the sight of the woman had been a gift, that in witnessing her arrival he had in some sense witnessed the arrival of his own mother, Eva Laubenstein, so many years before, and that in these circumstances his mother would have been just as blind to him as had been the woman. Then, staring into the glass and feeling the return of confidence, he made his final silent admission to himself: that secretly, deep within, he approved of the chains.

Poor Konrad, she said, addressing him sweetly, gently, from the deathbed where she lay with her eyes already closing, her smile fading, her breath expiring. Poor Konrad, knowing at her very

18

moment of death that he would never cease to grieve for his loving Claire, and at this moment being concerned, typically, not for herself but for him. To the end she was the maternal as well as the conjugal Claire, though at the outset of his grief and in the midst of his gratitude it did not matter to him that the object of Claire's pity was the child secreted inside the man of fifty. Poor Konrad, she said from the depths of her strength and gentleness, and died.

His friend Gagnon consoled himself with his collection of birds, which he kept in wooden cages stacked and hung in his otherwise nearly empty room above the café. Gagnon was obsessive in his love of birds, in the attention he lavished on seed, water, light, and the movements of the little creatures and their bursts of song. Except for his daily glass of beer at the café below, he had time and energy for nothing but the care and enjoyment of his family, as he called it, of bright birds. Konrad Vost took a distant pleasure in visiting his friend who was also a widower whose only child had been born a girl. Though Gagnon's daughter was imprisoned in La Violaine, and though Gagnon did not refer to her in any way, still she was a bond between the men. As for the birds, they were colorful, active and amusing.

Gagnon was never disturbed when one of them died. Eagerly he visited the railway station, where replacements arrived in cardboard cartons, filling a dismal baggage car with the sounds of faint music.

Mirabelle was no longer enraptured with Gagnon's collection and for months now had in fact refused to join her parent in the cell-like room devoted to the myriad cages of captive birds that were rare, common, cultivated, aboriginal. The significance of this narrowing of his daughter's interests, as he thought of it, was one of the whispering voices her father could not hear.

19

In retrospect, well after the disordering of his world had suddenly commenced, only then did he understand that until the eruption of unpredictable incident on a public axis that was also his own personal axis, he had passed his days in time uninformed by chronology. Of course he had lived in the shadow of La Violaine. Of course his life had not been without significant events. Thanks to their random accumulation he had come to prize his superiority, his irony, his self-condemnation, his intractable belief in his identity as Konrad Vost. After all, he was ordinary but at the same time exceptional. How many men were capable of knowing, as he full well knew, that the artificial limb, the imitation of a hand in a black glove or the replica of a missing foot in a real boot, adds splendor to the body presumed to be merely maimed? How many professed, as did he, the amateur's unexpected proficiency in the area of what he called the psychological function? Or could suffer the understanding, as could he, that smashed glass is preferable to the pure plane? He had his theory of memory, his theory of clear sight, his theory of travel, and who else in La Violaine could claim even the faintest intuition of being embarked on a journey, let alone admit to consciousness the blankness of the way? He approved of precisely everything that caused other men pain or bafflement. He knew that the world was man-made and that the world was dressed in its best when it was clothed in tatters. Yet he too was delighted when he heard the word Papa on the lips of his child.

Only in the midst of the disordering of his small world did he come to learn that without chronology, without unexpected events suddenly manifesting themselves in series like the links of a chain, a person could never uncover the sum of his own secrets or profit truly from the lessons of devastation. When the time

20

arrived, and disorder surrounded him with the force of shattered morality, he was stunned to discover how rigorously he clung to his former self and how bestial he had in fact become.

Laubenstein was his mother's maiden name. To allow it to consciousness was an ordeal he seldom undertook, assigning it, and the reasons she preferred that name to his own, to that interior place where he concealed the images of the man who had fathered him as well as the images of himself as a small and innocent trumpeter in the children's marching corps in the poor village of his birth. But even now, in the complacency of his middle age, he was sometimes startled awake by the blasting chorus of those terrible distant heraldic horns.

The flowers were recalcitrant in yesterday's newspapers. He was stooping, alone in the cemetery, the center of the dead city, and he heard the sound made by the soles of his shoes on the gravel and that of his fingers against the paper and flowers. He knelt; he was aware of the sensation of the gravel against his knees and through the black serge of his trousers. The distant silhouetted derrick that was never in use, the cemetery like a replica of the city itself, the utterly dry stone monument, the tin flower holders that were themselves hammered into the shape of the fluted bells of lilies: everything was muted in the dull light of finality that illuminated with terrible clarity the smallest detail of that stricken scene. He was precise yet clumsy, only an actor in a film long since destroyed, a waxen figure kneeling in clumsy obeisance at the head of a grave.

Even as he knelt before the grave, the unwanted and unimaginable scene emerged: he saw the familiar room, empty except for the cheap metal bed, the enormous chiffonier that was metal painted to resemble a bright veneer of wood, and the man standing uncomfortably in that bare room in which she, his seductress, had never slept alone in her married life. The woman herself, large, smiling, incapable of guilt, now in silent animation approached the chiffonier and from its scented interior swept together an armful of warm and rubbery corsets large enough to contain the weight, the size, the beauty of her own torso, and turning and in a gesture of superb and innocent salutation, thrust upon the bulky man this profusion of intimate apparel, this undeniable expression of her girlish expansiveness and matronly desire.

Then it was gone. He refused to move, refused to wipe the perspiration from his face now raised in defiance of the waiting judgmental eyes. But he calmed himself by recalling for an instant his theory of memory: that memory was an infinitely expanding structure of events recollected from life, events that had been imagined, imaginary events that had been recollected, dreams that had been recollected, recomposed, dreamt once again, remembered. Yes, he told himself, the storehouse of memory was like a railway terminal for trains of unlimited destination.

The dead light was gone. He rose and walked away as usual on the narrow path between the tiers of graves. Even now, five years beyond the time of her death, he was still not responsible for his involvement in Claire's life. And no guilty mental image, he told himself, could ever quiet the clamoring of his grief for Claire.

As usual the little dog had once again deposited the wet clothespin next to the tip of his shoe. But as usual he refused to give the wretched creature his slightest attention. He refused to acknowledge even Gagnon, who was sitting three tables away and propping his head in his hands, as if he were waiting hopelessly on a bench in the courtyard of some dusty asylum in charge of nuns instead of sitting alone, as usual, at a table beneath the faded street awning of La Violaine. Today he, Konrad Vost, could not contend in any way with the ugly dog or the sentimental friend.

The glass of beer was cold and tasted of salt. On the front of the newspaper was a murky photograph of three children sitting on what appeared to be some kind of iron death machine in the black sandy oasis where they were meant to play. As always he was sitting rigidly upright in the garb and posture of what he thought of as his contemptuous dignity, attempting to ignore the noon traffic as he was ignoring dog and friend. In his two rigid hands the folded newspaper was already beginning to absorb out of the atmosphere the dampness of the gray day.

Over the rim of his raised glass he stared across the street at the wall of the prison. There were the remnants of a poster on the wall, a shutter was moving behind its bars. But why could it not have resembled a fortress? Turrets, massive walls of gray stone, giant slabs of wood and iron; and imposing, ominous, smoke-stained with time, dark with the implications of physical pain inflicted in the labyrinths of its buried cellars: at least some such grandeur of horror might have cloaked in romance the thralldom of the habitués, who spent their hours attempting to disguise themselves at the tables of La Violaine. But for them there could be no grandeur, no breath of unmerciful history. The high ordinary wall with its torn poster and crumbling surface, the gate with its climbing vine and cobwebs in the iron mesh, the shuttered windows, conventional except for rusted bars which, along with the old watery green tiles of the roof, were visible above the walls, the close resemblance between the prison and a decayed public building in a poverty-stricken village, these reminded the habitués in the café of what they did not wish to know: that the degradation concealed within La Violaine was no different from that implicit in the city in which the prison thrived.

He put down the glass and felt the heavy opalescence of impending rain filling the air. He stared at the façade of La Violaine; he leaned forward and clasped his hands on the table. The hour was noon, despite the darkness and heavy air.

There was activity behind the tall gates across the street. He was intent on it; momentarily his view was obscured; then, as did those around him, he saw the woman emerging from the narrowly opened gates. No guards, no few assembled inmates to wish her well, no hand waving from one of the windows above. Only the single figure of the woman walking out of the prison without a backward glance, and deliberately, without expression, crossing the street. She carried a small new suitcase that might have been weightless. She had no regard for the traffic. With her empty hand she wiped the side of her face, as if the rain had already begun to fall. She was wearing a small red brimless hat perched on the top of her head.

It was the hat, rather than the woman herself, that held his attention, though he had known from the outset that this very woman was crossing the street and approaching La Violaine to sit at no table other than his own, to talk with no one except himself. But never before in his life had he been so approached, so singled out. Never had he felt so timid, so elated. But he detested the small bright red hat and even more the fact that it was perched on top of the woman's head at a crooked angle.

Noontime of what would be a day of rain, and the woman came directly to his table, put down the suitcase, gave the little dog one deft vicious kick that sent it scurrying, pulled out the other chair at his table, and seated herself. The hat was molded of red felt, the hair was dark, the face was that of a woman who had supported herself by attending to the needs of other women: hairdresser, beautician, perhaps masseuse. Everything about this face was

24

hardened: the skin without the shadings of cosmetics, a latent puffiness contained in the flesh of the cheeks, the thick wings of the nose, the mouth that was neither sullen nor tender, the chin bearing its telltale scar in the shape of a barb. Hardened, colorless, indifferent, the face of a woman who had once received the first level of training in some crude profession, and nothing more.

The proprietor appeared with a glass and a small dusty dark green bottle of sparkling wine on a tray. He filled the glass, from the same tray produced an unopened package of cigarettes which he placed near the woman's hand beside the glass, and in the darkness behind the bar someone switched the radio from its customary sound of voices to a popular song. Hastily the proprietor's wife entered La Violaine through a doorway draped with strings of tinkling beads and at once began to make fresh coffee. And he, Konrad Vost, felt the pleasure and concentration of those who were gathering around himself and this woman who, for all of them, was an envoy from La Violaine. The proprietor reappeared with a fresh glass of beer and a napkin. On the radio a girl was singing the popular lyrics in a quavering voice. Here, on the narrow sidewalk beneath the shabby awning, the unusual darkness and heaviness of the impending rain were conducive to the feeling he now had that actually he was seated alone with the woman, despite their audience.

"To your good health," she said quietly, matter-of-factly, and took a drink of her wine and opened the package of cigarettes.

"Your health," he answered formally, with all the reserve that betrays acute embarrassment. Noticing the hairlines of dirt in his fingernails and seeing himself as the woman must see him, a lonely man turning toward her his face that might have been composed of white wax, he realized at that moment that he had not been so concerned with a woman since the day he had wanted to accost the chained woman in the railway station and had not been so intimately related to any woman since the death of Claire. Yet

25

here he was, drinking quickly from his glass of beer and waiting to look directly into the woman's eyes.

She drank again. One of their silent audience proffered a lighted match for her waiting cigarette. She accepted but did not acknowledge the sulfurous flame. Her face was impassive. Then apparently without intention she looked directly, firmly, into his eyes. He returned her gesture that was a steady unhurried communion of sight, and was startled by the directness of her gaze and the brown or nearly amber color of the woman's eyes.

"It's a good day for me," she said, looking away and tapping the cigarette into a chipped glass ashtray that had appeared on the table. He could feel her breath against the exposed skin of his wrist, he knew that he was both smiling and pinching tight his lips as the woman glanced over her shoulder and back toward the gate, the wall, the dim blue-clad figure slouching in the sentry box.

Again she looked him full in the face and nodded, as if she were not only accepting him as her companion on the day of her release but taking him also into her deepest confidence. A permanent band of discoloration on the finger of the left hand betrayed the long absence of the missing ring, of the marriage dissolved upon her entrance into La Violaine and perhaps forgotten. She began to talk and though her eyes were on his own he knew she was speaking for the benefit of anyone who wished to hear.

"Paquet is well and safe," she said, drawing smoke from the cigarette but not inhaling it. "And Berenger, Kimski, Servelle, Roterman, Jouffe, Le Touze, Laubenstein, Spapa, Hauptman, Nerval, all are well and safe." The voice continued, the catalogue of names increased in length as if it were a roster of survivors or of those dead in the charred arena of some intensive combat, while the woman held his attention with her eyes and with the tone of voice that was conspiratorial or more remote and stiffened with the cadences of reportage. He held the glass of beer halfway to his mouth and stared back at the woman but no longer listened. He

26

realized that she was reciting only family names, as if those named were men rather than women, and more important, in the harsh music of her recitation he had heard unmistakably the name of that woman who had destroyed his childhood, tormented and destroyed his father, and deprived himself of her maternal love. He had never doubted that she was there, across the street, hidden somewhere inside La Violaine. But to know it as fact, to find himself suddenly counting the years of her imprisonment, to hear the sound of her name in the midst of many, to think of her as living, to be so relieved and yet alarmed made him wish both to strike and to embrace the woman who was wearing the red hat and was now regarding him with her expression of intimacy and complicity. There, he realized, there exactly was the source of this woman's singularity: from the outset she had assumed that they were comrades, he and she, and had behaved as if her life now deserved at least the comradeship of men if nothing else.

"I wish to know something," he said, interrupting the woman. "I must know exactly why you chose my table instead of another's." He drew back, he was shocked that his own voice could sound so false. But the woman nodded. Apparently she was quite unaware of his discomfort which had been so easily prompted by the name of his mother and by the closeness of the woman herself. He looked at the finger that bore no ring and thought of the order of motherhood, from which the woman had been long ago expelled. The faint lines in her face were like those in his own, despite their difference in age; he was aware of the bosom beneath the dark shiny material of the dress. His own skin was growing moist. He smelled her breath, he heard a sound as of wind blowing steadily across flat fields of sand.

"But you were the most distinguished man in the café. I could tell at a glance."

He did not move. He waited. Somewhere the wind was flattening itself to the sand. She had spoken as though discussing a route on a map, and yet there was no mistaking what she had said, and now her eyes were the color of amber licked to moistness by a child.

"So Eva Laubenstein is well," he said, inclining his head and crossing one leg over the other. "And the rest you have named, they too are well." He was pleased that all around him his compatriots were leaning forward and straining to hear.

"Safe and well," repeated the woman, as she finished the last of her wine and disposed of the cigarette. "But it cannot last. Things in there are worse than they were. Much worse. Do you know what will happen? They will revolt. The women in that place are going to revolt. Very soon. In a matter of weeks. I could almost regret my own freedom today. But what is one woman more or less in their ranks? Though I am gone they will revolt. I promise you."

She reached for her suitcase. She rose. Her waist was at the level of his eyes. Even then he was hearing shouts, hearing a shot, seeing smoke issuing from the gates and windows of La Violaine, though he reassured himself that what the woman had said was impossible. For a moment he wanted to denounce the woman and at the same time put his hand on her waist.

"And you," she said, waiting, looking down at him, causing him to shake her hand, and turning so that her dress twisted in the tightening waist, "you shall have your reunions, thanks to force. You shall join them in their revolt. I promise you."

Then she was gone: to the railway terminal, to the child she might yet conceive. As for himself, he drank the last of his beer and watched as the now falling rain began to fill the darkening air. He shook his head, thinking of the woman and her waist, her bosom, her consoling eyes. But could she in fact have been so deceived as to think him pleased by the prospect of violence? Could she think that he, Konrad Vost, could ever ally himself with the maenads?

28

She was gone now into the rain. Across the street the sentry was perfectly dry in his box. Now the passing motorcyclists were hooded in sheets of rubber. Behind him the popular song had already given way abruptly to the familiar monotony of the arguing voices. Then he too left La Violaine, retrieving his newspaper and walking off bareheaded into the bizarre noon-hour darkness and heavy rain. His black shoes became immediately wet; he walked as close as he could to the concrete walls and iron shutters drawn as if forever across the faces of small shops with their single dead light bulbs and sparse shelves of dusty merchandise. Even he began to wish for an occasional linden tree or the flight of a wet bird.

He was thinking of Gagnon, who like himself had also received encouraging news in the hour just past, when suddenly in an opening like a dark mouth he caught sight of the red hat. Clearly the woman was taking shelter. It was a garage, he recollected, a cold black concrete cave where trucks and automobiles were dismantled and subjected to the hissing of blue flames or hoisted into the air on chains.

He drew near, he smelled the wet smells of grease, oil, gasoline, the prevailing rain. But the woman was not alone. As soon as he approached close enough to distinguish her wet body from the surrounding blackness, he saw that just inside the open doorway of the garage stood not one person, as he had assumed, but two, and saw that the woman was clasping in her arms the figure of a man whose hands and denim shirt and pants were wet with grease, and who was returning the woman's rapturous embrace by squeezing her to him with one blackened hand on the back of her neck and the other pressed with spread fingers to her buttocks. The woman's head was thrust backward and to one side; her right lower leg was lifted in the tension of the wet embrace; her arms were clasped about the neck of the man, who had apparently dropped a heavy wrench in order to grasp the woman's body against the length of himself. The two mouths were enjoined, as if each were at the same time devouring the other and being devoured.

Abruptly Konrad Vost crossed the street, in the face of the traffic, and continued on his way through the rain. He felt that beneath his wet clothes his entire person was bound in broad shrinking strips of leather. The sight he had just seen could have served as a warning, but it did not.

In the photograph, which existed now only in his mind, like the dream already dreamt or the day once lived, he was standing with his ankles crossed and his right fist gripping a gnarled walking stick on which he leaned. Large, sepia-colored, mounted in a silver frame, the photograph depicted the little walker surrounded by a vast indistinct whirling diffusion of light no doubt intended to suggest clouds. There he was, leaning on the black outlandish stick and smiling, oblivious to the costume which even now, in a moment of distasteful memory, induced in him a certain shame as well as incomprehension. The short leather trousers with the leather halter adjusted to the shoulders and fastened across the birdlike chest were merely grotesque on the thin boy they clothed; the shoes were worse, since they were constructed of leather so thick that they appeared to encase the feet in lumps of highly lacquered wood; but worst of all was the shirt which, in contrast to the stick, the shoes, the trousers, was tailored of an elegant white fabric, linen perhaps, and was short-sleeved, pearl-buttoned and decorated with an open flowering collar whose ruffles lay on the shoulders, finally, like soft curls. But who could have contrived such a costume in which masculine debased feminine and feminine debased masculine and both were subjected to a kind of silent mockery? Yet he himself was unmistakably por-

30

trayed in this photograph that dominated the lavish family collection in the poor village: the pants and shirt and stick only exaggerated the thinness of the little torso and arms and legs that were his; and there, in the head of the smiling child, was already evident the elfin head that was his own, with the large eyes and ears and the smile much too broad for the narrow almost transparent face. How could the handsome features of his later youth have emerged from such a face? My little mountain walker, his father would say, while his mother polished the glass of that photograph with happy vengeful energy. Even he understood, though dimly, that the shame induced by this photograph was the result of his innocence —innocence that had unfurled its sickening gauzy wings and exposed itself, like some poisonous moth, to the thick eager lens of the camera.

The weaker the child, Claire used to say, the more fanatical the man. And my dearest, where is the woman who does not love a fanatical man? He would nod, smile, incline his protruding jaw. But never once while she was alive did he understand that he himself was the subject of this the rarest of Claire's aphorisms.

The poles of his most general theory of the psychological function were these: that the interior life of the man is a bed of stars, that the interior life of the man is a pit of putrescence. Of course the two poles could be easily reconciled by discerning in putrescence its natural radiance. But he, the pedant, recognized the danger of such a reconciliation, which all too easily became the sleight of hand of the optimist, who employs light to blind us to the fact of darkness. So he preferred to keep these two poles apart, leaning toward now the one, now the other. But no matter the argument, it was essential, he knew, to cling to the first observation: that every man contains his psychic pit, and that each such pit is filled with slime.

In retrospect he was not able to discover the source of the well-being he felt that day or of the realization, upon him once more, that again the day had arrived when, as many times in the past, he would devote his entire afternoon to Mirabelle. But there it was: the good feeling, the benevolence, the exhilaration of seeing the day through a sheet of ice, and the determination that he would now refuse the ordinary demands of his daily life in the pharmacy and undertake the long familiar walk in order to greet Mirabelle at the end of her day at school. The satisfaction attendant on this decision was immense: the students would emerge from the several gray buildings behind the wall on the top of which were strung the long strands of protective wire. The students would fill the sandy compound with the life of their bodies; the moving students would remind him of Gagnon's birds. He would see Mirabelle; he would stand still and wave; Mirabelle would return his greeting, surprised, happily understanding that once again her father was taking the trouble to walk home with her from school. Arm in arm they would set off together as they had done less and less frequently in these five surprisingly bearable years since the death of Claire.

He was breathing exactly the same clear cold air as would soon fill the lungs of the dispersing students. He was alone and walking eastward into the shadows of exactly the same street he would soon be traversing westward into pale fading light with Mirabelle. It was the route of the small infrequent trolley cars, those doorless vehicles of gray riveted metal, and the sight of the narrow rails embedded in a field partly of cobblestones, partly of concrete, and the sagging overhead cable and the tin-roofed shelters where waited no passengers, no parents with children in hand: the sight of this thoroughfare on which he alone was proceeding could only evoke, as he strode along, the sound of Mirabelle's voice at his side and the vision of the entire schoolful of students swarming toward him suddenly with arms in the air and shoes and boots clattering on the empty stones.

He reached the landmark of the fountain, an amateurish replica in concrete of a dolphin from the mouth of which trickled not a drop of water. He turned the familiar corner where now, as always, he was both vindicated and offended by the smell of sewage pumping upward through an iron grate in the stones; he approached within sight and hearing distance of the low darkening school. But he heard nothing. He saw no one. He quickened his pace. With misgivings, with the utmost of disappointment, he entered the sandy square intended for recreation and calisthenics. But it was empty, except for a single girl who was walking listlessly in his direction and who was not Mirabelle. The impossible had happened. He was too late. He who was always correct, precise, punctual, was now too late. Nevertheless he decided to speak to the girl, who evidently meant to speak a few words to him.

"I am looking for Mirabelle," he said, "the daughter of Konrad Vost. Is she here?"

He inclined himself slightly from the waist, he relaxed his face, he assumed a pleasant quizzical expression, all in order to put at ease this girl who, except for her clothes, was strikingly similar to the girl he was seeking. The same rather large size, the same dark hair cut to shoulder length in imitation of an adult style, the same unformed quality of the face that still belonged to the child. Of course instead of wearing skirt, blouse, shoes tied with laces, this girl was dressed in pants of faded blue denim and, clinging to her torso, a thin white collarless and sleeveless shirt that was like a

33

sweater. Across the front of the shirt and conforming to the shape of this child's womanly bosom was printed in block letters the message WE AIM TO PLEASE. He noted the boldness of the letters but did not understand the pathos of the double meaning, since the message on the shirt was couched in that language he had never learned to read. He noted too the wooden sandals on the bare feet, the goose flesh on the arms and upper chest. Mirabelle would not approve of such a costume. And she was perhaps too shy to stand this close to a stranger in the lengthening shadows of an empty schoolyard. But the incongruity of the lone girl was appealing, as was the directness with which she was looking up at his face, so that he found himself bending again from the waist and attempting to disregard the tightness of the pants, the shirt.

"Well," he repeated, knowing the uselessness of the question, "and Mirabelle? Is she here?"

"No, she's already gone," said the girl, inclining her shoulder vaguely and drawing still closer. "If you want Mirabelle you must come earlier. But I'm available. And I can give you more than she could. And for less."

He waited. She said nothing more. He listened intently. And was someone else, someone very like himself though with briefcase, topcoat, cane, face in the shadows, now approaching this same empty place to pause at the gate, to draw back, to stand quietly watching a tall middle-aged man already conversing with the obscured figure of the very person he, the imaginary stranger, had come to find? Had he visited this same schoolyard weeks in the past? Had this same girl been waiting? For a moment longer, he, the actual man, the living father, he who had come on his innocent mission, stood darkly within this institutional enclosure creating a dream, escaping a dream, clinging as best he could to incomprehension. But then his entire world fell from him, like a facing of ice from an immense cliff, so that he was left with only defeat instead of disbelief, with the intolerable pain of sight after blind-

34

ness, with the feeling of young fingers on the sleeve of his coat. So the school was in fact visited by men who were not at all the fathers of the concerned students; so she who was now waiting beside him meant what she had said and did not know or care who he was; so in an instant he had discovered the true uselessness of inquiry about Mirabelle who was already the genie who knew how to escape from the bottle. He was cold. He felt annulled. He was able to think of nothing but an armful of corsets. He was inflamed. He was annulled.

"Now," said the girl at his side, recalling him to the young fingers and the voice he would never forget. "Now, are you coming?"

He nodded. She requested his billfold. He complied. After she had transacted her business, alone, impervious to the fading light, oddly considerate of the man who possessed a steel tooth and who had made her friend her competitor, she stepped around his rigid figure and led the way out of the sandy enclosure and through the cold streets toward the building that concealed the shuttered room in which he knew she would again confront him with what he had hardly thought of since Claire's voice faded and the deathbed contained only her still form.

Between the schoolyard and the shuttered room there were only the determined clattering sounds of the wooden sandals and the cold blanketing knowledge of himself as a single anonymous older man in pursuit of the illicit services of a girl who was still in fact a child. Within the caverns that were now himself, even this knowledge was a form of oblivion. The girl made no attempt to conceal their passage together. He found that he was neither alarmed by nor dismayed at the loudness of the sandals that protected the bare feet from the stones.

But it was precisely the sandals that she removed first in that small room with its single shuttered window and its empty walls of whitewashed concrete. One narrow door opened into the cubicle that was the toilet, which the girl now used, while the other opened into the cubicle containing the stove, the iron bottle of gas, the meager tins of food, the outmoded refrigerator on the top of which rested the radio of blackened Bakelite. In one corner of the room stood a table and two upright chairs; along one wall was the sparsely padded couch that obviously folded out into the bed for both mother and daughter; from the corner opposite the table and chairs, and positioned so that it bisected the corner exactly, there protruded the shockingly incongruous sight of a gaunt narrow chaise longue which, with its gilded lion's feet, its gilded frame, its upholstering material stitched with the enormous brown heads of flowers in bloom, might have been dragged from an abandoned chateau that existed only in the pages of a moldy volume bound in green leather. Clearly this shabby overly rich piece of furniture, situated in concrete and emptiness, represented the unattainable taste and vision of the mother; here she rested whenever she returned from working in bakery, dry goods shop, laundry, rested in poor splendor while the girl, no doubt, played the radio in the cubicle that was filling with the smell of meat boiling in a steel pot on the stove.

No sooner had the toilet flushed than the girl reappeared, zipping her trousers, disregarding him where he stood fully clothed between the chaise longue, the bare table, the couch. Through the slats in the shutters the light entered the room as through the skeletal ribs of an animal long dead. He had not moved since entering this place of nakedness, and when the girl returned from the cubicle of the kitchen bearing a small glass filled to the brim with a clear liquor, he found it difficult to raise his arm, extend his hand, seize the glass. But he did so, while the girl stood watching him, and at the precise moment he coughed on the last of the liquor, the girl, in an easy gesture, and with both hands, pulled the white shirt over her head and free from her body. He coughed, he felt the burning in his nose and throat, the wetness in his eyes, and in the midst of this condition induced deliberately by the girl as preparation for the sight of her nakedness, he attempted not to think of Claire but instead gave himself the full benefit of what in his lifetime he had never seen: the thick and womanly breasts of a young girl.

She took the glass from him and replaced it not in the kitchen but on the bare table, so as to keep him in sight. The room smelled faintly of garlic and bottled gas, in the puckering of the naked waist he saw a scar that might have been inflicted in the fury of some childhood beating. Through the open door he could see the black and white toilet stark and waiting like an instrument of execution, and still wet and noisy from the girl's use. Around her neck was a thin chain bearing a small golden heart for a pendant.

Then, taking his hand in hers, she directed him, as if he were a walking invalid, not to the couch as he had expected but instead to the anomaly of the chaise longue that extended into the room like an ornate tongue, like the narrow prow of an entombed boat, like the reclining place of a courtesan with feathers and painted skin. He could hardly bear to stretch himself out on it. But he did so, as she directed, allowing her to straighten his legs and, with her hand on his brow, to push his head gently backward into the cushion. She did not remove his shoes or spectacles; against his forehead her hand was as dry and naked as the bare feet, the bare breasts.

She remained at the head of his half-seated, half-prostrate form, retaining the single childish hand on his brow, until patient, un-hurried, staring down at him, she extended her other hand and touched him behind the ear, on the back of the neck, and then inserted two fingers between the collar of the turtleneck shirt and the skin of his neck and slowly, in gestures that were now circular, now probing, worked the fingers downward as far as she could comfortably reach. He felt that those fingers were exalting his bones and flesh and buried spine. Fully clothed, hands at his sides, he felt himself imperceptibly reaching upward with the top part of his body toward the upright heaviness of the girl at his side. Her breathing deepened: the fingers probed, he allowed his head to incline gently to the right so that through half-closed eyes he could see the armpit, the surprising hair, the shape of the ribs like curves of light beneath the skin, the rounded bottom of one large breast. Hearing the girl's breath and his own, he allowed himself to raise and maneuver his right arm and hand so that his forearm was extended between her legs and the hand was clutching to himself the tightly denimed weight of the girl's leg and thigh. The zipper was half open, the thigh in its skin of cloth was hot.

He felt the fingers withdrawing from the neck of his shirt, he felt the bareness of the girl as she leaned over him and, with the fingers that only moments before were on the pulse of his neck, began to massage his chest and abdomen through the black shirt. He was not moving, and yet in his entire upper body, from his hips to his head, he felt himself straining to arch his back. Without looking he was aware that the girl's trinket, the small golden heart, was sliding in little fits and starts down the black expanse of his shirt, and knew that the girl's spread fingers were working insistently into the secrecy of his hard chest.

Slowly she dislodged his hand and arm and momentarily disappeared from the darkness in which he lay. He waited; on the chaise longue he was like a man fallen to a narrow ledge; never had he known what he now recognized as the beginnings of the state of ecstasy. Then with relief, with anxiety, he realized that the girl was kneeling at the foot of the chaise longue and was gripping his ankles in her two hands and pulling apart his legs so that he had no recourse but to comply, to bend his spread legs at the knees and to allow both feet to drop to the floor on either side of the flat narrow bedlike portion of the chaise longue. The position, that of lying backward with legs wide apart and feet on the floor, like a survivor upside down on his back and awkwardly straddling in reverse some enormous wet black beam of a ship, exposed him suddenly, unmistakably, to the total mercy of the nameless young half-naked girl who was herself now straddling the flat narrow portion of the chaise longue where his outstretched legs had lain.

For a moment he looked down the partial length of himself and into the eyes of the girl. He confronted the steady eyes, the hanging hair, the naked breasts, the tight fat triangular area where the strain on the girl's spread thighs was causing the zipper to creep increasingly open of its own accord. Then, as she moved closer and leaned forward and reached for him with her two hands, the small golden heart swinging free of her naked chest like a plumb line, then his entire person underwent a moment of brief spasmodic revulsion which, in the next instant, collapsed and gave way to a wave of trust and desire. Even before he closed his eyes he felt the girl's fingers flicking loose the tongue of his leather belt and unzipping and pulling wide the mouth of his trousers.

His eyes were shut, he gripped the edges of the chaise longue; his breath was short and helpless in his mouth. The girl's fingers were inside the now invaded clothing of his loins which were flat, rigid, tumultuous in both concealment and accessibility. In his darkness he could feel the belt no longer buckled, the shirt pulled free from the trousers, the sensation of unexpected air. He could not have felt more naked if she had removed altogether the black trousers and the severe and modest underpants. But he was clothed and unclothed at the same time, and the girl's fingers— gentle, warm, cool, always in motion—seemed to be multiplying inside his clothing and next to his skin. Somehow he was aware of the fingers all together and individually, detecting now the careful circumvention of a tight seam, now a smooth endless tickling or caressing sensation in the most vulnerable portion of his anatomy, now a rushing of all her fingers together inside the private tangle of his groin. In the midst of this pleasure, suddenly he became aware of the girl pushing one of her fingers into his rectum, and he gasped in a silent cry of joy and humiliation. How could he have been so ignorant of this experience? How could the girl have the knowledge and daring to do what she was now doing?

But then, as he knew by the sudden pressure and the profusion of hair, then the girl's face was buried in his disheveled groin. It was as if her head had become suddenly the head of a young lioness nuzzling at the wound it had made in the side of a tawny and still-warm fallen animal. Her face, her head, her mouth, her tongue, and suddenly he was confronted with his own unmistakable flesh—flaccid, engorged, he could not tell—aroused and moving in the depths of his clothes, in the mouth of his open trousers, in the mouth of the girl. Bright blood, golden hair, and now the girl's head swerved once in a large circle of violence, tenderness, and then abruptly stopped, became fixed and rigid so that all her determination was concentrated in the now fierce sucking activity of the hot mouth. The rectal pressure was increasing, the sound of breathing ceased, in the midst of his shock and pleasure he was now refusing what he knew was inevitable inside himself, fighting the greedy mouth as the child fights his bladder in the night. But then it began, in darkness and in the midst of what sounded like distant shouting, that long uncoiling of the thick white thread from the bloody pump, that immense and fading constriction of white light inside the flesh. Whom could he thank? How could he admit what had happened? He wanted to breathe, his head had fallen to one side, for a moment he did not even know whether he, like the poor child, had soaked his clothes in the futility and brightness of that emission that was now, finally, at an end.

He could not move. His eyes were closed. But then—after how long? and how soon before the mother would turn the corner and approach the silent building that housed this room?—then he felt the girl stirring and lifting her head from his lap. But she continued to move, not climbing indifferently to her feet, as he expected, but moving forward, keeping her body close to his own,

40

until suddenly he felt her two hands pressed gently to the sides of his head, turning it, straightening it, and felt her mouth pressed against his own in the kind of protracted youthful kiss he could not have expected and had never known. Then as she continued kissing him with lips, tongue, jaw, slowly into his exhaustion, his joy, his mortification, there came the realization that now the girl was returning to him the gift, the taste, of his own seminal secretions, his own psychic slime.

When he finally reached the doorway, adjusting his clothes, attempting to stand at ease, he could think of nothing except that the discoloration between the girl's buttocks had reminded him shockingly of a blown rose, and that the girl had in fact removed his spectacles and hidden them safely in the right-hand pocket of his black coat, where he now found them.

In the doorway and clothed again in pants and shirt, the girl spoke to him at last:

"I've never done it before with an older man," she said, as his age and station came thundering down upon him once again. "But this is just the beginning. I promise you, just the beginning."

In the dark street there was no sign of the returning woman, the deceived mother, as rapidly and with set face he turned his back on the scene of his awakening, his degrading, at the hands of a dissolute child, and walked away into the night. The streets were empty yet everywhere he heard the sound of clattering sandals.

He knew exactly where he was going, and he walked on as swiftly as possible until at length he arrived at the Prefecture of Police, where, blinding himself to raised eyebrows or faint leering expressions or the disrespect of open tunic collars and kepis tilted backward on heads of thick greasy hair, he, Konrad Vost, formally reported his own daughter for prostitution. When he returned to the empty streets he noticed immediately that he no longer heard the cheerful or accusatory sounds of the sandals.

In the late night, sitting beside his radio in the glow of a single bulb, he heard the first interruption of normal broadcasting and learned that the inmates of the women's prison of La Violaine were in revolt. With these words firmly lodged in his head, he sat bolt upright on the wooden chair, put both hands on his knees, and in this position waited out the otherwise uneventful night. Even then, in the drabbest and cruelest of those night hours, he had only the first and faintest intimations that his life had collapsed into chronology, that private axis had coincided with public axis, and that the disordering of his small world had in fact begun. But so it had.

Oh, my dearest, Claire used to say, you must avoid despondency. If nature yields to intelligence, as you insist it does, if the natural world is understandable so that in the loneliest of trees we are able to see its remarkable plan or in the bloom of the flower to discover its origin, then why, my dearest, is human consciousness the terrifying thing you claim it is? The chaos of nature is only a deception; nature is not at all chaotic, as you yourself have explained to me. But consciousness does not lend itself, apparently, to inclusion in the schemes of ocean, sky, mountains, the little animals. Poor Konrad, you cannot understand how you achieved consciousness, and you are always detesting the enigma, refusing to believe it, assigning it a place far off the edge of the astrological charts, finding in it only the source of your despondency which makes me so unhappy, my dearest. But you, my poor Konrad, are the cause of your own discontent. Human consciousness is only the odd flower in the unbounded field. It exists in the natural world and as such is natural, whether it is enigmatical or not. If logic fails then reason is required. So, my dearest Konrad, no despondency. Please.

But why could he not believe her then? Why was he not able

to believe her now? If he cared to suffer his inner torment, and if he was willing to deny Claire dead or alive, the answer was simple.

The first premise of his theory of the psychological function, that which preceded even the initial evaluation of the inner life of the man, could be simply stated: that in the storehouse of memory everything is retained. All perception, all psychic life, everything remembered, everything dreamt, everything thought, all the products and all the residue whatsoever of the psychological system are retained, down to the last drop, the last invisible hair, within the storehouse of memory. Nothing is lost, nothing discarded. Every image, sensation, concept, has its own invisible track. There is a track for everything, for the flames that flicker into sight or remain in darkness, for everything the psychic life reveals and all that it hides. And this multitude of tracks is not only without limit, crossing and recrossing through the tunnels, through the marshes, but is ever increasing, lengthening, multiplying, silvery minuscule track upon track, giving rise to the paradox that within the fixed and unchanging shape of the storehouse itself, its content, nonetheless, is forever swelling.

There was not a day when the truth of his theory did not once, more than once, consume him in momentary awareness. At such moments amazement came into his life like a blade into his body. At such moments he, a mere clerk in a dismal pharmacy, was filled with dread.

In a corner of the room, in a large square of sand contained by a wooden border, stood the large white glistening ceramic stove, a fearful beautiful monster as tall as himself, the only child, with

43

its thick white candylike surface decorated with little flowers and in its middle bellying outward in the shape of a great white egg. When cold it was something he could secretly approach and touch with his hands, his face. When hot it became the dangerous pink color of scalded flesh. In front of this stove his mother gave singing lessons to the village children; in front of it his father waited patiently in a wooden chair; in front of it he himself sat alone and holding on his lap his silent horn. Slowly the white stove would begin its discoloration, sending out through its iron chimney the smoke that smelled like burning leaves, burning trees, on the night air that was waiting to be filled with snow.

Now, if he could, he would destroy that stove with a hammer.

All night long he waited, sitting fiercely upright with his hands on his spread knees and his back straight, the mask of his face shrinking, tightening, becoming increasingly painful on the bone that gave it shape, sitting throughout those hours in bitter loyalty to the crisis that had announced itself through the dusty mouth of the radio at his elbow, and during this time, when in his mind he again heard the sound of shots and the sound of distant shouting, he did not once lose sight of himself as the warm waxen figure of the seated man awaiting his fate. He was refusing himself explicit knowledge of the disordering of his life; he admitted the journey but had yet to recognize its object or that it was taking him in fact from woman to woman in a disarrangement that would finally effect his change. He saw himself only as a representation of the seated man grimacing in the face of unseen events, or only as a large rubber puppet dressed in black, a figure that could exist without bread, sleep or water and yet possessing, in its rubber face, two eyes that were alert and living. In his exhaustion and in the darkness, beyond the glow of the bulb, he thought for a mo-

44

ment of the small golden heart dangling in all its innocence from the cheap chain. But why had he failed to demand the name of its wearer? Surely he should have denounced two persons instead of one.

When the light of day inside the room was about to fade and was thus most intense, revealing at its clearest the path of the spider across her field of white concrete, magnifying as if under glass the orange plastic webbing of the sack containing a handful of dried potatoes hung from the wall, it was then that the radio broke off into silence, remained silent, and just as abruptly throbbed again to the vibrations of an official voice: conditions in the prison of La Violaine had worsened; the revolting inmates were beyond the control of the authorities; the call for volunteers to aid in the suppression of the revolt at La Violaine was being issued; the need for volunteers was urgent. He listened, he heard the dead insects on the strips of paper, he had no further need for the radio and turned it off. The body of the rubber puppet would soon be as alive as its eyes.

The wall, the protective wire, the gate. The dark and empty school. In the sandy enclosure the civilian volunteers standing together, the half-dozen blue vans waiting with rear doors ajar or swinging wide, a small group of men in uniform, and, massed at the gate, a crowd of curious or angry spectators. But no dogs? He noted the absence of the trained ferocious dogs, he wondered if the nameless girl was hidden somewhere in the crowd, in another moment he had shouldered his way through the crowd and had joined the eighty or ninety men who, ill at ease, clearly separate from those in uniforms and those at the gate, and standing closely together, having no idea of what to do or what was expected of them, readily identified themselves as the volunteers. He joined them, he gave his name, he noticed the clear bright splinters of a bottle broken and gleaming in the sand. They milled tightly together, this group of men who disregarded the shouts of the crowd and whose ranks included several physicians, an engineer, a large assortment of those men who operated shops and stores, a reassuring number of men who worked with their hands and who had come directly to the schoolyard from ditches, cesspools, building sites. Again he gave his name and again he looked at his fellow volunteers, recognizing, warily, that this band of anonymous husbands, fathers, bachelors, included three of the habitués of La Violaine: Spapa, Roterman and himself. But no word passed between them, no gesture of recognition, and each of these three was careful to stand well away from the other two.

The unexpected sound of the engines of the six blue vans, the arming of the volunteers, the assignment to vans, the departure from the makeshift staging area of the schoolyard: it was all accomplished swiftly, with much more ease than he had expected, and accomplished in the last cold orange light of the day. But tall, rigid, cold, uncomfortably aware of the bodies of others, in this situation and from the instant he first heard the radio proclaiming his fate, at no time had he thought of himself as being armed, as holding in his hands some weapon to be employed against the women of La Violaine. The sudden jostling, the confusion of feet, the shouts of the men in uniform, who made it clear that they, the volunteers, were now lining up so that they would not be forced to subdue a horde of rebellious prison inmates with empty hands: it was at this moment that he, faltering for the first time, found his mouth filled with the wetness of yellow bile.

But sticks? Mere sticks? Brutal primitive sticks? Was it possible? He was moving forward through the line, shuffling, turning to complain against the truckdriver who stood directly behind him and never once ceased his pushing, and it was indeed clear that one by one each man at the head of the line was having thrust into his hands a stick, a long stick seized from a pile, and was then being shoved in the direction of one of the vans. But then he himself was standing there at the head of the line and, from the tall gray-haired man in faultless uniform, was receiving into his own two hands the cold unfamiliar stick. It was as if he had never before held in his hands a simple stick; he did not know how to hold it, how to carry it, this object that was merely a piece of wood dark in color, a meter in length, square in cross section instead of round, and tapering somewhat from one end to the other. Yet holding it awkwardly in both hands, he knew that without question this thin length of wood was as hard and unbreakable as a rod of steel.

All around him men who had never in their lives inflicted injury were beginning to perspire in the sudden realization of what they were now taking upon themselves, or were beginning already to tighten their muscles in anticipation of the strong and ugly blows they would soon strike. But under this startling orange sky and in this now darkly shadowed sandy enclosure, there was not a man, whether reticent or eager, who was not fully or partially aware of the fact that the blows he was about to strike would fall on the flesh and bones of a woman. It was this fact alone that produced in each one of them such guilt or such eagerness to be under way. The engines were turning over, the air was filled with the presently faint and harmless clattering of the sticks. Someone laughed, blue lights began to flash on the roofs of the vans.

But just as his foot touched the metal step, just as his free hand took hold of the open door, just as he was on the verge of climbing inside the van, it was then that he was arrested by the shouted sound of his name. He paused, he looked over his shoulder. For a moment the face of Gagnon emerged from the angry or jeering faces of the crowd.

"Konrad!" he shouted. "Konrad, don't go!"

But he was helpless and could only turn, stoop, and enter the van. Once seated on the bench that ran the length of the vehicle, he adjusted his spectacles, gripped the stick between his knees, tried to obliterate from his mind the image of Gagnon and to avoid the eyes of the man directly across from him who, he noted, was clearly afraid. As for himself, he was pleased to discover that his own anxiety had quite disappeared and that now he was aware only of the smell of long-dried vomit that filled the van, and of the hardness of the bench, and of the cobwebbed metal grilles that covered the small windows in the two rear doors, and of the irony that vans used ordinarily to transport women to La Violaine were now employed to carry free men to the women's prison.

By the time the convoy of six vehicles drove out of the gates and into the city streets, the terrible two-toned horn of each was sounding its alarm in insistent accompaniment to the whirling of the cadaverous blue lights already in motion. There was little to see; the speed of each vehicle was registered in the soles of the shoes of each passenger like an electric current entering the feet of a deranged man on a dark and empty avenue; among those crowded around him inside the van there already existed those several men who would not emerge unhurt from the prison. Who was to say that even he might not become one of the casualties of La Violaine? Perhaps he himself would be carried back by the arms and legs to the refuge of this same official vehicle from which, in a moment, he, like the rest of them, would disembark. Yet he was not afraid. His moment of anxiety had already passed. Now his serenity was a matter of whatever dispassionate strength he would be able to summon. He was prepared to accept the worst of bodily pain.

Someone coughed; someone lit and immediately extinguished a cigarette; sinister lights and ugly horns proclaimed the danger and urgency of this expedition.

Minutes later, in the twenty-fourth hour following his submission to the naked schoolgirl, Konrad Vost alighted from the last of the blue vans to enter the main gates of La Violaine. The vans were parked side by side with their open rear doors facing the gates and, beyond, the street, from which the traffic had been diverted. Through the high rusted bars and iron mesh he could see the crowd that had slowed the entry of the convoy into the prison. Across the street the steel shutter of the café was down; inside the prison yard, where he stood now like the rest of them, with his stick held in both hands and raised as high as his chest, suddenly the horns fell silent while the blue lights continued grimly to revolve and flash. For each van there was a driver and one additional member of the official force: these men now drew their automatic pistols. Behind them, on the street side of the gates, the small cadre of uniformed men guarding the gates also held in their hands black automatic pistols ready to fire; similar groups were posted at the other and less important entrances to La Violaine. Thus the inmates, deterred by shots in the air, had been so far unable to escape from the prison, within which, however, they were still roaming destructively at will. If they were not soon subdued, clearly they would accept a few deaths in their midst in order to gain the street or lesser alleyways surrounding the prison.

Now the civilian men were massed at the innermost edge of the central prison yard and Konrad Vost was aware of their concentric order: the street, the gates, the vehicles ranked side by side like a barrier, the dozen men holding drawn pistols, and finally the volunteers themselves who, sealed inside the prison and with the armed guards at their backs, alone faced the field of sand around which, in normal times, it was intended that the women walk for the sake of exercise. Now smoking remains of fires littered the sand; in the center an archaic flower bed had been trampled so that it resembled a palette of smeared and lifeless colors. An iron bedstead had been pushed from an upper-story window, through bars battered aside, and stood upended against a mustard-colored wall; from another window a dark blue kepi, no doubt snatched from the head of an injured guard, hung like a flag from the tip

49

of a broom handle thrust between the bars. A toilet bowl, torn from its fixtures and dragged into the yard, lay on its side near the trampled flowers; fragments of green roof tiles glittered here and there in the sand. Shouts, screams, sounds of female laughter, filled all this desolate area from far and near as did the hard silvery light from which the last traces of the fiery sunset had disappeared. A face stared momentarily from a smashed window; smoke rose from one of the stone and plaster buildings that were so arranged as to form between them narrow dark entrances to the prison yard through any one of which and at any moment the women of La Violaine might charge.

Would it be necessary to pursue fleeing women into those ravished buildings? Would inmates and volunteers grapple with each other in dark rooms where ordinarily and under lock and key these same women slept during their endless and unnatural nights? In the midst of his fellows and standing inside the walls of La Violaine at last, suddenly he began to feel that he recognized the yard, the buildings, the catacombs and labyrinths of this world of women, as if he too were a prisoner in this very place and had always been so. Carefully and with one hand he removed his spectacles, placing them, as had the girl, in the right-hand pocket of his black coat. Still he could see with perfect clarity the distant inclined ramp in its tunnel of barbed wire through which the women daily marched at the sound of a single shouted command, and with the same clarity could see the distinguishing details of the men around him: a leather jacket, a red neckerchief knotted about someone's throat, blond hair stirred by the breeze.

From one moment to the next the cold silvery light remained unchanged, fixed in an intensity characteristic only of dead light. Again he thought that he recognized the prison and that he would never leave the space that was guarded or pass through the way that was barred. He would remain or he would be brought back endlessly. He began to see the interior of the nearest building:

50

above a narrow bed was tacked a crude childish picture depicting in thick colors of black and orange a horse waiting beside a moonlit pool. In a tiled corner stood a porcelain sink bearing green stains and long disconnected from any supply of water. It was familiar, all of it, and he had been waiting months, years, to enter into this forbidden place where he too belonged. It was his mother's prison, after all, and here he would find her.

Shots rang out. The guards were turning back the women at one of the lesser entrances. Beside him a man wiped his face on his sleeve. The faint wind smelled of burning rubber. A puff of smoke rose from the small black orifice of a doorway that had been beaten open with the top of a scarred table. From the distance came a crash of metal against metal, a long thin delirious cry of joy or pain.

"Look," somebody shouted, "a woman!"

She was directly opposite the mass of men, a lone woman not a hundred meters away and carrying a torch and wearing, over the gray prison dress, a tunic which clearly a band of them had stripped from one of the guards: the same, perhaps, whose kepi dangled from the tip of the pole thrust out of the window above the woman's head. The torch hung from her hand, the hair was loose, the dark blue tunic with its red chevrons and silver insignia was much too large for the figure it draped. He watched her, feeling the weight of the stick in his grip, aware of himself as utterly motionless yet touched by the breeze, and it was then that his reverie of a few moments before gave way to instinct and practicality so that he found himself wanting nothing more than to beat the woman first to surrender and then to unconsciousness. He was not given to physical exertion, the bones in his hands and long thin feet were delicate, his weight was abnormally slight for his size, his age a weakness. Yet he was determined that he himself would administer the blows that would fell this woman who had become victorious in a man's clothing.

51

"Ready!" cried the same voice from somewhere to his left. "Ready! Here they come!"

The woman wearing the dark blue tunic disappeared in a swarm of women. The single emblematic woman became a mob. In an instant the entire area on the other side of the flower bed was filled with jostling women who, laughing and shouting, entered the prison yard in aimless haste and then stopped short, packing themselves abruptly together, at the sight of the silent and waiting men and the vans, the guards, the revolving lights. The dead laughter was still passing from woman to woman; arms rose above the heads of the crowd; in the cessation of random exhilaration, they held each other about the shoulders, about the waists, while a few weapons—knives, the leg of a chair, a pistol from which all the shots had been fired—were brandished and forgotten in a tableau of astonishment and suspended fury. Several of the women wore kepis cocked on their heads, so that clearly they had overpowered more than one guard. Someone was carrying by its neck a chicken from which exactly half of the feathers had been plucked; another was silently waving an empty hand back and forth toward the waiting men. Had it not been for the revolving lights, the inmates, in that instant, might have mistaken the purpose of this sudden assemblage of ordinary men in the yard of a prison that had already fallen to a mutiny of women. But there was no mistaking the message of the blue lights, and in the next moment the women began to shout, to jeer, to cry out in anger or derision. Throughout the day they had had nothing to attack but the prison that was only an extension of themselves, like insects devouring their own glossy feelers and antennae in their hunger. But now the enemy was in their midst and they were doubly betrayed since they were not only opposed, as they were, but opposed by the very men who might have come to their aid.

The shouting increased. A shard of roof tile came through the air. The crowd of women undulated in rage, contempt, indecision.

In another moment they would break into a run and fling themselves, young and old, upon their betrayers.

But the men, rather than the women, were the first to move, stumbling, shoving, gaining speed, so at the outset initiative and momentum belonged not to the inmates but to the volunteers who, despite inferior numbers, were confident in their purpose, in their masculinity, in the power of the sticks that they held aloft and shook as they charged. Workers, shop owners, professional men, together they were sweeping forward into the violation that had been sanctioned and the conflict they could not lose. Foremost among them, holding his position in the ragged front line, Vost was himself carried along by the moment's unspoken elation, running and shaking his stick like the rest of them.

He stumbled. He regained his footing. All around him men were calling out words of encouragement. His mouth was dry, he was baring his teeth. The red neckerchief flashed somewhere to his left, to his right the young man in the leather jacket was smiling a radiant smile, despite his exertion, and had tears in his eyes. But now he saw that instead of dispersing, as they might have, the women too were charging, running directly toward the onrushing men, running heedlessly into the path of the men when they might have fled. Even in midstride he found the spontaneous action of the women puzzling, self-defeating. He found himself thinking that these rapidly approaching women, whose screams could only be heard as the high-pitched piping of irrationality, as lyrical cry transformed to screech, were flinging themselves into conflict without protection, unadorned, wearing no individualizing rings or lockets, carrying no papers of identification, risking their persons in utter nakedness, except for the gray dresses and the stolen kepis and the massive blue tunic worn by the torch-bearing woman, who now loomed before him, suddenly, like a monster from some doomed horde of renegade foot soldiers.

They clashed. The half-plucked chicken came hurtling over

their heads and into their midst. Men and women were crushed together, standing or falling, forearm jammed into open mouth, legs tangling, a small head buried in the immensity of a broad chest. But he was still on his feet and for his entire length was locked against the body of the woman in the blue tunic. She struggled to escape the weight of him; the torch, which she had dropped, lay at their feet and sent up its thick smoke as if he and the woman had been bound together and set afire; his stick was wedged horizontally between the two of them and was cutting into his own flesh and hers. He too was attempting to move an arm, a leg, to thrust himself away from the woman, to gain leverage. He did not know whether the fingers clawing slowly at his ribs, as if to work their way to the bloody place of his heart, belonged to the woman or to an old white-haired man who was pressed to both himself and the woman and whose face, elongated like that of a horse, was blindly rubbing his own.

Then he heard but was unable to locate the voice that continued to speak its simple childish declaration throughout the time between the first blow he struck and the last. "Ah no," came the words clearly, without emphasis, without variation, spoken in a high soft voice that might have belonged to a female child but was in fact a young woman's. "Ah no, ah no," she said in the voice of someone who wishes to express her pain without imparting it to her listener, or who loves her antagonist as strongly as she suffers the pain he inflicts. "Ah no, ah no, ah no," came the appeal in the voice that could not have belonged to boy or man, as at last he was able to free himself from both the woman and the old man and stepped back, raised his arms, and prepared to drive the stick into the face of the disbelieving woman.

He felt the abrasive sand through the thin soles of his shoes. His feet were spread, the stick was high above his right shoulder, against his will he perceived the numerous components of a vast incongruity: a distant hanging shutter partially aflame, an old woman staring down into the prison yard from between the bars of an open window where she rested with her elbows on the sill and her chin on her clasped hands, streaks of soot climbing a wall, the shouting and noise through which the voice of the young invisible victim was all the easier to hear, the unchanging silvery light that magnified the combatants, men and women alike, where in small groups they were now assaulting each other, exchanging wounds. And now, looking into the eyes of the woman in the blue tunic, he knew that to her his face was as unnaturally strained and gray as that of the old man who was already lying prostrate in the sand.

He swung his arms with all the strength he could manage and brought the stick crashing against the side of the woman's head. He felt the blow in his arms, palms, fingers; he heard the sharp cracking sound as if he were alone in the empty and silent yard of the prison. The woman fell, she lay at his feet, he waited for blood to form at the temple. He saw nothing but the great lifeless sleeve of the tunic from which emerged an inert wrist and hand composed, it seemed to him, of white china. "Ah no, ah no," the voice was still saying behind him, close to his ear, and for a moment he wished that the rioting all around him would never cease. A woman with short gray hair and heavy arms and legs passed him at a run, and he was in time to give her a glancing blow on the shoulders and to see her brought down, a few paces away, by none other than Roterman with his crooked nose and brow wet with sweat. Beyond Roterman a squat man was belaboring a small fierce woman about the upper body: even after he had struck her head and she was pitching forward, falling, he managed to strike her twice on the upended buttocks.

Again he turned, instinctively, and again braced himself, spread wide his legs, raised high the stick. The woman bearing down upon him was young, as small as a child, and was carrying dagger-like in her fist a long thick splinter of glass. For an instant he could

55

not move, fixed as he was on the sudden beauty of the oval face which was tinted and darkened as by the sun. How could a person of such diminutive and perfect features be an inmate in La Vi-olaine? How could such a face be the vehicle for such intense hatred? But so it was, and stepping aside to avoid her first vicious but inexpert thrust of the glass, he was fortunate enough to strike the wrist of the offending hand so that she dropped the long shard of glass. She staggered a few paces and stood still. With the oppo-site hand she clasped her injured wrist. But now his rhythm was established, he was again rooted in the sand in the position that best afforded him strength, speed and accuracy. He struck this small would-be assailant on her other arm so that she freed her wrist and, in the pain now infecting both useless arms, stood with her face distorted in a scream that was only the faintest quavering tone in the general sound of violent voices and clattering sticks. Then quickly but with no loss of strength he held his breath and swung the stick in a horizontal plane, aiming for the center of the small and rounded hip which was revealed even in the looseness of the prison dress. Again through the medium of the unbreakable length of wood the young woman's pain leapt to his clenched hands; in his hands and arms he could feel the small perfect body losing its form. In the midst of this encounter, as he scuffled and angled himself precisely, and as the childlike woman took random useless steps, cowering and dangling her arms, the dress fell and exposed one shoulder while on the oval face the lips began to glisten with a wetness rising from deep within that miniature anatomy. Then unaccountably, all at once, even as his arms and upper body were reaching the middle of another arc, suddenly there was Spapa behind the woman and swinging his stick into the frail back at exactly the moment that he himself landed his own stick with full force against the belly. Together they chopped away at her, he and Spapa, like two boys beating to death a bird or like two wooden figures striking a bell. What sense could he make of

56

the fact that he and Spapa, whom he had always disdained, no longer avoided each other's eyes and, without meaning to do so, achieved a curious unison in their paired assault, so that like the wooden figures wielding their mallets high on the clock tower, they struck each other no crippling blows and kept their two sticks from entangling? Yet it was true, he thought, that the ungainly dance of the victim made collaborators of the most unlikely men.

"Ah no, ah no," came the pure voice, and the sound of it only caused him to grimace and fight on all the harder.

But something was wrong. With the passing of time he could not measure, aware of the heads of hair flying like the tails of horses, hearing a new tone in the cries of the men, feeling in his throat the constriction of all the shouts he had kept to himself, seeing that his sleeve was torn, aware of a stiffening in all the joints of his body, finding himself without breath, feeling through the sole of one shoe the head of a fallen flower which he had ground to a yellow paste: in all this he knew, suddenly, and beyond a doubt, that something was wrong. Were those men, rather than women, who were now weeping like children? Could that be Roterman staggering in circles with his hands to his face? And Spapa? Spapa kneeling over his palms cupped into a bowl for his vomit? And one of the white-haired men wandering out of the smoke with blood in his eyes? As for himself, why did he not know which way to turn? Why were his hands empty? What had become of the stick he had used to such advantage and without which he could not possibly defend himself against any attacker armed with burning torch or piece of jagged glass? But then from behind him there came a fusillade of pistol shots, the urgent popping sounds of the guards firing their pistols into a crowd. With the sounds of the shots he knew immediately what was wrong: that there had been a reversal, that the women had overcome the men, that the rebellious women of La Violaine had routed the invading men.

When the tall handsome woman drifted in his direction, smiling and holding aloft a rusted hatchet, and when the woman embraced him, or so he thought, and he began falling into the hands of darkness, he was able to think only that he had not caught even a single glimpse of his mother in La Violaine.

He was in the hands of darkness. He was lying face down on his bed of stars. But it was not the darkness of night, which is always brimming with the implicit light of the impending day, but rather the eternal darkness of that interior world into which no light can shine and whose nomenclature can be found only in the formulations of the psychological function. Here the star is a matter of neither light nor time. Here the spectator is never allowed to forget that the illumination occasionally and slowly gathering, like a fog on a marsh, and in itself becoming the "daylight" necessary to the experience of the interior world, is not in fact the light of day or the light of dawn, but is only a reflection of that light-in-time by which a certain day once existed, or will in the future exist, or now exists but as imaginary without a genesis in either the past or the future. By the "light" that appears in the eternal darkness, the spectator has the sensation that for him actual light, natural light, light-in-time has been extinguished. No day will come. Now he himself is only a figment of his own psychological function within the only domain that is eternally dark, even when "lighted," and eternally insubstantial despite the sights and sounds with which it is either suddenly filled or emptied. It is here, when he has all but lost it, that the spectator knows the dread of consciousness.

He was seated on the velvet-covered seat of a train that was traveling at the pace of a walking man. Cinders were beating against the glass of the windows, the coach rocked back and forth on its ancient trucks, from below came the terrible sound of the wheels grinding against the rusted tracks, from the invisible engine a long dark arm of smoke was slanting across the marsh like the low flight of a goose. Yet if he had lowered the window he could have reached down and taken hold of the upraised hand of a man who might have been walking beside the train.

The compartment where he sat was cold. He smelled the cinders and the furious smudge of the smoke lying back across the marsh. The sternness of his posture was his only defense against the incongruity of the train's motion and its slow pace. He carried no luggage, he was not dressed for travel, he knew that he was alone on the train though he had no recollection of boarding it and had not walked the length of its coaches searching the empty compartments. Yet he was also convinced that one of the empty compartments contained the smell of a freshly smoked cigar.

Through the window at his left shoulder, and through the glass panel in the door to his right and the window beyond, he could see that the marsh stretched to the horizon on either side of the train in a flat expanse of water, thin ice, sea grasses, a vast field for the wind, a landscape waiting, he realized, for approaching snow, and in its texture exactly appropriate to falling snow. He had only to glance directly downward to understand the complexity of the dead marsh, composed as it was of salt, patches of ice, rivulets of black water, masses of sharp flowerless grass in which no creature nested, bits of wood that may once have belonged to fences or the prows of shallow boats. He had only to raise his eyes to suffer again the extremity of the marsh, its coldness, its yellow light that had no source and beyond which lay the eternal darkness through which he was in fact traveling. Jolted by the motion of the crawling train, rigid, clasping his knees together and his hands in his lap, constantly he reminded himself that the fearful noise apparently coming from everywhere in the marsh was actually the noise of the train in the agony and arrogance of its funereal pace.

59

The snow crystal, the marsh, the cold and antiquated train: they were all the same, each was a version of the other, together they composed the darkness that was himself.

In the seams of the black serge suit the threads were loosening. The cloth of the trousers drawn tightly on his knees was wearing thin and had the appearance of being polished. There were patches of frost on the walls of his compartment along with intricate designs of cobwebs filling the corners and holding in place the overhead light fixture that contained no bulb. The glass in the windows was rattling; outside, the slowly passing marsh was etched in mercurial poison while the cinders now raining against the windows were still livid with the glow of the tiny flames they had sustained. He had never been so stiff, never had he so ached in his joints.

Slowly, bracing himself against the lurching of the ancient train, slowly he rose to his feet, opened the compartment door and stepped out into the empty narrow corridor with its brass handrail and large partially frosted windows. Tall, angular, cold, staggering now and then and clutching the rail, slowly he made his way toward the rear of the train. With every few steps he found the view from the windows on his left suddenly obliterated by the fuming black smoke; he could not prevent himself from glancing into the empty compartments on his right, feeling, with each glance, a brief sensation of guilt as if he were peering at the most exposed of intimacies, when in fact there was nothing to see except the velvet of the facing seats, the frost, the cobwebs like threads of ice, the emptiness that had been left behind, deliberately it seemed, by all those who had ridden this train before him. Then he felt prompted to try the door handle of the next compartment: it was locked. Then another: it too was locked.

With difficulty he passed into the next coach. He braced himself against brass and wood. All about him was the sound of rattling, the smoke and cinders were becoming ingrained in the marsh. The darkness that lay beyond the yellow light was filling his head, his eyes, his nostrils, the long narrow corridor of this empty coach. He knew that he was traveling inside himself. But then he stopped, adjusted his spectacles, listened to his own shallow breath and the clanking of iron and, following a sudden premonition, refrained from looking into the compartment he was now approaching. There was something inside that compartment that he was meant to see, but in a moment, he told himself, in a moment. He kept his back to the glass in the waiting door instead of facing it, and took great pains to lean down, with both hands on the vibrating rail, and to gaze again across the marsh, where now the snow was beginning to fall. He waited. Faintly, from behind him, came the smell of a freshly smoked cigar. Then, still unsure of his footing, carefully he turned, took the simple awkward step across the corridor and, bracing himself with both hands spread wide on either side of the door, looked directly through the glass, from which dark velvet curtains were tied back on the inside, and into the compartment. He stared, as he knew he must, and felt, despite all the evidence of the slow labored passage of the train, that he was standing still and would never move again. There, on the other side of the glass and resting head and foot on the facing seats, suspended in a sense between the seats, was a coffin which he could not help but recognize immediately. It was made of metal, perhaps silver, and was smooth and unadorned except for the handles and the impression of flower blossoms embossed in the heavy silver metal around the entire perimeter of the coffin where the top was sealed to the bottom. He stared, he smelled the faint smoke, he pressed his face to the glass and stared at the silver coffin which he had seen once before, as a child, but which was now resting head and foot on the edges of the velvet seats and rocking between them. He watched, he pushed his face into the glass, he remembered with a painful childish thrill those same black han-

61

dles and the blossoms that were only shadows in metal. Even now he might have been looking through the glass side of the hearse. But now, in this train that was like a mausoleum laboring along its endless rusted tracks, now he knew, as he had not in the past, that the darkness filling the body inside the coffin was also filling himself. In another moment he would begin to live all the life it contained.

Slowly, keeping his face to the glass, slowly he lowered his right hand to the door handle and waited, filling his eyes with the sight of the flowers, then exerted pressure on the brass handle. But the door was locked, like the rest of them. There was nothing to do but make his way back to the cold compartment that was his own.

In the village he had been known as the little trumpeter of the silver hands.

He could not move. He was bound hand and foot by lengths of stiff rope and bound also about the chest and lower legs to the frame of the massive straight-backed wooden chair on which he was seated as for some form of execution. The black serge of his suit was bunching under the tightness of the ropes, his hands were not free to adjust his spectacles, which were crooked and slipping on the bridge of his nose. He was hooded. But the hood covered not merely his head, which would have been a severe enough indignity. No, it was an enormous hood of burlap covering head, body, and even the massive chair as well, so that he was entirely and helplessly concealed where he was positioned in the center of the vast stone floor, as if the others in the room could not bear the sight of any part of him, or could not bear to look at a man who deserved to be so roped to the chair of the penitent. However, there were slits for the eyes and against these slits he attempted to press the unruly spectacles so that by looking straight ahead and upward he was able to see both judge and accuser, who were seated side by side on a dais, the judge somewhat higher than the young woman who was now making her formal testimony against him. Inside the enormous hood, whose skirts were crudely draped about him on the stone floor, covering even his pointed shoes, there was nothing but darkness and a stifling atmosphere in which he could not breathe. With concentration he could see the judge, whose heavy face had been wiped clear of features like a slab of white wax caressed by the heated iron, and also the young woman, who was as small as a child yet clothed in a tight gown of a sparkling mauve material which, more than nudity, exposed the diminutive anatomy that could belong only to an adult woman. She was smiling, she was seated with her small perfectly formed bare legs crossed at the knee, she carried her head cocked slightly to one side in an habitual expression of charm and attentiveness. The judge and young woman alike were looking down at himself, the accused, though he knew they were staring only at a large ominous sackcloth mound bearing two slits in which glittered fitfully the spectacles of a man deemed unworthy to be seen. They could know nothing of the humiliation that was prickling his skin or the perspiration in which he was already steaming. For a moment he imagined that to the judge and woman he must have the appearance of an ancient horse and warrior so draped and concealed in a single sheet of armorial cloth as to look not like man and horse but like some loathsome tented monster condemned to death by fire.

The vast chamber in which judge, accuser and accused were arranged as in an inverted triangle was empty except for the three of them. The cells of the condemned were in proximity to the chamber of judgment and filled it faintly with their characteristic odors of lye and urine. From his stifling vantage point his view was restricted to the judge and young woman, whom he had not seen before, and yet he was as aware of the labyrinthine architecture surrounding him as if he himself had invented it. Water was trickling in a stone conduit along one wall of the vaulted room, the young woman was sitting with her right leg crossed over the left so that the right calf was pressed firmly to the left and the right foot was pointed toe downward beside the left. In this rigid position, in which modesty became an explicit form of prohibition, she was nonetheless working her small right leg up and down against its mirror image.

". . . Oh, I can tell about this man," she was saying, addressing herself to the judge but all the while looking directly at the person, himself, concealed within the enormous ugly mound at her feet. ". . . Oh, I can tell about this man easily, without any trouble at all," she was saying, confident of the judge's attention and even his belief, while staring at himself, at the flashing lenses of his spectacles in their narrow slits, and working the superior right leg tightly against the inferior left. "This man," she was saying, "is a man who does not know the woman. . . ."

He could see her only through a slight film over his eyes, through the perspiration that was dimming his sight, and yet in all his discomfort and humiliation his attention was fixed on the young woman with an intensity approaching rapture. The woman herself was smiling, cocking her head, gesturing with one shoulder toward the judge, while enjoying the pleasure and prohibition of the top leg rubbing against the bottom. Her voice was light, cheerful, animated, deliberately filled with the music of casual speech, which she knew only too well would most please the judge and most incense him against the accused. Yet he too, the penitent dripping inside his hood, was also thrilling to that voice.

". . . Oh yes," she was saying, "the man who does not know the woman. It is quite true. He is nice enough, this gentleman, and he is tall, he has a certain attractiveness in the face. It is no wonder that the poor woman invites the attentions of this sort of man, only to suffer when nothing comes of it. Yes, yes, that is true enough. But of course he is a rarity, this man. He is quite unlike his brothers who already know the woman and whose attentions give what they promise, or even more. What else would we think? But what did he do, this man? He commented on my size! My small size! Exactly! He said that the smaller the woman, the greater the capacity of her organs of love. . . . He did! He used those words, he spoke to me in just that way! He dared to admire me for my small body but could not lay a hand on me. What could he know? Many men larger and stronger than he have begged me to remove my clothes, or inspired me to remove my clothes, and have held me happily against their nakedness. What else would we think? But not one of them ever talked about my body. How did he dare discuss such a subject? . . . But I have other things to say about this man. . . ."

Still she was smiling. Still she was cocking her head like a lively bird on a branch. Still she was speaking in her light cheerful voice to the attentive judge while continuing to look into the dimmed appreciative eyes of the penitent she so enjoyed condemning. But now she was straightening her spine and squaring her shoulders in a graceful but determined expression of her injured pride. Yet now she had also placed her hands on the roundness of the hips and with her hands appeared to be inducing in her hips a faint circular motion complementary to the vertical motion of the top leg on the lower. As for himself, the smothered penitent, now he knew precisely what he should not have been able to know about this person who was to him a stranger: that her hair smelled of lemon soap and that her hands smelled of onions; that the skin of her body was as hard and smooth as skin that has been severely burned; that all the agreeableness of her mannerisms concealed a petulance even more desirable than the legs, the hips, the musical voice; and finally that what she accused him of saying was exactly true. But now, against his will, in the darkness of a condition that could not have been more contrary to that of erotic excitation, now he was overcome with the knowledge that in his locked and inaccessible loins the army of mice was beginning to run through the forest that was filled with snow. It was impossible and yet it was happening, and there was no way he could prevent the charging and spreading of that army of little feet.

". . . There were those who thought this man might be my boy friend," she was saying, while twisting her hips appreciatively in her two hands, "but he was not my boy friend. With him I was not aroused. Who does not know that it is the boy friend who must arouse the woman? Everyone knows that that is the responsibility. But not this man. With him I was not aroused and so I was insulted. Of course I was. This man did not even use his lips for kissing. He told me my mouth was a little golden wasp, but he felt no responsibility for kissing. Such language! With words like that a person can only drink her wine and sulk to herself. What else? But this man did nothing. He did not take the lobe of my ear in his big fingers or breathe on my neck or smoke a nice cigarette like other men. He did not offer to brush my hair, he did not lift me off my feet in his arms, he did not take me to the chair and sit me on his lap in the way that most of my boy friends seated me on their laps with my skirt above my knees and their beautiful big fingers inside my pants. That's a good position, on the lap. It makes me feel even smaller than I am. But there was nothing from this man. Nothing. He did not give me a bruise or make me take his thumb into my mouth, or touch him on the trousers like my other boy friends. Oh no, with him I was perfectly calm: no laughing, no wiggling, no big surprises. He did not even try to force me to allow him to put the tip of his finger against my forbidden place, like some of my boy friends. But I would have slapped away his hand if he had! But he said he knew all about my forbidden place anyway. He said it looked like the nostril of a dead bird. A pretty thing to say to a woman! But in that place, which only a few of my boy friends ever found, I was not at all as dry as he thought. . . ."

His eyes were closed. For some time he had seen nothing of the smile, the cocked head, the hips, the legs. For some time his eyes had been closed so that he had seen not the woman on the dais but that same woman who, lying across his lap, had borne an enormous blue starlike bruise on her haunch. Now he heard nothing and saw nothing. Now he was exerting himself only to disguise the shallow pumping of his lungs and to forget the shameful wetness left behind in the white forest by the fleeing mice.

Thus the stationary traveler was moving slowly and in total darkness down the road within.

SKIRMISHING

He awoke to the knowledge of a constellation of thoughts and perceptions so arranged in his mind as to conceal the most important fact of all. He was aware of the self-deception yet conscious only of the bright elements of the constellation: that he was in the hospital, that it was dawn of the second full day following the birth of the revolt at La Violaine, that outside in the purest morning air the gigantic red cross on the roof of the hospital was only the faint pink color of blood washed in rain. He was lying on a narrow hospital bed in the gray light filling a long corridor; he was fully clothed; on a chair at his side was sitting a small woman wearing a gray dress, a white apron that shielded the entire front of the body, and a white hat resembling the spread wings of a great bird in flight. He knew that as soon as he turned his head in her direction she would rise, close her book of prayer, and abandon her vigil.

He was awake at dawn in the hospital and knew that only the intervention of a short obliterated night now stood between his present consciousness and the abrupt cessation he had experienced at the very edge of darkness in La Violaine. He could not determine the source of morning light, yet it was all around him in clear fresh streaks of illumination; his bed linen was as stiff and wrinkled as his clothing. All around him the sounds of dawn had the intensity of the noise in an iron foundry, as he lay listening to the trickle of water against enamel, the breath catching in the throat of an awakening man, the distant sound of shoes on tile, the tinkling of a knife's edge against a tube of glass. The hospital was filled to more than capacity so that a certain number of the sick and injured, including himself, were accommodated in makeshift beds lining the damp walls of the otherwise empty corridors. Now he was here, awake, in a place oddly suggestive of the railway terminal; and lying on top of the wrinkled bed linen he noted that the light touching the tips of his shoes might have been shining on the feet of a corpse. The observation aroused in him no emotional response, though it was of the same magnitude, he realized, as the grainy face of the handsome hatcheteer, which he could summon at will, or the sound of the turning pages of the prayer book held by the as yet unseen young attendant sitting beside the head of his bed.

He understood that what had occurred in La Violaine was both far and near, and that now, like the stationary traveler, he was listening to the sounds of awakening made by people who could not move.

But what was he hiding? What was so much clarity concealing? What was the one fact now essential for him to know?

He was alive, he was awake, he had fallen in the ranks of the victims of La Violaine as he had thought he might. When he summoned it, the face of the woman who had struck him down was long, white, handsome, benevolent, and framed in a mass of dark reddish hair. Of his hours of darkness he could remember nothing, though the likeness between the hospital and the railway terminal was, he understood, a clue. That he would recover them all, his waking hours and hours of darkness, he also now understood. He would spare himself nothing; he would discover complete illumination in blinding light.

Her hatchet had been thick with rust. He had marveled that so handsome an assailant had employed so primitive a weapon. Her left hand, the hand that had held aloft the wooden shaft of the hatchet, had borne no rings.

For one more moment he defended himself against the fear, the fatigue, the relief that would come with comprehension. In the suspended moment he concentrated on the unnatural aching he felt in all his joints, and on the coldness that had hours before sunk into the depths of his body. Without turning his head he knew, suddenly, that within those past hours the man lying in silence on the bed to the left of his own had been surreptitiously smoking a green cigar. To his right the small woman who he knew was clothed according to the prescription of her order was slowly turning the pages of her book while studying his own rigid features, as she had been doing all the time of her vigil. Someone passed by the foot of his bed; the walls of the corridor were darkened here and there as if they had been charred by fire; again he was thinking of the railway terminal, of a train, of great distances that could not be traveled without the loss of blood.

His left forearm had been carelessly abandoned at an awkward angle across his chest. About the left wrist was tied a paper tag bearing the victim's handwritten name: Konrad Vost. His right arm was concealed from his view along the crumpled side of his body. By raising his head and tilting downward his line of sight he was able to see the left hand, the loose cord about the wrist, the dangling tag, the several smears of dried blood staining the whiteness of the hand that was lying inert on his chest. He waited, then slowly he allowed the back of his head to sink again to the pillow. The effort produced dizziness and certain knowledge: he had undergone a great loss of blood.

With his eyes toward the ceiling, and imbued with a certainty as definite as the pallor of his face or the coldness inside himself which was so painful that it was entirely appropriate to a man in

70

his condition, slowly he concentrated on the concealed right arm and its dependent hand. His task was not merely to lift his head but rather first to elevate the concealed forearm and the hand without feeling. Slowly he contracted the cold muscles, demanded of himself a total disregard of time, forced himself to set in motion the arm and hand as one might operate the mechanism of a rusted motor-driven crane at the edge of the marsh. Slowly the arm began to move, he himself was lifting into sight the unwieldy arm from the end of which there appeared to be suspended a great weight. When the forearm was at last vertical, a condition weakly signaled by a system of nerves long out of use, or so it seemed, he then concentrated on elevating somewhat the upper arm, which responded to his will power, finally, and began to rise from the pivotal aching joint of the shoulder.

He raised his hand. Cold as he was, he began to tingle in the first shock of what he saw: the upraised right hand, in a relaxed open position with the fingers gently curved, was encased in a skintight glove of black leather. He was tingling, he continued to hold upright his hand and arm, he noted the contrast between the strain of the immobility maintained in neck, arm and back muscles, and the serenity of the immobile hand in its black glove. The vigilant woman had stopped turning her pages. Still he looked at the hand that was his own and not his own, at the leather that gleamed as under a black polish, at the symmetry of the hand that had become an object all at once emblematic of terrible loss, mysterious gain. But its weight? Its lack of sensation? Its solidity?

He closed his eyes and waiting, forcing himself to move in time he himself determined, slowly and carefully he lowered his arm until it was again stretched full-length at his side. Then he allowed his head to fall back to the pillow. Still there was only silence. His breathing was easier, he was warmer, against his right thigh he could feel the unmistakable hard touch of the foreign hand. But the essential fact? The secret concealed inside the glove? Suddenly he understood exactly what the glove contained: he was both dismayed and elated to recall the village street, the bare legs of the boys, the scurrying dogs, and to hear again the pure horns of his childhood. He was dismayed and elated to understand that inside the black glove was a silver hand.

He saw nothing. He heard nothing. He was both maimed and adorned. His character was now externalized in the gloved hand. Inner life and outer life were assuming a single shape, as if to conform with one of his theories. He was crippled, he was heraldic, soon the rest of him would follow the way of the hand until he could be mounted upright on a block of stone.

He turned himself to his right side. He raised himself to his elbow. The woman, who was watching him intently and sympathetically, closed her book and leaned down to him, so that the wings of her white headgear fluttered and the beauty of the small oval face was clearly evident.

"This hospital has no morgue," she said, and smiled. Then she rose quickly, as he knew she would, and disappeared from the corridor lined with the prostrate forms of unattended men.

He left the hospital, without authorization, seeing no one, speaking to no one. The hospital was waking, not where he walked but elsewhere, in distant white rooms, in cubicles where the gas could be lighted and the day begin. He hurried. The name tag was still tied to his wrist.

The street was as empty and silent as had been the corridors through which he had just passed. The surfaces beneath the soles of his shoes were still fresh from the night's dew, and yet there was trash in the gutters. The sun was rising to his left, filling the sky and silence with a light so new, cool, vast, without purpose as to be the very landscape of disquietude. In this light, through which

72

he alone walked and at so rapid a pace, he found himself more contradictory than ever: he was proud yet wild-eyed; he was serene and yet on guard against every menace of the desolation around him. His figure was formidable, yet he was disheveled and had not toileted or taken off his clothes since the schoolgirl had opened the front of his trousers. He was walking with such determination that he might have been marching and yet his determination was so pointless that he felt himself staggering with every step. But on he went, fiercely, loosely, chin upraised, right arm and gloved right hand pressed to his side and hence partially concealed from the view of anyone approaching, just as once he had attempted to conceal his steel tooth behind a corner of the upper lip drawn down in what might have been the disfiguration of a childhood paralysis. He had fought, he had fallen. The silver hand disguised in the black glove was tapping steadily against his right thigh in the rhythm of his long urgent stride. He felt that he was a tree stump blasted in electrical fury. He was thinking that only the hero is awarded the magnificence of the silver hand, and that he himself had become living proof of his theory about missing and artificial limbs. On he strode.

When he reached the cemetery, where in the rising light the dead lay in their marble houses, he decided that today, this morning, he would not stand a moment before Claire's grave still wet with dew, but instead hurry on toward the pharmacy, where he now knew he was going. He had lost his daughter or was rid of her; he must now take leave of the old pharmacist for whom he worked.

For some reason he stopped and listened. He took several breaths, with his naked hand he wiped his brow. What could have caught his attention? A bird? But here in this city there were no birds, just as there were no flowers except the pathetic few already destroyed at La Violaine. Here in this cemetery there was not even a caretaker to rake the gravel, set right the tokens of grief

73

blown down by the wind, or apply new mortar to the fissures in old and fallen monuments. And yet there had been a movement, unquestionably. Above his head the wingtips of the soot-colored iron angel were beginning to glow in the dawn light; from even this dry ground was rising the scent of a new day.

But again he heard the sound and even as he realized that someone had entered the cemetery unconventionally and with no concern for the dead, at this moment the hidden figure rose into sight and from behind the headstone of none other than Claire's grave. Slowly, in wary silence, the intruder assumed a standing position protected and still half concealed by the very headstone before which he himself had so often knelt or stood for long minutes in awkward reverence. They faced each other, he and the violator of Claire's grave, who suddenly retreated a few steps, crouched slightly and raised threateningly or defensively one of those same wooden sticks employed so uselessly in the debacle in the courtyard of La Violaine. The weapon and the ill-fitting trousers, the khaki shirt, the dark hair tied back in a length of string, the agile body poised for attack or flight: in all this the intruder's identity, as one of the rebelling women of the sacked and smoking prison, was clearly revealed, and the sight of her filled him with anger: the prison had exploded, so to speak; interior and exterior life were assuming a single shape; rebellious women appeared to be arising even from the graves of the dead.

The woman stared in his direction and shook her stick. Without thinking he abruptly raised aloft his black hand. But he refrained from passing through the gate, entering the cemetery and attempting to drive off the woman, simply because an obvious thought occurred to him: how could he know which of the slowly brightening monuments concealed still further crouching women awaiting only the briefest signal to show themselves and strike? It was obvious that the woman armed with the stick was not alone. It was not for him to engage in violence in Claire's resting place.

He lowered his hand newly lost or newly acquired, taking a certain comfort in the sure knowledge of the silver light that would flash from his hand's shape if, all at once, he stripped away the black glove. Then he pulled shut the gate, turned on his heel and again strode off in the direction of the pharmacy. The noise and fuming of slow traffic, the crowds of gray-faced citizens, each following his invisible thread, horse-drawn wagons sagging rearward under loads of concrete piping or wet potatoes: in a breath the life of the city had emerged in its usual immensity of congestion, as if the teeming interior of an outwardly silent hive had been laid open with a single blow. But hatless, with no coat to deflect the morning chill, and exaggerating even more the severity of his military bearing for the sake of the hand that to himself was both claw and wing, in this condition and pushing his way through the crowd, again he was confirmed in one of his primary beliefs: that the day's "reality" is merely the extent of the displeasure it brings to consciousness, that calamity is the fuel of time. All around him were packed together the bodies of creatures naturally rather than artificially misshapen: in the streets were the old men with their swollen handcarts, and the old women haloed, so to speak, in the vapors of their terrible coughs. But how was he to discern which was the escaped prisoner, which the aged grandmother? Who was to say that he, who walked in darkness and traveled nowhere, was any different from the hunched or limping figures surrounding him? They were all drops of water; they were all maimed. He listened to the dead weight thumping against his thigh, and its message was clear: nowhere in all these streets or alleyways, in all the labyrinths, was there another Konrad Vost.

Door ajar, locks forced and steel shutter halfway raised, plate-glass window shattered, sidewalk littered with broken glass and the remnants of what had been displayed in the window (empty cartons of herbal medicaments, shattered vials of golden syrups for the cure of muscular disease and inflammation of the lungs, spilled white powders and a cracked bottle of violet gel for use on the skin, a red box of artificial chocolates crushed beneath a flee-ing heel), and old Herzenbrecher on his hands and knees in the midst of this debris and blocking the progress of all those strug-gling north and south in the dawn hour: thus he discovered the wreckage of his place of work and the groveling person of the pharmacist himself. Daughter, grave, pharmacy, four empty concrete rooms he could no longer bear to inhabit: was there anything left?

"Konrad," cried the pharmacist, sifting glass and powders through arthritic fingers, "look what they have done to us! Can you believe the sight of it?"

"The women, Hermann?"

"The women, the women. The fury of such vandals. They only laughed at my tears."

"But at least I am here to help. . . ."

"Never mind, Konrad. I will restore the pharmacy myself. You might as well have a vacation for a day or two. But, Konrad, are you in good health? Is something wrong?"

"Nothing. A few disturbing dreams which I cannot seem to remember. . . ."

"Dreams, you say? But you are white of face. Have you been sleeping out of doors in the rain?"

"Only a few bad dreams. Nothing significant."

"Well, then, take aqua vitae. Enjoy your rest. And, Konrad: beware of the women!"

Jostled by the passers-by, oddly reluctant to part from the old man there on his knees, nonetheless he nodded, made a sign of respect with his left hand, and took his leave of this old Herzen-brecher whom he would never see again and who, despite his extreme age and the looseness of his soft skin, still bore on his upper right arm a tattoo of a balloon in flight with two plump naked women waving from its basket, as if this aged and gentle pharmacist had once known virile days in a distant part of his young manhood.

As for himself, now, for some reason, he knew precisely where he was going and what he would do: alone he would hunt down those women who, in twos and threes, were already taking refuge beyond the edge of the city in the wilderness of the salty marsh. The sight of the old man innocently sifting the refuse of the gutted pharmacy had something to do with the reason he was now committing himself to the marsh.

Konrad, dearest Konrad, came the voice that was growing gentler, softer, harder to hear, you must not grieve for me when I am gone. You know what I think, my dearest: that no life disappears, that nobody dies, that the person you have lost today reappears tomorrow in a different place, in different circumstances, not in your own family but in someone else's. How strange it is, Konrad, how beautiful, that every person is repeated endlessly. The new life appears to be not at all the same as the old: the woman whose face turns gray at the moment of death is rosy-cheeked in less than a week; he who was firm of step now walks with a cane; the person who had no children suddenly goes in a swarm. What do we do, my dearest? We exchange our wigs, so to speak, we exchange our spouses, the wife of the dentist now wears an apron and sells fruit at a stand, the person whose nakedness was like a map of your heart now turns the corner arm in arm with another. The pity is that we cannot remember our former days. The lifelong bachelor would bask in the memory of his years of marriage, the old woman crouched in her cellar would remember the glory of taking her dog on a leash. So each person is really an entire population, my dearest, increasing, ravished, increasing again, if only we knew. And are all our selves so very different, each from the other? No,

Konrad, no. That is the point. We are all the same. So one day soon after you put me into the ground you will exclaim to yourself: There she is, there, beside the driver of that automobile. Or again: There, that lovely woman pushing her twins in a pram, is it not she? And it will be so, Konrad, though we may not meet and never speak.

She was wrong, of course. That much he had learned in the empty church on the day of her death. And yet if his own theory was correct, then why not Claire's? Why shouldn't the railway terminal house the trains and tracks of more than one life? But if it was so, then a single person would know in his hour of joy or hour of dread not only his own life and former lives, but the lives and former lives of everyone. It was a monstrous thought.

His fingers on the valves of his trumpet were like mice in a forest filled with snow. By day the sounds of his trumpet filled the village streets, in chorus with the trumpets of the several other members of the boys' marching band. By night those same sounds came faintly from the stars, the planets, unceasingly, until light and sounds together faded and disappeared in the darkness yielding to the falling snow. By day the marching band included drummers, two small boys who carried and beat upon great snare drums that were ancient, wooden, scarred, and that rumbled and crashed as if to the rite of an execution or to the slaughter of untrained soldiers shooting each other in an empty field, in contrast to the trumpets that sang with the high shrill voices of flying souls. By night the drums of the day were still: only the sounds of the trumpets continued to cry and careen in the dark heavens until at last and as usual the snow fell.

Every night was the same. Every night the child who in daylight hours assaulted the ears of the villagers with chords, harmonics, crescendos, that were spiritual and martial both, awoke alone in the coldest and darkest hour in a small crude wooden bed and, without shivering, though he could not be colder and was dressed only in the ankle-length white gown that provided no warmth at all, again lay open-eyed and waiting in the grip of the mystification that called him silently awake in exactly this same way every night. It was all imperative: his listening, first to the hot uneasy sleep of the creatures bedded together in the outbuildings, then to the silence of these small frozen rooms of wood and stone, then to the silence of the night in which more snow was gathering. Every night he rose from the pile of rags and furs in which he slept and crouched waiting and dressed in nothing more than the white gown that hung free of his body, thus entrapping between cloth and skin a layer of the utmost cold. Finally, when the cold was so deeply set in his bones that he could hear it, then, as always, he began to creep along the invisible wall, away from his bed, in the only direction he could take.

Every night began with mystification: he did not know why he awoke, why he climbed from his cold bed into the colder vacancy surrounding it, why he made of himself a fluttering moth in an abandoned icehouse of blackened logs, why he crept away each night into the darkness. But after the passing of an appropriate time, when instinct warned him that he had gone as far as he could down the corridor beyond the alcove that contained his bed and also beyond the door to that large room where slept she who was the fearsome heart and mind of this household, and in fact was now crouching before a crooked wooden door barely tall enough to admit even a person of his small size, it was then that every night mystification gave way to the pleasure of mystery. He knew then exactly what he would see when he opened the door, and knew in advance how much he would enjoy the sight. The frozen air was already thick with the telltale smell.

As always he would reach as quietly as possible for the latch, as quietly as possible draw open the little slanting door, and then, without entering the cubicle that was both a storeroom and a place of nighttime exile for the man it contained, then he would stand unseen and frozen in the doorway giving him an unobstructed view of the smoker in his makeshift bed. By the brightness of the night that entered through a narrow window overhung partially with thatch from the roof, he could see the room, the man, the burning cigar in a clarity of detail that could not have existed in the light of day. There in the open doorway he would stand, so cold that not a shiver passed through his body, and in that cold light see everything: the jumble of tools, the long-dead wooden machine for making cheese, the iron-bound wooden chests piled one on another, and in the midst of it all the narrow makeshift bed which had been somehow forced into the storeroom between a great wooden wheel and the window that was a mere sliver of glass. He could see dark knots in lengths of wood, the sheen on an earthenware jar that hung from the slanting wall like a large bird on a length of cord, the silhouette of an old pair of boots, coils of wire like tangled hair. And there, wedged tightly in the midst of retired farming implements and domestic relics, there for the pleasure of his endless scrutiny stood the tiny bed with its quilting and blankets, its pillows filled with shavings, its occupant who instead of sleeping in the dead of night inevitably sat smoking his cigar that smelled like fields and cold fireplaces. The thrill of every night was to observe, as always, that the mysterious occupant of the little bed was sitting upright rather than lying upon it, that he was seated cross-legged at the head of the bed, that as always he was totally unprotected from the cold, having flung aside his dusty coverings and being dressed only in a gown much like the one worn by the boy himself. The small round face still wearing its eyeglasses, the apparent absence of neck between head and body, the roundness of the upper body in its delicate sack of white cloth, and then the raised plump arm, the hand with three short tapering fingers held curving like the legs of a child dancer while thumb and forefinger gripped in a horizontal position the living cigar: this was the spectacle that every night awaited the eyes of the admiring boy.

It was always the same. Inevitably when the boy opened the door he found the smoker in this stationary position, holding the cigar horizontally and away from his face. The knees were always visible beneath the hem of the gown, the tip of the cigar was pink in color, the pungent sweetness of the smoke was everywhere. The man looked like a round porcelain doll immune to the cold; his only signs of life were the smell and dim pink light of the cigar. But every night the small unseen boy was patient, and waited in the doorway until at last the cigar began to move, slowly, bearing its dim coal along its majestic path, until it stopped and head, chest, arm, hand, cigar became a single mute assemblage for the inhalation that was now inevitable. Then it would come: the light of the cigar would change from dim to bright; the glowing of the coal would fill the room; from the ceiling would hang a shuddering mass of livid crystallization of white light; fragments of molten red honeycomb would be lodged in all the crevices and empty spaces of the room for one long fiery moment in the freezing night. Then it would die in a splendid massive puff of white smoke which in its turn consumed light, room, cigar and seated man, and upon which the boy would quickly and silently close the door and, suddenly overcome with the cold, run shivering to his own bed hidden away in the darkness. It was then, while still shivering and waiting for warmth, that he would lie alone listening to the faintest metallic voices in the distant heavens and for the approaching snow.

Thus night after night the boy trumpeter accepted as magic what was in fact no more than his father's cruel inability to sleep. No wonder that years later he, the son, regulated his own deep nightly slumber according to the dictates of a loudly ticking clock.

81

No wonder that he at last succumbed to all the phantasmagoria that had been denied to the sleepless and dreamless Konrad Vost the Father, as the small cigar-smoking man had been known to the son, the wife, the villagers.

How could such a child be the seedling of a man who lacked all the redeeming qualities except self-esteem?

Was it then the child who was worthless of soul or only the man?

Both, he cried to himself in his worst moments of pride. Both.

A bright red dragonfly on a half-sunken post, the claw of the small yellow earth remover clutching the air, the rusted treads of the abandoned machine resting partially on the torn soil and partially in a pool of clear sun-filled water, his thin black shoes appropriate only to city streets but already bespattered with the mud of the marsh: thus he paused in that area of contested desolation where both marsh and city met, faltered, struggled, flowed and ebbed in the rhythm of natural infestation. For all his walking, he had never before stood exactly here, though the yellow machine was a familiar monster and the dragonfly, its transparency gleaming with the color of blood, was catching the light and quivering as if adorning not the rotted edge of the tilted post but the black surface of the back of his gloved hand. Never had he stood beneath such a distant sun; in the brightness of the ferns at his feet he saw only the strangeness of vegetation that grows in the wake of a holocaust, while in the shell of the small upturned automobile that lay nearby in a bed of silt he recognized the remains of the vehicle Claire had spent her life desiring. Everything was here and nothing. A wire dangling from the iron claw contained the power of

82

electrocution; an empty concrete conduit emerging from a lip of clay had been meant for sewage; a black shoe cupped in a clump of marsh grass might have been his own. With every breath he smelled the salty fetid smell of air that is always fresh, never confined, always stagnant, forever drifting in random currents between layers of water, layers of light. He stared at the marsh that receded in all directions like an immense pebbled sheet of purple glass. He could see nothing of hut, barn, haystack, cluster of young naked trees, yet these too were embedded in the distant glass. Konrad Vost was alone and unable to move in a landscape without shape or meaning, belonging to neither city nor country-side: it was worse than bearing his disfigurement through the dawn streets and indifferent crowds. For him there was only sun, emptiness, the smell of salt and putrefaction.

But then the air around him, vagrant, powerful, cut adrift from tides, earth, light, shifted its fetid currents and brushed aside the grass, rolled aside the still marsh water, and exposed momentarily what otherwise he could not have seen: the curling iron rails of some anomalous narrow-gauge railway track long ago destroyed and long unused, long buried in the flat and shifting marsh. Through the parted grass and water shone the deep orange light of the bent and splintered rails that now consisted of nothing except the splendor of rust which even while he watched was flaking, burning, as the iron itself continued its slow process of disintegration in the light of the sun. But a severed train track across an empty marsh? Rails and bonelike ties rising into sight from beneath blankets of sand, sludge, drifting water? He shaded his eyes and smiled. The sight before his eyes was unaccountable, but suddenly he remembered Claire and understood what previously he had merely feared: the unaccountable is the only key to inner life, past life, future life. From the silence of the purple distance came the rattle of couplings, the sound of gunfire, the chugging of a locomotive that did not exist. Air, rust, water, grass:

83

had he not once ridden a train on these very tracks? And hidden himself in village streets now buried beneath the city streets at his back? He listened. Here, now, alone at the edge of a marsh, suddenly he knew that he had once been a child in flight. The sounds of the locomotive were coming no closer. But he was comforted.

He nodded to himself, compressed his lips, and without hesitation stepped into the water that lay between the shelf of mud where he stood and the section of railway track, once again hidden beneath the water, behind the grass. The tracks were gone but he had seen them; they were there, for his own use if not for the use of any actual train.

The water rose to midcalf and, as he could not have expected, was as cold as a blade. It dragged at his trousers, he felt the mask of his face reflecting the shock in his legs. The water eddied away from him as he pushed on toward the brackish spot where he had seen the tracks. Silt, water, algae clogged his shoes, his socks, his trouser bottoms, his nakedness. He would never again be dry or free of the dead smell of the marsh. But what did it matter? The inner landscape had become externalized. He would cross it with the ruthlessness of a police patrol following leashed dogs.

At precisely the moment when the smell of natural decay and artificial decay was strongest, and when behind him the dragonfly quit the safety of the rotten post and disappeared, leaving in its place only a droplet of shimmering water, then simultaneously he found his footing and climbed aching and dripping onto the all but concealed bed of ancient tracks. Again he shaded his eyes, waited, felt the water descending his calves inside the trousers now heavy and shapeless from his wading. The horizon was empty. He knew that he was becoming more gaunt than ever; he knew that behind the steel shutter of La Violaine, the shutter that was still down and would remain so until calm was again restored to the prison across the street, the silent figures of those men loyal to the rebelling women were gathered already for morning coffee or beer. He

84

knew also that there was no longer a chair for Konrad Vost in the closeness and darkness of the café. So much the better, he told himself, and started off down the tracks that led, apparently, to the deepest easterly recesses of the marsh.

The tracks had been constructed on a roadbed nearly level with the deceptive surface of the marsh, so that occasionally he found himself again walking through sheets of water. Now he was totally exposed to the sun and was, he knew, an all too visible target to anyone lying prone and watching him from no matter how great a distance out there in the purple or deep green spaces; now he was well hidden behind walls of yellow and undulating grasses that rose higher than his head and whispered like thin blades sharpening each other. As he progressed, stumbling and adjusting his stride to the ties, it became increasingly apparent that the marsh was not merely flat. Shallow ponds concealed the wide mouths of wells that dropped downward for immeasurable distances; stands of pale trees suddenly sprang up from the mud; he could see the vestiges of an immense canal undulating through ribs of sand; off to his right lay a geometric arrangement of wet stones where primitive buildings, long since dissolved, had sheltered both men and animals. More fence posts, the rotten ribs and backbone of a small boat, brightly colored marsh plants festering in sockets of ice, the fragments of a shattered aqueduct gray and dripping where moments before there had been only flatness and emptiness, abrupt discolorations that revealed quicksand or underground rivers: it was all an agglomeration of flashing mirrors, the strong cold salty air was impossibly heavy with the smell of human excrement and of human bodies armed and booted and decomposing under the ferns, behind piles of rocks, in the depths of the wells. Had it once been a landscape of nighttime skirmishing? Was it then the terrain of at least some kind of history? At any moment an iron ship might loom before him, or the vast trench of a communal grave.

He stopped, wiped his face, looked back in the direction from which he had come: the city was now only the faintest line of little concrete teeth littering the horizon. Soon when he turned again to look there would be nothing. He felt as if he were walking on the crushed or broken bones of the world's dead. His shoes, socks, lower trousers were still damp and dripping; his upper body was growing warm in the sun. When he again paused and looked backward down the length of track at the distance he had already come, the city was gone.

Not a bird. Not a scurrying animal. Not a fish to leave bubbles or ripples on the clear or purple glass of the water. No insects. Nothing but the light, the swollen breath of life in decay, the muddy plains and fissures of the deceptive topography.

Toward midmorning he heard the unmistakable sounds of men's voices. Later, before he had time even to conceal himself within the shelter of a growth of high yellow grasses rising suddenly on his left side, he watched as three men, who were wearing the familiar kepis and dark blue uniforms and carrying weapons hung from straps on their shoulders, passed in single file across the line of his vision far down the tracks. In another moment they were gone, these representatives of the Prefecture of Police, disappearing abruptly as if into a tilted mirror. But he had seen them. He was not alone in searching the marsh. Again circumstance had borne him out, again he had been proven correct: where else to hunt down the fugitives of La Violaine except in the marsh? Still later, from a different direction, came the faint snarling of brutal dogs baring their teeth and straining on their leashes of black leather. Then again there was silence, with only the sounds of his own breathing and walking to scratch in his ears.

How long it had taken for the sun to climb directly overhead he did not know. But the hour of cessation had arrived; the light of the marsh was stronger, more evenly diffused than ever, as if it could not possibly intensify or fade; and in this hour of midpoint he felt suddenly safe, disarmed, stiff and fatigued from his walking, curiously freed from the purpose that at dawn had impelled him to enter the muddy, crystalline, uncertain reaches of the marsh. He rested, sitting on the edge of the track with one knee drawn up and the black hand lying inert at his side. He was on top of a low embankment from which he could see on an island of black soil a stone hut oddly intact, a threadlike road that might have been made with the tip of a finger, a long glassy stretch as of the sea. He clasped his raised knee with his active hand; he was conscious of the breath of decay that was in his clothing and the pores of his skin; he was at peace with the incongruity between himself and all this low wilderness. In face, neck, arms, chest, his muscles and tendons were slackening, coming to rest. The smell in his nostrils was like that of a naked human shoulder green with mold. He felt himself in a waking sleep, suspended between clear sight and silence: this was the landscape that had swallowed legions; everything and nothing lay at his feet. It was then that he heard the one sound that even he, in all this wet or spongy vastness, could not have anticipated: laughter, the shrill tones of what could only be an old woman in the grip of laughter. He listened, he held his breath. For the first time since leaving the hospital he was on his guard. The pleasures of the high sun had evaporated. In this place what could be more alarming than the sound of an old woman's laughter?

Carefully, propping himself on his left hand, disengaging his right from a circlet of thorns that had sprung up beside the rails, slowly and quietly he descended the embankment and entrusted himself to the shadows and sudden light of a thicket he had failed to notice from his vantage point above. The earth was silent beneath the wet soles of his shoes. He moved between the slender white trees with all the stealth he could summon, and despite fear and urgency he was entirely conscious of how the tall young trees dispersed and focused the light so that now, all at once, the thicket was warm and filled with star-shaped patterns of bright flashing light. Again came the sound of the laughter, high-pitched, close, trembling with the broken music of an old woman long confined among other old and laughing women. He knew without thinking that it was a sound to fear, that loud sounds of unreasonable pleasure were not to be enjoyed vicariously but to be feared. But he could not have imagined that within this thicket of flowering warmth and whitened light he himself could be so violent.

Her back was to him in the narrow clearing, and yet he recognized her at once. Despite the deceptive clothing, the black gown and, on the head, the black shawl holding the hair, still he recognized at once the same old woman who, from her barred window, had stared down happily at the chaos of men and women in the yard below. Now she was laughing to herself, without reason, here in the gentleness of shadows and light, as if she were not one of those condemned long ago to La Violaine.

He reached the small black figure in a single stride; she turned; the astonished face was staring up at his own. Now they were so close together, he and the old woman, that they could have clutched each other's clothing with angry hands, and though she was bent and though her face was far below his shoulder, still it was shockingly upturned toward his own in one of the brightest rays of light to pierce the leaves overhead, so that every feature was thrust upon his consciousness and sealed there in heat and light. He and the old woman were stock still, he tall and at the mercy of his fury, she bent and twisted in her attitude of vanished laughter. The two of them might have been about to embrace or to grapple together in unequal contest there in the new growth of trees. Within easy reach the ancient face was turned up to his own and brought alive, though unmoving, by the focused light. He stared down at the warmly tinted expression of fear and surprise, and there could be no question of identity: it was she, the old woman who had savored the chaos of La Violaine as a private

88

spectacle. The open mouth with its three amber-colored teeth and the breath of a great age, the small twisted ears that appeared to have been sewn to the sides of the skull with coarse thread, the skin that was shriveled tightly to the bone beneath and cured in sun and salt until the wrinkles were deep and permanent, the soft facial hair that flowered around the lips and on the cheeks like a parody of a bristling beard, and above all the yellow eyes, which alone reflected the ageless crafty spirit in a face that otherwise was only a small torn mask of leather: these were the elements that made his recognition a matter of certainty, and that inspired in him a rage which, even to him, bubbled and frothed in excess of what the emotion, the time, the place or the old woman herself might have justified. But the very texture of her age affronted him, as did the cleverness that burned so youthfully in the yellow eyes of someone who should have been confined to an iron bed or rickety chair in a prison for women. He was appalled by her disguise, her freedom; he was infuriated that someone so old was still a woman. But in this instant, when warmth and speckled light cushioned the proximity of gaunt bony man and shrunken woman, suddenly he understood that the old creature's eyes were telling him that she knew full well that in her he despised the pretty bud that has turned to worms.

When he raised his arm he had no intention of letting it fall. He had not even meant to lift his arm, but when he felt his right arm moving upward and backward until it was higher than his head, he did so in the knowledge that he intended only to frighten the old woman, nothing more. Yet he too was shocked at the length and breadth of the gesture that carried the arm that had been inert at his side to the top of its arc so that the black hand was poised at its summit, prepared with greatest strength to strike its blow or fling a great weight to the ground. In the extremity of his vision he had seen the upward passage of the black hand, and when it was no longer in sight, raised at arm's length above and behind his head, still he saw the uplifted hand as did the old woman: black, clawlike, murderous, some interminably heavy and destructive weapon that would travel at a great speed down the terrible distance from its place in the air to her own small weight-less self, at which the blow was aimed. But he intended none of it. He did not in fact swing down his arm.

For the old woman, however, it was otherwise. Before he could move and while the black hand was quivering high in the air, at that very moment she must have felt that the black hand would fall and must have felt the inevitable rush of air and the breathless pitiless impact of the blow itself. In that instant his own body was as unwieldy as an awkwardly drawn bow; his black hand was still in the air; he stared down and in disbelief as the old woman's eyes squeezed shut and the face gradually changed its expression from fear to girlish supplication to the pinched and luminous grimace she had saved for her doom. Death lit up the old woman's face as from within. She dropped at his feet.

Slowly he lowered the black offending hand to its place at his side. He heard a voice shouting and noticed, a short distance beyond where the dead woman lay, a great pile of fagots tied with a rope. He could not move, his scalp was bristling, he felt as drained of blood as was the small deflated body in its heap of rags. Obviously the old woman had been carrying the fagots on the little saddle of her bent back; obviously in this sunny spot she had decided for no reason to throw down her burden meant for the hearth. It was for this that she had been laughing to herself in the speckled light. Now the querulous voice was calling; now he felt as if he had been seized from behind by powerful bare arms locked around his waist. He thought of himself as that Konrad Vost who had again been wrong. He turned and fled.

For Konrad Vost, he told himself, the world was now in a con-stant state of metamorphosis, duplication, multiplication; figures deserving existence only within the limits of the dream now sprang alive; the object of least significance was inspired with its secret animation; no longer was there such a thing as personal safety; in every direction there rose the bars of the cage. What could be worse?

He gained the tracks and immediately, without wiping his face or glancing backward and downward toward the tranquil stand of trees where he himself had committed an act that had erupted only from his own contemptible imagination, and without waiting for a glimpse of the old man who was now discovering the sack of rags in the clearing, he broke into a clumsy run which defied his characteristic bearing and which he was able to sustain until his pained chest brought him again to a walk. He forced himself along, despite shortness of breath, the swinging arm, the clamminess of his legs and feet. As he hurried down the lengthening tracks, not in flight from evildoing, as he reminded himself, but only in pursuit of legitimate or even heroic ends, still he formulated what he had learned in the grove of laughter: that whatever his own previous misconceptions, nonetheless age never obliterates entirely the streaks and smears of masculine or feminine definition. Never.

He longed for water. Slowing his pace but walking on, he found it ironic that he who was making his lonely and treacherous way across a marsh, which was nothing if not the residence of a retiring sea, that in such a place a man as determined as himself should suddenly be compulsively concerned with drinking cold cups of water, immersing himself in water, when there was none. The hut where the old woman had lived with the querulous man would have had its well, its ladle, its ancient bucket on a length of dripping chain; even here, now, the light through which he moved was like a bright clear fluid which he could almost cup in his hands and drink. But it was light, not water, and for some reason the vista now surrounding him was dry, murky, muddy, barren, without any trace of water that might cleanse him, quench his thirst.

Now the light was changing, the mirrors were tilting, the tracks

91

were lying exactly at sea level, and now the light that had so filled his eyes was spread in a miragelike sheet of water across the entire landscape, which, before, had consisted merely of parched grass or mud. The level of the roadbed so perfectly matched the level of the surrounding water that now the way of his journey appeared to be carrying him through the water itself.

Again it was a sound that brought him to a dead standstill in the midst of the emptiness. Suddenly his perspiration disappeared in a cool breath; the brightness of the light diminished to normal intensity; the air became clear; the mirrors of the marsh were again adjusted so as to be conducive to the ordinary sight of his eyes: still water, islets of crab grass and, to the left, a frieze of tall thin pale green trees aligned exactly parallel to the rusted tracks which lay now like broken lines of fire across the water. Behind the trees something was wetly gleaming. But also, and more important, the sound he was still listening to was coming from behind the trees.

Small but unmistakable, it was the sound of splashing. It reached him faintly, musically, yet without rhythm, like a bell deliberately tinkled to destroy rhythm and prevent anticipation. Again it came to him, the sound of water disturbed, water tossed into the air, water set randomly and sweetly in motion behind the trees. But dare he risk again leaving the solidity of the tracks? There was no way of knowing, for instance, the depth of the water between himself and the tall green trees that were spaced evenly and closely together like the stakes of a fragment of a gigantic fence. Yet here, after all, was the substance of what he himself had been desiring: the calmness of green trees, the freshness of water.

Abruptly and with a few awkward movements he hid his right hand from view in his suit coat pocket, attempted to judge the distance between himself and the trees, and then decisively and silently entrusted himself to the flat water. He felt as if he were gliding toward the screen of trees; underfoot there was firmness,

92

the water rose only to his midshins. The splashing sounds drew closer, the structure behind the trees was brightly shimmering. The trees appeared to be clothed in pale green skin and, as he approached them in haste and silence, revealed the webbing of white vines that, never climbing more than a meter from the water's surface, laced the trees together trunk to trunk. His thirst was intolerable, he was surprised at his eagerness to see beyond the trees which, he knew full well, were watery replicas of those other trees, which had proven to be a grove of death.

He stooped, held his breath, with his left hand seized the green thinness of the nearest tree, and then bracing the side of his head against the tree, and crouching like a phantom in the still water, he stared at the spectacle that some master stroke had surely fashioned only to feed the needs of his own psychological function in this instant of suspended time. The crumbling remains of the old mill, for such was the structure that had gleamed through the trees, consisted of a high partial wall of jagged and blackened stones and a great iron wheel rusted into the antithesis of motion, and stood before him at a small distance like a dripping theatrical backdrop before which a single young naked woman was enjoying the water. The enormous wheel could not turn, could no longer bear water to the top of its arc, and the air itself was a dry transparency, and yet both wheel and wall were, on all their surfaces, totally and freshly wet as if from some invisible but constantly replenished deluge of clear water.

But the small young naked woman? This childlike creature quite unaware of the dripping ruin which, behind her back, could only exaggerate her nakedness, her small size, her dripping skin? But even in the first glimpse he knew conclusively that she who was now splashing herself in the pleasure of natural privacy was the selfsame person whom he and Spapa had beaten into unconsciousness in La Violaine. He could not be mistaken: the very bruises that blurred his own elation in a flash of shame gave absolute identity to the young woman who had in fact survived the combat in the prison only to experience now the privilege of being herself in her skin. The black and blue welts were all too visible, the eye puffed shut gave him a stab of pain, in particular he recoiled from a star-shaped bruise on the little haunch. She was disfigured, more so than he, and on her body bore the livid signs of his own righteousness. But her beauty remained: the freely hanging dark hair, the sun-darkened tan and pink complexion of the wet skin, the shocking symmetry of a body so small that in its childlike proportions it exceeded the beauty of the life-sized woman it was intended to represent: in all this his powers of recognition were even more confirmed than in the physical evidence of her injuries, the sight of which so offended, suddenly, his proud and sentimental eye.

She was facing him, she was close enough so that he could study as if in the magnification of a large and rapturous lens the eye that was open, the scarred stomach he could have contained in his hand now clinging to the tree, the naked breasts which had somehow escaped the damage inflicted by Spapa's brutal stick and his own. Facing him, in the water that reached above her knees, and in silence, without either song or laughter, merely reaching down and splashing her hands against the water or scooping it up and allowing it to trickle on the shining hair, the oval face, the waist where the skin was tightening in the exertions of her self-absorption, on the wet thighs that, together, preserved her modesty. As for himself, surely he who had beaten her on head and body could now be allowed to spy on her innocent nudity; after the first violation, peering at her through green trees was nothing. So he watched as the hands fluttered, as a knee rose, as one thigh crossed the other, as the shoulders dipped, as the muscles played beneath the skin about the navel, as the water flew from the fingertips and the mouth smiled. Alone, turning toward him her diminutive naked profile with its curves freshly dipped in light, it was she who

94

imparted to the sinister ruins behind her back a lifelike pastoral completion. The wheel might have been steadily revolving, the water might have been coursing in its productive fall, the grain might have been gathering in its stone bowl, while on the other side of the building the old men might have been lounging among their waiting donkeys, unaware of she who, naked in the millpond, was causing the wheel to turn, the grain to flow.

Not once did he blink. Standing fully clothed in the same water in which her nakedness was flowering, now he was suddenly aware that the object of his spying had turned her back to him and was bending down to stir the waters. The sight of her body bent down from the waist in precocious but unconscious self-display destroyed in the instant his tranquillity so that loathing the repetition of the sensations that had been aroused in his trousers only days before, and determined to preserve in his mind the vision of the bather, he loosened his hold on the tree, turned away reluctantly from his secret view of the pond, and crouching, silent, stealthy, waded back across the water to the dry tracks.

He paused once to hear again the splashing. He noted that his thirst was quenched. He told himself that he could not have harmed her person for a second time or dared to interrupt her bright bare immersion in air and water. Abruptly he set forth again and the sounds of splashing faded, his own unwanted sensations faded, while only the vision of honey, light, water and dark hair remained. He could not have been more soiled in his dress, or in his blood, his bones, his tissues, and yet he carried with him the clear indestructible sight and, despite discomfort and weariness, was now increasingly animated by self-satisfaction: he had looked at her, but he had not harmed her.

If he had known the identity of the little martyr of La Violaine, as he soon came to think of her, he would have suddenly understood his own death the day it arrived; and if he had not allowed himself to be consumed by the vision of the bather he had spied on through the green trees, he in turn might have prevented her martyrdom.

As it was, he walked with a fierce exhausted pleasure, he walked while bearing the entire millpond inside his head, he had eyes only for the nudity of her whom he had spared, he towered and staggered along bemused and unaware of the dangerous tracks and making no effort to recall his dream: he who knew better and should have concentrated on the path of his journey. But it was of course too late.

The snarling of the black dog destroyed the vision as swiftly as the fangs of the beast would have seized his thigh were it not for the leash. The terrible lean creature lunged at him from no place of hiding that he could see, while the loudness of the weapon being prepared for firing came to him exactly as if the dog had not been snarling but had instead been frothing and straining at the leash in silence. They came from nowhere, the vicious dog and the armed unkempt man wearing the familiar blue uniform and, on his head, the kepi cocked at an arrogant angle. From nowhere, man and dog, yet suddenly his way was obstructed; the muzzle of the gun was aimed at his chest. The beast was straining so fiercely on its leash that its front feet were free of the ground and its snarling jaws were not a hand's length from the center of his own body where lay the living entrails the animal clearly wished to rip and masticate while still steaming in the heat of his blood. As for himself, he fell back from the murderous pair, he raised his left hand in self-defense, in supplication, and managed to restrain himself from flight. He could hear the dog's breath and the guttural wet tones of its lust and hatred; he could hear the creaking of all the wrinkles in the thick uniform of the man who was leaning his weight backward against the pull of the leash wrapped several times about his left wrist and leveling with his right hand the weapon suspended from his shoulder by a leather strap. The stub of a yellow cigarette was caught between the lips, the careless stubble of beard on the coarse face glistened with the exertions of his search through the hot marsh. Even while noting these details he, Vost, was thinking that in a moment or two he would be shot by the man and eaten by the dog.

In shocked and cowering haste he heard the sound of his voice in his rancid mouth: "But I have discovered one of them, there, in the pond behind those trees where she is in the nude. She's alone. She's yours for the taking. . . ."

The silent yellow eyes of the thick man cloaked in his barbarous officialdom stared into his own wide eyes as steadily and ruthlessly as the eyes of the dog. The man said nothing, holding both gun and dog, while the animal continued to choke and gnash its teeth. Perhaps the escapee naked in the millpond was not enough enticement for this man who bore on his body the smell of his dog; perhaps he would take the woman captive and, even so, fire his weapon into the tremulous breast of himself, Konrad Vost. But the image of the naked bather seemed to form at last inside the thickness of the broad cranium; the man in his suspicious but slowly growing interest lowered his gun; he jerked once on the leash and gave the quivering animal an incomprehensible command. Darkly this cruel pair circled around him, where he stood crushed in his shame, and set off toward the screen of trees.

But what had he done? Was it possible? Had he sacrificed the purity of his vision and the freedom of his former victim merely for the sake of his own well-being? Or merely because he had been so taken by surprise by the brute maleness of the man and dog that he had simply collapsed in the stench of their intimidation? But there was no excuse. With a word he had snatched the bather from her clear pond and imprisoned her once more, in some makeshift cell in the city. And who could say to what further mistreatment she, who had already suffered enough, might be subjected by her wordless captor once he had tied the leash to a tree?

It was then that he heard the burst of shots. Not a single shot but several. A sound like the dog snarling. But they were shots from a gun. He heard them, they hung in the air, they faded, he swung wildly around and then, in the stillness of the echo, seeing nothing of trees or man or dog wherever he turned, then in the silence and failing light he stood alone to bear as long as he could his incomprehension, his complete understanding. He did not know what had contrived the terrible correctness of his knowledge. But it was true: he himself had killed the little martyr of La Violaine.

His shoulders sagged, his head was bowed, his grief was centered in the pain of the face he dared not expose to the darkening air. When at last he took his hand from his face, he found that the formerly brilliant light of the marsh had given way not merely to dusk but to fog. Gauzelike, thick, tinted here and there with a wet pinkness, it lay in strips or massive handfuls on the tracks, on the nearby water, between blasted stumps and hummocks of cold grass, covering the entirety of his now subterranean world wherever he looked. Two thoughts came to him at once: that he could not determine which direction led back to the city, or which away from it; and that now the fog was smothering the small naked figure as it drifted, face downward, in the pond. But she too was gone, the millpond was gone, while for himself there was only the sightlessness that resulted from the paradox of the increasing whiteness of the fog and the growing darkness of the approaching night.

As soon as he freed his right hand from the pocket where it had been concealed, and raised it as if for the first time to his defeated scrutiny, the fog settled immediately on the slick black surface of the glove so that the upright hand, in all its sculpted solidity, might have been clawing, for long breathless minutes, the wet air. Slowly he revolved the glistening hand to the left, to the right, noting the hard leather beneath its wet atmospheric skin and noting too, with the faintest return of pleasure, that the physical part of himself that was most distinctive was of course without feeling. The famil-

98

iar muscles were tightening around his mouth and in his jaw and neck. He was able to lower his hand and begin walking, though he did not know which direction he was taking or how, without shelter, he could survive the night.

Never had the sounds of his own movement been so loud; never had he heard the echoes of his own footsteps as he now did behind him and on his either side. But why was it that the fog reminded him of snow? In a sense the entire fog-covered marsh was in itself a morgue. But in this instant, before the darkness became complete and while the fog still rolled and shifted, rose and fell so that the light was purest and so that his field of vision was constantly changing but was not yet totally obliterated, now he saw that the marsh was an immensity of cobwebs: in passing ferns, leaves, forks of stunted trees, hoofprints left behind as by beasts of the field, in all this he saw a flowering of prismatic cobwebs which had remained invisible in the dryness of day but which now, in the last of the day's light and touched by the fog, were suddenly wet in every thread and filament and thus caught the last of the light and were as clearly visible as the black hand with which, in passing, he rent as many of the frail constructions as he could. But why did such a vastness of cobwebs so quicken his exhilaration? Because they too were unaccountable? Because they were visible proof that the eye was never totally to be trusted? Because in all their various sizes and designs they duplicated, though many times enlarged, the crystal of snow?

For the fourth and final time it was a sound that interrupted his speculations, and it caused him once again to abandon the railway tracks stretching onward through the darkness and fog. Again he stopped. In the darkness the bright intricate webs were no longer visible. He had come from light to water to night and was alone and shivering; what was not hidden from sight by the fog was concealed by the night. Everywhere the fog was silently dripping. But through it all the sound persisted, close at hand, innocuous, small, placid: the sound, he realized, of a barnyard fowl scratching the dirt.

He listened, and suddenly indifferent to quicksand, deep water, strands of barbed and rusted wire, the uncovered mouths of wells sunken into the earth in another age, suddenly indifferent to whatever dangers awaited him in a world he could not see, he quit the tracks for the last time and groped his way toward the sound of what was apparently a starving hen clucking quietly to itself as well as scratching for seed. The tortuous ruts of a former road, a fallen gate, the heavy wet stones of what had once been a large enclosure, the remains of an iron pump that rose from its flat stone base in the shape of a tall and empty pitcher, these he discovered more by touch than by sight, though the smell of the long-abandoned farm, for so it was, still reached his nostrils through the smothering fog. By touch he entered the stone enclosure: hands on wet rocks, he waited without resistance for snarling dog, flash of light, the singing iron tines of a pitchfork flung like a spear in his direction. Unexpected suffering had been contrived for him at the millpond and grove of death; why not here? But there was nothing, not even the scratching of the hen which, he decided, must have returned to some familiar roost for the night. But he too could shelter himself where the bird took shelter: there must be a barn.

When he found it, as he did by following the slimy roughness of the enclosure, and when he entered the darkness of rude beams and heavy stones, inhabited only by a single creature of gauntness and black feathers whose existence in this place he merely presumed, he knew again the satisfaction of his own peculiar bitterness: what could be less appropriate to the stringent character traits of Konrad Vost than an empty or nearly empty stone barn in a drifting night?

No matter how long it had stood unoccupied, the barn, for all its black space, was curiously warm. He submerged himself in its seductive temperature by progressing along the right-hand wall, where, at every few steps, he discovered a ringbolt protruding from the dry stones. Immersed in blindness, lulled by the warmth, carefully and silently he traced his way along the wall until he reached the first corner. He had encountered nothing, no stone gutters for the flow of urine, or blades or iron claws or blocks of wood or tall wooden racks with spikes for teeth, nothing to cause him sudden pain, sudden alarm. He stood in the corner, waiting, contemplating the softness under his shoes, the scent of previous animal life that had dried to dust, and contemplating also the fact that he was safest where the two walls joined. He forced himself into the security of the two walls. He heard nothing, not even the uncomfortable sounds of the dreaming hen; with sudden relief he inhaled long slow breaths of the herbal sweetness, of the ancient animal skins and manure that had turned to dust. How could the warmth of former life be so pronounced? How could he, a pharmacist's assistant, take shelter in an abandoned barn? It was in this way, he told himself, that the bespectacled designer of a holocaust would preserve his own existence amidst the violence he had unleashed. For the first time since he had awakened into his condition of discovery and disability he was at peace, cushioned externally in warmth and sightlessness and inwardly in his favorite product of the psychological function: the thin serum of irony.

He needed sleep, he expected straw. But when all at once he understood that he could remain on his feet no longer, recognizing the imminence of that collapse of the system which he could enjoy only at the end of a day he might have dreamed and only in the warm darkness that was the residue of life that had died, and when he felt his way downward, expecting to lie like one of the missing animals in a bed of straw, he found that there was nothing at all to lie on except the thick lumpy carpeting of animal droppings on which he had in fact been walking or standing since he had first entered the barn. The waste of dead animals, the fecal matter derived from cold water and flowering grasses and ex-creted through the labyrinthine canals of the dark beasts waking or sleeping: here at last was the final irony. Konrad Vost, he of the purest habits and coldest turn of mind, was to sleep on dung. As best he could, he forced his aching angular body into the space where the walls met, and without removing his eyeglasses and holding his silver hand against his breast, he prepared to survive his night in the wilderness. It was the dung in which the heat was secreted, along with the smell of soft hair and distant flowers. But why was he now so comfortable? After all, dung and snow were the essential ingredients in the crucible of his innocent and de-tested childhood. His eyes were closed, he was drugging himself on deeper and deeper breaths of the anal elixir of horse, cow, beasts of the field. Already the hated smile was becoming fixed in the paralysis of the sleeping mouth.

But was he not even to be allowed to embrace sleep's dubious specter? In the next instant he had locked himself partially upright on the elbow of the arm that was capped like a column with the silver hand, and was holding his breath and staring with useless intensity into the blackness that bore not the faintest trace of light. He had not been sleeping, he was sure of it; his wet feet were cold; the smell in his nostrils was not of dusty pollen but of ammonia. He felt as if he himself were chained by the neck to the stones at his back. He was alerted to one indisputable fact: inside the very skull of darkness he was not alone. It was not breathing he heard but simply the sounds of mammoth existence. There were soft erratic footfalls, heavy, desultory, and a whispering that must have come from the great tail being drawn through the air. The crea-ture was slowly approaching the corner where he lay in cold and bitter wakefulness, unable to move, unable to breathe, listening to a concert of sounds he had never expected to hear: the snakelike distending and contracting of sinews, the sluggish flow of the blood, the slippage of enormous blunt bones in their sockets. Then through the darkness, and even closer than he had thought, there came to him the thick watery sound of what could only be the snorting of a horse in the blackest part of the night. Closer still, the shuddering sound of a great hoof coming to rest in the dung and not an arm's length from where he lay entrapped in his corner. Then another, and another, the hoofs softly and unevenly detonating around him like heavy explosions in a charred field. In the slowest possible motion, unwittingly, the old invisible horse was nonetheless bearing down upon its prostrate victim who was now suffering the extremities of his adult attentiveness and childhood fear.

But was the horse moving or not? Had it stopped where he lay? He listened, he heard the shuddering of an ancient flank high above his head, suddenly his own extended left hand was pressing against one of the hoofs, which, to his fearful sensitivity, was like a sullen block of chalk or bone crowned with dead hair. Quickly he withdrew his hand, though he knew full well that the mere touch of his fingers could not possibly signal his presence to the horse that was as heavy and stationary as a horse statue on its pedestal in an abandoned village. He covered the side of his head with his forearm; all around him were implanted the shaggy legs of the beast. He could hear the ponderous monotonous breathing that stirred the immense and rubbery nostrils and then ceased and commenced again, closer, transmitting the very dimensions of the animal's great vacant breast and the living power of the creature that existed only to inspire fear. Its smell was filling the darkness; even while stationary it was raining down a fine sifting of dust, hair, flakes of skin.

It was then, with no warning except the increasing loudness of the solemn breath in the hollows of the skull, that the nose of the horse, broader than the spread hand of a man, suddenly struck him a firm sightless blow in the chest.

"No," he said involuntarily. "My God, no. . . ."

He was surprised at the sound of his own futile exclamation. But he was more surprised at what followed immediately upon the sharp but muted tones of his voice: the nose of the horse breathed once on his face and disappeared. From close by in the darkness, from a position that lay also within the aura of the towering horse, there came the abrupt and unmistakable sounds of suppressed giggling. Female giggling. So he was not alone with the monstrous horse in the darkness. His few sharp words spoken more to himself than to the deafened beast had betrayed his whereabouts to those who, like himself, were seeking sleep in the barn. At least in the accompaniment of women who were unknown but were also amused at his presence in the vast and otherwise empty barn, he himself could be in no grave danger of pain or harm.

"You are there?" he heard himself saying in tones intended to be neutral, even receptive, but which to his own ears had the ring of an officious whisper. "But who? Who are you?"

Again the eruption of giggling behind hands they must have been holding flat to their mouths. Then a brief whispered exchange he could not decipher, then a bar or two of overt laughter.

"Well," he said again into the darkness, unable to control himself, "I am Konrad Vost. And you?"

For answer the two women, for such he was now convinced they were, gave him another brief example of outright laughter that was friendly, it seemed to him, and not mocking. After a moment, during which the horse appeared to be taking a few lumbering steps in their direction, the women again whispered together. But they were refusing, he understood, to speak aloud.

Had they, for just this night, deserted husbands or fathers at a nearby farm where the men were already drunk and vomiting into their leather boots which they had removed in order to warm their feet at the fire? Bloodshot eyes, half-empty bottles, a fat male child naked from the waist down and relieving himself into the flames and embers of the dying fire: no wonder the women had

104

fled hand in hand into the fog and darkness of the endless night. No wonder they had no fear of a stranger such as himself. As for the horse, to them it was nothing.

The horse snorted heavily, quietly, but almost directly above his head. It gave him pleasure to think that now the unknown but undaunted women must be preparing for sleep, no doubt holding each other in their sturdy arms. His own fatigue returned, his own need for the relief of sleep. Irrational though it was, he felt that the nearby sleeping women gave him immunity from the destructive weight of the horse; no matter its closeness, he would not awaken to his fingers caught beneath the edge of a hoof, or to find that same hoof crushing his chest. Thanks to the sleeping women he was safe. In the morning the women would take one look at the stranger sleeping in his black suit of clothes and then, without waking him, return to their farm. He was safe.

But the women were not yet asleep. The whispering commenced again, drawing him back to reluctant consciousness. The giggling, when it came, was louder, closer, and suddenly flushed with a coloration of intimacy that caused him again to prop himself on his elbow and frown into the darkness that was more than ever frustrating his perceptions, burning his eyes. He turned his head; his face was conforming to the severity of his frown. But there was no mistaking the quality that had now crept into the wordless music of the two women: their giggling was now meant explicitly for him. How could he stop those shy inviting sounds? How could he prevent the two country women from approaching him on hands and knees, as they were now doing? How could he preserve himself within the boundaries of sleep? A fearsome horse was preferable to the approach of unknown women who were not in the least interested in the sleep into which he himself so wished to sink. But perhaps he was once again mistaken; perhaps the women wanted only additional warmth and the closeness of a man in the night.

105

After the passing of another moment or two, marked by a few more sounds of wordless pleasure and the undertones of speech too faint to understand, he discovered that he had not been mistaken. He heard the movements of their arrival next to him; even the anxiety he experienced when there could be no doubt but that the two women had arranged themselves on either side of his body and were pressing against him, even this anxiety was uncertain and might dissolve in a moment. When cool unfamiliar fingers began to explore his face he stiffened, resented the investigation, and then slowly abandoned his suspicion and relaxed into the kindness that the woman's hand conveyed to his face. But in another moment or two he discovered that he had been initially correct: the hand that had lain lightly against his face seized and held his jaw in a thoughtless grasp, while a still bolder hand, which surely belonged to the woman lying behind him, reached over his hip and, catching a handful of the trousers bunched between his legs, roughly shook him like a cat with a bird. He made a disapproving sound in his throat, the women giggled, he grew suddenly flushed in the realization that he was being robbed, not of wedding band, money, identity card, but of sleep.

He attempted to sit up but he could not. The women were feigning sleep; the horse had swayed once more in their direction and was close now, standing heavy guard over the two women who were wedging the body of Konrad Vost between their own. On the breath of one of the women was the smell of food that had spoiled; the feigned sleep of the women was slowly inducing the rhythm of the all too real sleep into which he longed to descend. The woman behind him was scratching herself briefly, the other was quiet. Again he was being drugged on what he was breathing: the smells of manure, dust, perspiration, unwashed hair, a rancid mouth. Suddenly, viciously, a hand was again gripping his jaw and shaking it, shaking his head, while the woman behind him raised herself and drove her pointed elbow into his side, then with her

106

other hand began squeezing rapidly the front of his trousers as if to both arouse and crush desire in a single gesture.

But why should he not sleep at any cost and simply ignore the tugging, the shaking, the elbow irritably poking his side, the deceptive periods of silence that were only hiding places from which the giggling inevitably leapt into sight? He went limp, his body slackened, the burning sensation increased in his eyes, the darkness gave way to the brightening colors that were always the prelude to sleep and dreams. How could the women rouse him if he was asleep? He wished only that his head would loll and that his aching angular body would soon be without sensation and incapable of movement.

The horse stamped in the darkness and abruptly the battering recommenced: the woman behind him was pushing and pulling on his trousers where the cloth was tight between the buttocks, while the other, she whose round breast must have cushioned the entire face of the child now crouching beside the fire, was lowering her great head closer and closer to his own and filling his mouth and nostrils with her hot and rancid breath. Without question she was attempting to persuade him to accept some gift of tenderness. Yet even now she was giggling and rapidly working her thumb and first two fingers in the crotch of his trousers as if she were trying to tickle the fat and listless boy at the fire. Despite the indifference and aggression of the thumb and fingers, nonetheless deep in his trousers they were causing him to feel again the first tremors of excitation, though against his will and though he wished for nothing more than sleep. But just as it seemed that his loins must open, like creaking doors, the woman removed her hand, and squeezing his cheeks, shook his head to the left and right playfully, violently, then released him as before.

Again he was confronted by the imminence of the woman's face and the invitation of the open mouth in which her bad breath was crouching. She who was forever yanking on his trousers without opening or removing them was now holding tightly his left hand, still tied about the wrist with the tag bearing his name, and forcing it beneath her raised skirt and against the coarse dampened material between her legs. At the same time the other woman, whose large face was now in the process of mounting his own, was imprisoning between her heavy legs none other than the precious silver hand itself. He struggled; he attempted to free the silver hand; he attempted to ignore the violent knee that periodically rammed his side. Yet he had no choice but to comply.

He opened his lips, he raised his face, he took into his mouth the woman's demon of bad breath which, in turn, was followed by her anxious tongue. Inside his mouth the woman's giggling gave way gradually to a diminishing cascade of little sighs. No sooner had he accepted the woman's gift of tenderness and engaged the woman's mouth with his own than the blows ceased, the hard knee stopped its plunging, hands and thighs relaxed their grip on him, the elbow slept, the two women sank into tranquillity on his either side. He heard nothing but the patient horse and the kissing noises of the woman that were filling his head and making the front of his face a sounding board for the woman's obvious pleasure. He allowed his hands to remain quietly captive, he returned the nudging and stroking of the woman's tongue with his own tongue, as best he could he welcomed into the cistern she had made of his mouth the breath of the woman which surely her husband never tasted except drenched in his liquor. The stillness was a warm sham of peace; in it he lay flat on his back and blanketed beneath the woman's kiss. He resisted nothing; he complied with everything. The fingers of his left hand moved as they were being induced to move against the coarse material that was blotting the pleasure between the stiffening legs; with wrist and forearm he aided the kissing woman's manipulation of the gloved hand between her legs. He went so far as to encourage, at least in thought, the responsiveness that was struggling now

108

in the bunched and to him inaccessible front of his trousers.

He was breathless, he himself was aroused. How long could he endure such passivity? He was choking on the woman's kiss, his fingers were slowly losing the sense of touch, he longed to expose himself as the women pressing their bodies to his had exposed themselves. Surely if he could open the front of his trousers sleep would descend.

He turned his head, twisting his mouth away from the woman's, and suddenly was relieved to be inhaling the smell of manure instead of the breath of the woman. For a moment he breathed freely, and then, slipping his tagged left hand from the grasp of its captor, hurriedly he reached down for the belt, for the zipper, thinking to find himself with his bare fingers and even to entice the women to touch him with theirs. But hardly had he begun to pull on the belt when the blows fell: against his chest, across his face, into his ribs. False light shattered the darkness. He felt the disappearance of his spectacles, which he would no doubt discover in the morning light half crushed beneath one of the hoofs of the horse. But was it possible, this overpowering of Konrad Vost, this mistreatment of a man whose only remembered intimacy had been with Claire?

But what could he do if not comply? Quickly he began to move his head, to search for the woman's mouth until once again the lips met, the tongues extended each to the other, and the kiss, if such it could be called, returned to its previous subdued condition of sucking and sighing. The blows stopped abruptly. He allowed his left hand to be carried again to its wet place in the folds of the undergarment tightly drawn between the naked legs; he observed that the woman whose passion was largely confined to the kiss was once again employing his gloved hand between her legs.

So the darkness was consumed in revolt, attack, submission. His jaws ached, his tongue was torn, his eye sockets were packed with sand, a large invisible monkey sat grinning in lewd prohibition on

109

the trousered loins. Whenever he could bear no longer the woman's mouth he reached for himself; as soon as the blows fell he returned to the kiss. Submission, revolt, attack, submission: how could he sleep? How could the conspiring women sleep? But shortly before dawn he had at least a few moments in which to embrace the dubious specter, as did the women.

Why was Gagnon the bird lover not asleep? Could he who loved his birds in their little wooden cages have left his shutters so carelessly ajar? Why in this same late hour was the bird lover sitting with the sleepless few in the dank and shuttered gloom of the café below? Why could he not have enjoyed his usual sleep and died with his birds?

But in this darkness of predawn oblivion, how could the fire bomb intended for the barricaded prison have gone so astray as to soar to the loosely shuttered window of a roomful of sleeping birds?

How could one man's sleep become the vessel brimming with the agony of another's wakefulness?

But it was so: the light that destroyed the birds of he who was awake engendered, simultaneously, sequential vision in the sleep of the distant friend. For some, sleep is a matter of unfamiliar sights and logical distances. Sleep is the natural medium of light that cannot be seen.

In an instant the light appeared and like a rush of silent wind burst open the shutters and filled the room with a stationary white brilliance which, in turn, contained a multiplicity of process: an entire layer of small wooden cages disappeared. In one corner a colony of green finches was subjected to such intensity of heat that each of the creatures was reduced to a charcoal droplet on the floor of its smoking and slowly collapsing cage; along the left-hand

110

wall, from floor to ceiling, the sky blue and golden finches exploded in the still pressure of the light so that there remained only masses of bright feathers spattered over the surface of the wall where the heap of now ashen cages had been stacked. As for the stunted rainbow canaries, which were farthest from the light-filled space that had been the imperfectly shuttered window only moments before, these lost their feathers immediately and, smoking and roasting, resembled tiny brown glistening and shriveling shoes for the feet of dolls. In the instant the entire roomful of flitting birds became a showcase of the variety of the destructive powers of light in a state of radiance. The singing of the birds was transformed into color; there were entire snowfalls of severed wings. The frequency of movement which had animated finches, canaries, lovebirds, was transformed from moderation to frenzy and from frenzy to the stasis of empty air; dead birds flew slowly about the room as in a glass tank of light.

But even in this first suspended moment while the birds were whirling, changing shape, disappearing, suddenly the disordering of the birds became complete, luminous transparency giving way to natural occurrence as suddenly the silent light was joined by its familiar companions of fire and sound. The walls shook; shutters, window glass and window frame dissolved; cages and dead birds began to burn. Scorch marks appeared on walls and ceiling as if some large and coal-dusted animal had thrashed about the room in its final agony. Smoke began to displace all the patterns and discolorations first produced in the blast; the room became an oven in which the noise was so great that it summoned the terrified bird lover from the café below.

But then smoke, light, concussion, noise, ashes, organic remains, everything was drawn off in a slow and milky stream through the ragged hole in the wall and upward into the last of the night. When the bird lover finally reached his room and tore open the door, he saw in the darkness that nothing was left to him of his precious birds. They were gone. But was he weeping for the loss of his birds or for the loss of his daughter who had suffered the explosion of La Violaine?

The light that had fled the room of birds was still lying bright and painful behind the eyelids of its sleeping witness. Surely extinction was preferable to such a light.

The village church. The snow as high as the head of a man. The midmorning sun like the breath of summer in the cheeks of winter. The mothlike child drowsing cross-legged in his nightdress in a shaft of the warm light. What can such a child expect to know? Yet even for him, in whom pleasure and premonition took the place of consciousness, the substance of that morning included the church of flaking plaster and squared logs, the choir of small boys singing that very moment inside the church, the emptiness which certain children crave and which, that very moment, was filling the farmhouse on the edge of the village where the little trumpeter of the silver hand was sitting alone with himself like a moth at rest in the light. The woman of the house was with her pupils in the church; the hour itself was warmed by the sun and by the livid porcelain stove which the woman had lit before setting off brusquely into the sun and snow. Behind the house a pile of freshly flung hay was a head of yellow hair bristling in the white snow; a goose was honking between the barn and well. All this the child knew in his peace and weakness, though if asked he would not have been able to say a word about a world in which he himself was the only child, despite the boys in the church.

Who can account for the impulses that begin to grow in the narrow breast of the frail child who is both adored and scorned? Who can account for the secret impulses of the child who knows and does not know that he is admired, ignored, treacherously photographed, and that he possesses the power of the hawk in the sky and the contemptible pathos of the moth between the fingers? But now, in the sunlight, such a secret impulse was growing like a little tooth in the breast of the boy.

He was warm but he wished for greater warmth; he was pleased in his own presence yet wished for another; he himself was winsome, yet without knowing it he longed for beauty. He was an image of stillness but now wished for something greater: stealth. What small illness had caused him to be left alone in his condition of vague and innocent desire and had spared him the coldness and poverty of the church and the singing of the boys who looked like short lascivious men? It was only some small illness invented unwittingly by a child who, unconsciously, wanted nothing more than to be always right and forever without the slightest guilt.

He began to stir. But where was it that he wished to go? To the porcelain stove with its white surface flushed in the silence of the flames inside? To the cell of the cigar smoker that he so often visited in the night? Or to that other room, in which the large undecorated bed would not be empty, white, and both inviting and forbidden in the still light of the midmorning sun? Though uninstructed in stealth he was now stealthy; he moved as if at any moment he might be apprehended, imagining to himself that the farmhouse was not empty. In his white nightdress he was a destructive angel, a harmless insect; he walked on the toes of his narrow naked feet which, for his thinness and small size, were oddly long. Before him on outstretched frail arms he held his long thin hands fluttering as in benediction.

The doorway, the enormous bed, the white pitcher and basin on the wooden stand, the sunlight made even warmer by the reflecting fields of snow beyond the window and, on the wall above the head of the bed, the framed portrait of the naked bright red heart trussed up in the green thorny vines chopped from some wild and frightening bush. How could the boy know that the naked heart

113

was an image of fleshless avowal and not, as he thought, an image of ill-defined temptation? But so it was to him.

But the bed was not empty, as he had hoped and expected. There, in the bed that belonged to the woman of the house and that should have been empty, lay the sleeping figure of Konrad Vost the Father. At first sight of the sleeping man the boy in the doorway crouched down in fear and wonder, listening to the silence as if for the shriek of a spider and watching the bed as if its occupant intended never again to move. Konrad Vost the Father had ventured from the storeroom clothed in nothing more than his nightdress: it was not allowed. He was lying alone and in the center of the vast white bed that smelled of soap and a woman's hair: it was not allowed. He who never slept was now asleep and at an hour when he should have been at work in the barn: it was not allowed.

The little trumpeter had approached this room with stealth, pleasure, sensations of tremulous languor; now he was clasping his hands to his stomach and crouching down. The sight of the man in the bed caused the trembling boy to understand that he himself had meant to usurp the forbidden bed precisely as the sleeping man was usurping it. Why then was the daring of Konrad Vost the Father so much more frightening than his own? He could not have said. But the sleep of the man was more dangerous than anything he had ever seen, that much he knew. He wanted only to arouse and warn the sleeper and then flee from the room. But he could not move.

Once at a still younger age he had seen the bed when it was occupied by its rightful owner; on several occasions he had stood in the doorway and spied on the bed in all its inviting and majestic emptiness. But now the sun was lighting the bed as never before, so that the blackness of the heavy wooden frame appeared to be oiled with light while the coldness of the hand-laundered linen was turned to warmth. There, completely covered except for his head on the pillow and one bare arm stretched along the surface of the white coverlet, lay Konrad Vost the Father in total comfort, in deep sleep, in brazen elegance. The flesh of the face and arm was tinted with the warmer tones of a flower with petals reflecting the color of sun and blood; the sleeper's tranquillity might have been that of a lifeless figure supported in the exact center of the great sinister bed throughout the days and nights preceding interment; the expression on the sleeper's face was in itself an irresistible temptation to all the pleasures of silence. The allure of the smile arose from its display of white teeth that were all but invisible between the parted lips.

It was then that the child entered the forbidden room. He crossed the threshold, stopped, fluttered, and suddenly began to return the smile of the man whose insomnia had given way at last to exhaustion. Again the child's hands were raised before him, thin and quivering. The heart displayed on the white wall might have belonged to the sleeping man who, as even the child could see, had gotten into the bed as carefully as possible so as not to disturb the formal arrangement of linen, pillow, white coverlet as heavy and unadorned as a shroud. But if Konrad Vost the Father could so defy the prohibitions of this room, then why not he? If Konrad Vost the Father had the courage to sleep in the bed that was not his own, then why not he? Konrad Vost the Father would protect him; side by side they could defend themselves against the demons.

On tiptoe the child approached the bed. On tiptoe he pressed himself against the edge of the bed. His narrow face and the fragile shoulders draped in white were on a level with the bed's tight surface and the enormous bare arm which it supported. The eyes of the little trumpeter were large and bright; the mouth that was much too large for the narrow face was smiling so openly and crookedly that the pointed cheekbones might have been bright with tears; on a level with the eager eyes of the child the rosy naked arm of Konrad Vost the Father was lying in sunlight so thick and liquid that the bare arm was swarming with invisible and silent bees. The bravery and goodness of Konrad Vost the Father gave his bare arm its gentleness and great size. Even asleep he smelled of cigars.

Now, like the silver horn, a single purpose commanded all the child's attention: to attain the surface of the bed without causing so much as a ripple in the mysterious and precious sleep of Konrad Vost the Father. Barefooted, on tiptoe, wearing like a mask the soon to be hated smile, moving with all the shocking agility of the creature who is slight and who devotes himself fearfully to hours of prayer in the darkness, and fluttering with pleasure that comes only from behaving for the good of others and from earning imaginary approval, quickly and silently the leader of the boys' marching band positioned at the bedside a wooden chair which, like a stepladder, provided him with exactly the undetectable access he desired to sunlight, bare arms, sleeping man. He stood on the chair, he attained the white surface of the bed on hands and knees, he curled himself against the warm and hairless arm of Konrad Vost the Father, he quivered at the success of a maneuver that was without sound and that reflected in the surface of the bed not a single indication of his nearly weightless body where he knelt and then lay beside the man who should have been banging the iron pails in the barn.

He curled himself against the arm that was as thick and soft and smooth as a woman's thigh. His nightdress rose around his little bony knees, he felt that he had become a small and happy animal, with both hands and the side of his head he touched as lightly and fervently as he could the gentle flesh of Konrad Vost the Father. What more could he ask?

Much later, when the singing teacher finally returned from the church that had been filled with the sound of tongues, the bed was once again empty and revealed no sign at all of Konrad Vost the

116

Father or of Konrad Vost the son. Outside the snow was higher and brighter than it had been when, in their sleep, those two had comforted each other against the demons.

What is the natural response to the past that is gone?

Shame and grief. Shame and grief.

So, Konrad Vost the Father. Do you dare?

The stove was cold. In the approaching dusk the deep snow was turning pale blue while the last of the red sun was crashing across the horizon like a sea that ebbs and tosses without tides, without natural order, drifting to shore or cresting suddenly into violent waves in accordance with a single negative principle: chaos. The ocean of dead light was as wet as blood; it tinted the hands and faces of those inside the farmhouse at the edge of the village and, outside, heaved in silent waves or sudden clouds of bloody spray across the horizon. The shadows born of such light were subdued, furtive, expectant; the blue color of the snow was impassive.

Could the woman preparing to light the stove have known that her child was seated in a dark corner? Had she any consciousness whatever of the cold and nearly invisible child whose outlandish smile, in response to the calmly spoken words of the woman, was shattering the narrow face not in pleasure but in an agony of fear and incomprehension? If so she did not care. In the instant her child had been skeletal, except for the head; from the head down he had been reduced to his bones that were fragile, bright, clothed in neither flesh nor wool; only the head with its fine hair, its pointed ears, its outlandish smile, remained of his familiar self. For the rest he consisted only of bones. He and no one else could hear their toneless music.

So, Konrad Vost the Father. Do you dare?

The stove was taller than the woman and white and cold. The

woman was stooping before the belly of white porcelain; in one hand she was holding a large rusted container brimming with fuel; snow was still clinging to her rubber boots cut off below the knee; aside from the black dress she was wearing only the lightest of shawls, invulnerable as she was to the cold. She was stooping in semidarkness though the dark was seething with the dead sun and though the glass lamp on the bare table beside her contained a fresh white wick that was burning with a bright flame. In the corner, disregarded, the little skeleton was trembling while his smile was silently imploring the woman of the house for mercy.

But what had happened to Konrad Vost the Father? The hour for sleep was distant, despite the approaching dark; it was so cold that in the snow outside the long shaggy coat of a pony drawing a silent swiftly passing sleigh was thick with ice. The tiny flowers on the porcelain stove were frozen. Yet there stood Konrad Vost the Father in his nightdress. What was wrong? And what shiny thing was that in his hand? What can be expected of a few brittle bones in the sunset?

The woman of the house glanced over her shoulder, straightened up from the cold stove, and spoke. Konrad Vost the Father took two gentle steps as might a heavily booted man gliding forward among the dancing villagers; the sleigh passed into the night. In the dark corner the creature who was like a small animal that has been held by its furry head and dipped into a pot of acid until the bones of limbs and body have been cleanly stripped, this creature, contorted into its crooked smile, was unable to speak, to move, to intervene. The sea of red light was lapping and crashing against the farmhouse embedded in deep snow. The shadows moved furtively, with nothing to fear.

So, Konrad Vost the Father. Do you dare? said the woman of the house as slowly, without a moment's thought, she emptied the iron can of fuel so as to cover completely her victim, drenching his hair as well as his nightdress, and with her free hand seized the crystal

118

lamp and in one deft gesture made of Konrad Vost the Father a human pyre. He exploded in radiance which, in the instant, subsisted on his person like a mystical fire, allowing the man himself to remain perfectly visible inside the flames that imitated, though in a much larger size, the shape that was his.

Who would not admit that his presence of mind was immense? In order to spare the farmhouse and perhaps himself he turned and fled, the fierce light fanned by his haste and billowing and shimmering from all his surfaces. He managed to open the door of the farmhouse, to run several measured paces into the cold night, to ignite the darkness with his luminous presence, and then to fling himself hot and burning into the deep snow. But he was not able to extinguish, in time to prevent his death, the light he had at last become.

And what of the child in the corner inside the house?

Shame and grief. Shame and grief.

When Konrad Vost awoke at last to the sunlight pressing against the lids of his eyes, which he could not bring himself to open, he knew immediately that he was cold, that he could not move, that his body ached from sleeping on earth softened only with dung, and that his two tormentors now standing guard over him, one bearing a length of rope and the other gripping a wooden pitchfork in her two hands, were not at all from a nearby farm but from La Violaine. Without opening his eyes he knew that the hunter had been hunted down, and that he himself was now a prisoner.

The spectacles had been repositioned on his face but the name tag that had been tied to his wrist was gone.

THE PRISONER

Throughout his final days and hours, which were also his days and hours in La Violaine, there were occasions when Konrad Vost thought himself unable to bear the humiliation of being a hostage. Nonetheless he entered La Violaine feeling only recognition, relief, and the special pleasure that always attends the inevitable when it finally occurs. After all, the closing of the darkest gate is like a burst of light, and Konrad Vost found himself exactly where he had always wished to be without knowing it: in the world of women and in the world of the prison, where the more dangerous rudiments of common knowledge are unavoidable and where he would receive the punishment he deserved and desired, in confinement, for his acts of innocence as well as for his ultimate inability to be always right, always correct.

He had recognized La Violaine when he had fallen in the ranks of those storming the prison. Now his recognition of La Violaine was of double strength: he knew where he was, he belonged where he was. Four meager rooms of habitation, and pharmacy, school, cemetery, railway station: all these he was never to see again. The prison had taken the place of them all. Now he could dream at will, admit his shame and grief at will, suffer at will the presence of the women he had spent his life avoiding. He who had always considered himself the freest of men was now imprisoned. He who had always condemned the imprisoned was himself imprisoned. His penchant for irony had been fulfilled. What more could he ask?

Konrad Vost was led back into La Violaine like an animal on a length of rope exactly three days following the first public announcement of the rebellion in the prison, and at approximately the same hour when, three days before, he had first entered the yard of the school. For all his suffering, he was only too well aware, even then, of chronology, of the crossing of public axis and private axis like two rotten sticks. While small groups of women hooted and whistled at the once handsome but now ravaged black-suited figure being led across the yard of the prison, he himself was thinking of time, irony and stars. But did his theories of the psychological function apply to women? Could such a person as himself ever be brought to even rudimentary knowledge of submission, domination, the question of woman? As he lurched once again through the garden of ruined flowers, he was conscious of the fact that he did not know.

However, the first dictum of his notorious mother, whom he recognized immediately when at last they came face to face only hours after his arrival in La Violaine, was that marriage must never in any way become maternal. The truth of the pronouncement was like the removal of the hood from a man about to be hanged, and thus completed in the prison that annihilation of Claire which had commenced with her death. Thus Konrad Vost was able to learn his first lesson with ease, and at that moment lost the last shred of his grief for the woman he no longer needed.

Konrad Vost, condemned and justly so. The notorious woman revealed, though only as if her motherhood had never been. The tall and handsome woman of the transfiguring hatchet identified, though no longer as the nun she had once been. The woman of his married life replaced, though by two women instead of one, and by women who promised him not sentimentality but flesh and light. What more could he ask?

His captors, the one holding the end of the rope, the other still bearing her wooden pitchfork, appeared to have no memory of the torment to which they had subjected him in the darkness of the night and early dawn. That they had inflicted upon him sleeplessness and the pain of arousal deliberately and repeatedly denied left in them no residue of malice or self-consciousness. They were large and middle-aged, like himself; they were heavy and plain, their voices betraying not the slightest sound of girlhood or laughter, their faces and bodies betraying no sign of the wiles they had exerted on him the night before. With indifference, even tolerance, they led him slowly across the yard of the prison, among the groups of hooting and whistling women in whom victory had quelled rebelliousness, and up a high dark narrow staircase smelling of blood and urine. They unlocked a door, they thrust him inside a room containing shadows faintly edged with soft light. Here the smell was stronger, breathing more difficult, as if this room had been greased with the confinement of the woman who had preceded him. It was only after several moments alone that the first ugly realization came to him: the women had failed to remove the rope still tied to his neck.

He was disordered, demoralized, dislocated. Insects from the bed of dung in the barn had invaded his clothes. His long bones, the filth he had accrued on his journey, the rope that dangled down to his feet and beyond, the smells of the anonymous woman who in this very room had known the abominable enterprises of prison employees and inmates as well, the fitful shadows he himself was projecting into a cold space at once hospitable and forbidding: everything he felt and perceived only strengthened his gathering conviction that he would never again be free, no matter what happened.

He took the few necessary steps to the first of two windows and, after a moment of hesitation, thrust his left hand between the rusted bars and pushed open the shutters. The sun was dying like a florid deflated beast low in the sky; the window in which he stood was on the uppermost floor of the ancient prison building and faced the street where for days and years he had sat beneath the faded gold and crimson awning of La Violaine, glancing upward from time to time at these selfsame bars behind which he was now staring down; now, in the window, he was motionless with surprise and pleasure.

Below his dark barred vantage point where he stood in shadowed invisibility, breathing in the smells of the approaching night, smells in which those of the vanished woman behind his back were nonetheless faintly evident, below him the street remained empty of traffic, except for a single blue van parked opposite the narrow gates that were now guarded from within by animated women instead of from without by an indifferent sentry. Down there the café was still closed as if in mourning, its steel shutter drawn, its awning furled.

Gagnon's life, like his own, had changed. The charred hole in the wall of the room above the café, the smoke-darkened silence that should have been filled with the noise of the singing birds: it was a sight that confirmed the accident that had befallen Gagnon's room and that had come to him in the midst of his own torment the night before. Even now Gagnon was perhaps sitting alone and helpless in that blackened room as he himself was standing in the room to which he had been assigned in La Violaine. Grief and helplessness sway to and fro on the tide of the psychological function from friend to friend.

How then could grief, hostility and confusion give rise to joy? Gagnon was depressed, wherever he was. He himself had swung from maniacal determination to the sooty underworld of depression and there, according to reason, he should have remained. Yet he was rising on the dark tide. He knew where he was, he belonged where he was, never had he expected enough good fortune to find himself exactly where he most longed and feared to be: in prison. But so he was, and so too in the charred blackness of Gagnon's empty room he saw only the brightest colors. In the victory of the women, he, the captive, was victorious: his black hand was to his actual hand as the artificial aristocratic eye was to the face of the military leader proud in the pitted field: the recognition of this place, which he had always imagined, released from somewhere deep inside him a brief invisible spurt of elation as pathetic and valuable as the small single flame anchored to its dirty jet on a stove. The worst of life gives rise to its greatest pleasure. In his deepest convictions he was now confirmed. Perhaps his captors had left the rope attached to his neck so that, unable to bear these first few moments of silence, loneliness, imprisonment, he might the more easily become his own executioner. But all his sensations were the opposite of deadness: he had already been hanged, cut down, revived. The dead insects as thick as dust on the sill of the window from which there was no escape, the smell of vomit still faintly impregnating the cloth that covered his bony chest, the light that was now hailing the impending night for his eyes alone: in all this he discovered the restoration of certainty, a ravished joy. He alone was becoming witness to all those shadows ordinarily concealed. Mutilated railway trains were again running according to no schedule on the tracks of silence. Soon there would be no more punishment, even for him.

Suddenly he turned to the window in the other wall, and reaching through the bars and flinging wide the shutters, found himself flushed in the colors on the horizon and staring down into the yard of the prison. Thus the room in which he was now confined allowed him to look down both at the small secreted world of La

124

Violaine the café or into the yard of La Violaine the prison. Surely his captors had deliberately selected this high corner room in which to detain the only man alive in La Violaine.

This darkening room was filled with light that was by turns orange, purple, yellow, green. The rich light of expiation. The light of dead birds. He turned. He surveyed the room that was his. Wooden floor gray and splintered, small wooden table for a plate of food, iron bedstead with a mattress fallen partway to the floor, a lipless iron sink shaped as if to receive the most repellent of human waste, a porcelain toilet from which the seat had been torn, bare plaster walls covered with the handwriting of innumerable women, a single low wooden bench such as might hold the weight of the seated cobbler, and everywhere a profusion of scattered articles of clothing worn only by women: here at last was the splendor of deprivation, the pleasure that had been taken in the disordering of the familiar world, the excitation inherent in everything discarded, the joy of completion doubly evident in the ruin. Silent voices were crying in the gorge of the toilet; in an island of orange light at his feet lay a pair of soiled underpants that had been pulled from the loins of a woman shamed in her nakedness; and, just as he had thought, there were dark irregular stains of blood on the mattress. Never before had he so known the power of the physical object. Never before had he recognized the joyful indecency of wreckage. The broken vase, the bar of music already sung, what was there more? For the first time he recognized the trespasser inside himself. He had only to touch one by one the female garments left behind in this prison room or to read the various dates and messages scrawled on these bare walls by women, not men, to learn the particulars of indecency.

La Violaine to La Violaine, he thought to himself. For him the aphorism was now actuality. What was there more?

It was then that the night came suddenly to the world beyond the prison, and that the light died in the room where he stood, and that he heard the sounds of more than one person climbing the stairs to the door that was locked, chained, and covered with sheets of nailed tin. The sounds of the footsteps rose in the darkness, clattered abruptly to silence outside the door, and after a pause were followed by the noises of opening lock and falling chain that have always signaled food, reprieve, or death sentence to all those crouching in the dungeons forever sunken into the darkness of both the inner and outer lives of everyone. In this instant Konrad Vost discovered that he too was vulnerable: he could see little, he knew that the skin was tightening on all the surfaces of his body, the noise at the door was a loud and menacing chaos.

In the next instant, when the door had been flung back, he thought that three persons had come to interrogate him or to provide for his needs: the tall handsome woman who was now unarmed, the small woman he dared not hope to recognize but knew in the moment, and beside them a third figure, numinous, transparent, composed entirely of the fiercest light. But then the tall woman drew closed the door, the key turned, again the smells of blood and urine filled the room, with pained relief he saw that what he had mistaken for a third person was only the bright light of an oil-burning lamp held high in the hand of the small woman who was, as her only son well knew, the notorious Eva Laubenstein. The small size, the imperious and somewhat angled line of the dimpled chin, the smile implicit in the severity of the mouth and eyes, the black hair now a yellowish gray but as always bound at the back of the head in a slick tight almost fleshy bun: who else could she be but Eva Laubenstein? Bare knees, piled snow, thumping drum, cold trumpet clasped in the silver hands and pressed to thin lips, bell of the trumpet circling wildly in pursuit of its own frozen tones at the head of that childlike and meager march: who else had he played for if not precisely this same Eva Laubenstein who had destroyed his childhood and made

126

herself forever notorious? He had hardly dared look at her as a child, yet even now he loved the sight of her, though he averted his eyes.

"Hania," she said to her companion while inspecting their prisoner by the light of the lamp which she raised and lowered slowly, deliberately, shining the light fully into his eyes and up and down his rigid immobility. "Hania, untie the rope."

He was conscious that his upper teeth were clamped upon the entirety of his lower lip and that the corners of his mouth were drawn so tightly down that he might have been attempting to bite in half the hated smile before it could show itself once more on the ravished face. He was aware of the backward warping of his shoulders and spine, of the right forearm held parallel to the floor, of the black hand proffered stiffly from the wrist as if to receive in turn the welcoming clasp of the hands of the two women. He felt that nothing could pry apart his jaws, that no man before him had ever become, as he had now become, his own ridiculous effigy. He felt that his feet were bare and plunged into snow; he was listening to the cold martial chords and cadences of his childhood; he wanted to embrace the small bright figure of Eva Laubenstein but did not dare.

Even in his rigid indisposition, with eyes averted, he could not help but notice that the two women who had come to him were calm, efficient, and cleansed of the slightest trace of the smoke and fire of the rebellion. They had reverted to the gray dresses of the inmates of La Violaine, though Eva Laubenstein wore across her shoulders one of the captured blue tunics while her companion, the tall handsome woman who had smiled even as she had struck him down, was covered from chest to ankles with a long white butcher's apron tied about her neck and around her waist and bearing in a single pocket the great key to his room. So these were the women who promised him both flesh and light: the mother, whom he longed to embrace, and her companion, with red hair

127

so dark it resembled the meat of plums, whom he also wanted to embrace.

Eva Laubenstein put her glass-chimneyed lamp on the table at the head of the bed and turned up the wick, clasped her hands together palm to palm, fingers to fingers, and with head tilted to the side and small face severe yet warmly mocking, surveyed her prisoner. The tall woman stepped behind him quickly and, with strong cool fingers deft at needlework or brutal labor, untied the rope from his neck. He felt himself swaying though he did not move. Slowly, in a physical gesture like an exhalation of breath, he lowered his rigid arm and black-gloved hand, which had not attracted the attention of either woman. Eva Laubenstein, hands still clasped, had seated herself expectantly on the wooden bench; the tall and aproned woman was at his side.

As soon as he felt one of her hands on his left shoulder and the other on the sleeve of his right arm, he understood that whatever else they intended, he was to be undressed. The woman who had given him life was watching; the woman who had not hesitated to strike him down was already drawing open his stiff black jacket and pulling it off the shoulders. He assisted her efforts. The black hand caught for a moment in the sleeve. With no hesitation the woman steadied the inert black hand, freed the sleeve, stripped him of the soiled jacket which she dropped on the floor beside the rope. The serene fingers pulled the black shirt loose at the waist and removed it. His spectacles disappeared as did the shirt. The flame in the glass chimney was steady; the white apron smelled of lavender.

Shirt, rope, coat, spectacles, all were gone; the tall woman was as indifferent to the smells in the room and to the littered garments that were tokens of lust and torment as she was to his bare chest, black hand, waxen effort to retain some semblance of pride in the midst of submission. As soon as he felt the cool fingers on his arm he turned and took the few steps necessary to reach the bed, where he seated himself on the mattress. The tall woman knelt at his feet. To her, he understood, there was no such thing as indignity. But could he in fact allow her to expose his long naked feet as she had just exposed the whiteness of his glistening chest? However, the right foot was already gripped in her hand; the laces of the wet black shoe were yielding. He closed his eyes.

"Hania," came the voice from the shadows, speaking as the other woman's fingers tugged at the laces, the shoes, the wet stockings, "this man does not know that in the eyes of her husband a wife must never in any way resemble a mother. The woman who allows her husband to cause her to become maternal in marriage discovers the easiest possible way to pacify her husband while losing her womanhood. As soon as the woman tells the husband what to think, when he has no thoughts of his own, or comforts him in the kitchen, or rubs his back, she knows that she must turn to someone else for the companionship that she wants from a man. Oh, it is hard for a woman to be a wife. It is worse for the woman who finds herself not only married to a child but bearing children. We who spend our lives in prison know three things: that the family is the first prison; that among prisons the actual is preferable to the metaphorical; and that the woman is not a mother until she leaves her child. . . ."

His right foot was bare. He heard the shoe fall. Now the truth was unavoidable: his grief for Claire was finished; his marriage was finished, as it had not been even with the death of Claire.

The shoe of the left foot fell, the stocking tore, the left foot was now as naked as the right, though for this moment he felt it held in the two hands of the woman which were now warm to the touch. But how could the woman hold the naked ugly foot that was his? He did not need to open his eyes or listen to the tones of his mother's voice to know that his feet resembled long thin white fish and that on the toes the nails were like the yellow teeth of the horse.

129

"Hania," came the voice from the shadows, "are you listening? Do you agree?"

"I am listening, Eva," said the woman kneeling before him as if in prayer. "I agree. . . ."

She spoke softly, without turning her head, and yet her voice was so clear and strong, coming as it did from a lower register, that it was perfectly audible to Eva Laubenstein where she sat in the darkness watching, nodding, making her faint sign of approval with the two hands still pressed together. Despite her age, the voice of the kneeling woman contained all the depth and clarity of the boy who is on the verge of manhood and has been trained to sing. Her temperament was like her voice and body; of course she did not find his long bare feet repugnant; for her there could be no indignity, nothing repugnant.

Now, carefully, she released his naked foot, raised her head, placed her hand against his naked chest and pushed him back on the mattress. Still kneeling beside the rusted bed, though having risen upright on her knees, she untied the apron from around her neck so that the top of the apron fell to her waist. She unfastened the first several crude buttons of the gray dress. She drew apart the cloth of the dress as she might have the curtains of a children's theater. Then she placed her hands far apart on the edge of the mattress and, still tall on her knees, leaned forward and with her large mouth began kissing the cold white nakedness of his chest. In the light of the lamp he lay rigid, staring into the darkness beyond the light and listening for the brittle cracking sounds in his shoulders and in the top of his spine, receiving in this locked room of a women's prison the gentle deliberate attentions of a person he did not know. The smell of the kerosene was only another fragrance like the smell of the plum-colored hair. Never in his life had a woman devoted such attention and such concentration to the thin hard nakedness of his chest that was like the albino shell of a sea creature. But was this woman in La Violaine so very different from the nameless girl in the shuttered room? He had yet to know. Now he wished only that for a moment the woman might lift her long handsome face that he might dwell on the thought. But she did not. The movements of her face and mouth were continuous.

"Hania," came the voice from the shadows, "I too was a mother. . . ."

He listened, he knew that the tall woman had shifted so that one hand held his shoulder and the other was firmly pressed to his cold and scaly side. He could do nothing but wait for the large mouth to reach his dry lips, do nothing but attempt to listen to Eva Laubenstein acknowledge her motherhood at last. Now he would hear his own name on the wings of that voice. Or so he thought.

"Oh, yes, Hania, I too bore a child. . . ."

But now the tall woman was in fact raising her head, pausing, giving him the gift of the majestic consciousness that shone in her eyes. He looked so long into the eyes of the raised head that he was in fact prepared for the shifting of the woman's upper body. When she so arranged herself that the flesh exposed in the open dress was within easy reach of his face and mouth, and in the faintest motion was in fact brushing from time to time his forehead, his cold lips, his nose and cheeks, he in turn began to imitate the woman and deliberately to touch her skin with his cold lips, his untutored tongue. At last he was exerting himself to kiss the proffered flesh and yet was also exerting himself to listen to the voice in the shadows.

"Oh, yes, Hania, I was hardly more than a girl, though I had been for a long while in the wedded state, when suddenly my proud little belly began to swell. Exactly. Larger and larger. And at precisely the moment when spring arrived, the snow disappeared, and the entire village was covered with the blossoms of the fruit trees flowering in all the orchards. There was I with my little belly growing larger and larger, filling with the tears of spring, as the old women said. But what should have been my season of joy quickly became my time of deepest pain. Even the person who is unusually small and unusually attractive can suffer pain. . . .

"You see, one day the village doctor told me that the baby I bore in my body was already dead. A pretty thing to say to a woman who was no larger and not much older herself than a child. But the village doctor was a short massive brute who spent his life eating, drinking white wine, and causing pain. He disliked me on sight for my small size and attractive face. He told me that I must expel my dead baby, and in all possible haste. He told me that I too would die if I did not follow minute by minute his exacting regimen. So my season of sweet waiting for birth became instead my daily agony to induce expulsion. I was forced to visit the doctor once a day. I was forced to assume a squatting position and to strain, while pushing down with all my strength on my belly. I was forced to run in the mud after the snow-white pigs, to swallow roots and herbs and to engorge myself with platters of hot wet food. Daily vomiting and evacuation of the bowels were essential, said that doctor who had black hair on his hands. For hours I was packed in steaming blankets; about my belly I wore a rope which the doctor himself drew tighter day by day. Still I grew. The baby that was already dead, according to that brutal man, consumed more and more of my small life. The daily regime of exercising, eating, evacuating, vomiting, grew more severe. Wherever I went I wore my rope: the larger my little belly, the tighter my rope. . . .

"Finally, all these brutal efforts achieved success. At last the day of expulsion arrived. It was the hour of noon. I was naked. Even the rope was gone. In a matter of minutes the hungry doctor positioned me in a battered tin basin, low-rimmed but large enough for bathing. There I half sat, half lay, with my head and shoulders and hands and feet protruding over the tin edges while the doctor pushed on my belly and the basin slowly filled with my blood. Then I managed to expel my baby. I saw it emerge, that tiny hardly human creature, and watched as, small though it was, it began to crawl forward through the blood of its mother. I was in pain, I was shocked, I could not believe the sight of the life that inhabited the tiny creature whom I too had helped to punish so severely. It was not dead. I had been deceived. So when the doctor, who was late for his meal, suddenly reached out his hand, intending to seize the tiny creature and to crack its neck against the edge of the basin, as does the farmer who wishes to destroy the malformed newborn animal, I began to scream so loudly and also so obviously not from agony but in accusation, that even that brutal doctor fled for his midday meal. . . .

"So I saved my child. He lived. I could have no more. But I too was a mother. . . ."

How could a man born hardly human now be interested in a woman's kiss?

The red insect. The malformed child. The infant born not in love but in terror. The small red dripping thing that had destroyed its own mother's procreative powers, that had caused its own mother the utmost of unnatural suffering, that in its small deformed condition had managed to crawl from the sea of its mother's blood bearing in its minuscule impairment a single genetic inheritance: the instinct for innocence. No wonder she had not said his name. No wonder she had refused his father's name. No wonder she had disdained the cry of his trumpet while tutoring the voices of twenty boys. No wonder she had become notorious.

It was then that he heard the silence in the prison room, realized that the vision of the village birth was gone, and realized that throughout his mother's narrative the large warm mouth of the tall woman had in fact been pressed to his own. All the while she had in fact been kissing him. The words of his mother had come to him on the tongue of this woman.

That night Eva Laubenstein said no more. The silence grew.

133

The touch and breath of the tall woman disappeared. Behind his closed eyes the darkness returned. He heard the great key in the lock. In the darkness and colder than he had ever been, slowly he began to crawl into the pit of sleep.

Only the disfigured adult can properly care for the disordered child. . . .

So nightly shouted Anna Kossowski in her great stone kitchen where all the children, young and old, lay sprawled like dogs or dwarfs about the fire in the iron stove which was in the center of the kitchen of the long low farmhouse. Nightly Anna Kossowski walked among the children, some of whom were older even than she, shouting, laughing, and drinking from the half-empty bottle that she held by its neck. She as well as the children dressed in heavy discarded clothes supplied by the village. She was lightly bearded, heavy, passionate, with the thick large hands and feet of a man. From her left cheek grew a shiny brown toadstool in justification of her shouted rhetoric. Every night she walked in the kitchen among her charges and under the gaze of a small young woman known as Kristel, who was maintained by the village to assist Anna Kossowski in her care of the children.

The little trumpeter was always among those closest to the iron stove. He loved the light. He loved the drunken Anna Kossowski. He loved Kristel. Also he loved the other children, who were larger than himself or smaller, fatter than himself but rarely thinner, older than himself or younger. He loved those with hairless heads and faces as well as those whose faces were concealed behind mats of hair. He loved the sounds they made, or the bright red lips that never closed, the fingers without fingernails, the large round faces watered with the fluids of the mouths and eyes. But most of all he loved not the woman or the girl or the other children

134

but the fat horses roped side by side in the long low nearby barn of stone and wood. Gone were his trumpet, his marching comrades, the white porcelain stove, the cigar smoker, the singing teacher. But his life had improved, or so he thought. By night he smiled beside the fiery stove. By day he smiled beneath the massive legs of his favorite horse. What more could he ask?

The sagging barn. The long low corridor of wood and stone. The dust-filled darkness into which the day could hardly reach. The darkness, the heat and smells of the great beasts, the feeling of the hard shiny straw against his skin. Dust, straw, animal heat, the nest he made for himself in the straw between the legs of the largest and sweetest-smelling horse in the barn: here he was safe, here he was the happy insect among the monsters he could not imagine, and the heaps and swells of snow banked high against the outside of the barn only made the inside warmer and safer. In the straw at the horse's feet he could hear the cold snow creaking against the stones of the barn, while above him and in a long line to his either side the great monsters stood protectively at rest in the decay of the barn. The horses were no longer used. Rarely did anyone come to the barn to care for them. They were forgotten and left in peace. They were tall, heavy, massive, old, with shaggy uncut coats of hair impacted with month on month of gathering dust. The stone walls were sagging; the roof beams were sagging; the great beasts had lived forever and slept on their feet; up and down the long line of them he crept, looking, admiring, then returning to lie again beneath the horse that was his and that he thought of by the name of the woman he loved: Anna Kossowski. Above all the long hollow heads of the horses, which were as large as the coffins for children, the entire low ceiling of the barn was a honeycomb of cobwebs. Between the sagging beams, dangling above the twitching ears, up there the cobwebs existed in a thick silvery inverted mass of decay, desolation, time that was no longer time. Cobwebs above, straw below, here and there the dangling shrouded body of a small bird preserved as if by the art of a village taxidermist: it was here that he drowsed, hour on hour, breathed upon by the horses, forgotten, listening to the thudding of the great beasts near at hand or the distant wordless shouting of the clumsy children running aimlessly on the hills and in the fields of deep snow.

He stirred. The mice were running fitfully over the stones. He pushed off his blanket of straw, rose to an elbow, crawled out from beneath the monster he loved. He felt himself to be the animal's attendant; without thinking, he knew what to do for his great beast, she whose dusty ears and yellow eyes he had once inspected by climbing high on a broken wooden chair he had found buried under a pile of leather harness that had turned to stone. Water. She wanted water. He felt her blind thirst in his own throat. He groped for the wooden bucket, against his chest he carried the immense bucket through the shadows, down the length of the stones, and outside to the well that was cold and shimmering in the bright light and virgin snow. He shivered, cracked the film of ice, drew water, filled the bucket. A breeze intensified the light; his shivering had become a little dance. The water splashed against him, he heard the distant shouted grunts and cries of the children. He turned, dragging the water a short distance at a time, in puffs and starts, again he crept into the space between the high sagging wooden doors that were curved in age and frozen and ice-coated for three of the four seasons.

Slowly he made his way through the darkness, up the long line of forgotten horses toward the warm and slightly steaming place where the great ancient horse stood waiting. The water splashed from the bucket, from the other and far-off end of the barn came the sudden sounds of water beating down from one of the great beasts roped to the wall. The water carrier moved like an insect with his legs apart, the great bucket dragged and carried between them, his head flung back in the effort so that once again he was treated to the sight of the enormous glistening honeycomb of cobwebs that grew from the ceiling. But as he approached Anna Kossowski the horse, and despite his preoccupation with the sloshing bucket, he noted momentarily that something had changed: from a crack in the opposite wall a long thin finger of orange light was pointing directly at the neck of the waiting horse's immense black dependent tail. Something was different too about the great rear legs: they were farther apart than usual, and they were not relaxed as they usually were but rigid. The tip of the finger of light was becoming increasingly diffused over the neck of the tail that ordinarily reached down all the way to the straw but now appeared to be lifted and drawn aside. The light was diffused over the round curving buttocks and flanks of matted shaggy hair. Never before had the little water carrier noted such mild but oddly quickening changes in the immensity of Anna Kossowski the horse. But he did not allow himself to pause. Instead he squeezed into the narrow space between the rotted planks of the partition and the warm thick matted weight of his enchanted monster, until at last the lichen-covered bucket was properly positioned in the straw near the stones that bore the iron ringbolt to which she was tied.

He waited. With his own small breath he attempted to warm his fingers, still cold from the work of drawing water and still curved like transparent talons from the work of carrying the bucket. He waited. Overhead the cobwebs were stirring like sea grasses; again he thought of himself and, not in the least deceived by the baggy clothes he wore, again enjoyed what he knew to be his extreme small size and frailty. Though he could not have said so, he was aware that the frantic and ecstatic trumpeter had become, in the disguise of his borrowed clothes, the thin contented gnome who languished for as many of his waking hours as possible near or even beneath the living statue that was Anna Kossowski the horse.

The great head was now descending. From high in the darkness it came down, as long as he himself was tall and, despite its bony emptiness, much heavier than was he. The Roman nose was larger than his own white pointed face, the glistening eyes were as large as his fists, the sight that informed her eyes was more somber and comforting than anything he had ever seen. The head nudged him as usual and he staggered back in happiness, not fear, from its careless touch. As always he seized one of the great dusty ears and twisted it, waiting for the emergence of all the miniature creatures with wings, with many legs, with several heads, that lived inside. The creatures did not appear, as usual, but the ancient head dipped, groped downward for the bucket, and began to drink.

Invisibly, in single file, in long thin columns, everywhere the armies of mice were faintly running across the stones, running along the walls, tearing their way through the cobwebs, through the straw, and disappearing into the ears of all the horses that were not his. He waited. He languished in the touch of the horse, the sound of the mice, the sound of the nostrils breathing and the thick lips skimming the water. But still he was thinking of the light he had seen and the changes he had noticed in Anna Kossowski the horse.

She was drinking. She would not know that, for the moment, he was gone. Still pressing himself to the slow inner throbbing of the serpentine neck, he was consumed as never before with a curiosity that he did not understand and that was, as he somehow knew, forbidden. He did not know what he wanted to see or what he was going to do. But he who in body was among the smallest and weakest of all the children kept on Anna Kossowski's farm was now aware, for the first time in his life, of a dark wet craving inside himself for a knowledge he could not name.

He squeezed himself backward along the body of the great

silent horse. In the darkness, hesitating, baffled, performing his small and nearly motionless dance that always expressed his fear or eagerness, and recognizing in his indecision a sudden need for haste, suddenly he found himself searching for the broken chair and dragging it down the corridor of stones where he placed it directly behind the massive hindquarters of Anna Kossowski the horse. He was hardly able to contain his dancing long enough to position the broken chair: high above his head the orange light was shining warmly on the slopes and apex of the gigantic sculpted but living hindquarters that were now his to explore. He was dancing, he could not breathe, he knew that already the ancient horse was aware of his presence. But he did not care, he could no longer deny himself the sight that he craved. She was still drinking but she was aware of him: the great legs were oddly spread, the great neck of the tail was lifted and drawn slightly aside. He gripped the broken rungs of the chair, he smelled the straw and all around him heard the great jaws softly working; he tilted his head and stared upward at the steaming bestial hindquarters that were beckoning.

He climbed onto the chair. It wobbled; he straightened himself slowly and as best he could; eagerly he extended a small white timorous left hand and, barely touching the flesh of the horse, balanced himself on the ladder that would carry him to fire. The light was stronger, dustier, more diffused, more generous. He wobbled; with more reassurance he steadied himself by clutching with his left hand the hair that was thick and matted even at those slopes that were in the province of the sacred tail. He felt that in a moment more the smile would fly from his face. Now he knew that what he craved to see was concealed high in the somber darkness beneath the tail.

No longer was there need for haste. With his free hand he drew great shanks of the black luxurious hair of the tail against his cheek, his mouth, then allowed it to ripple away through the little transparent fingers. The rhythm of his stationary dance had reached him, suddenly, in the depths of the baggy pants, yet for him the tingling he could not have named existed only in the long thick strands of hair, and in the light, and in the love he felt toward Anna Kossowski the horse for allowing him to be where he was and to find what he craved. But perhaps what he sought was not forbidden to those who were ordinarily tall enough to see it in a passing glance; perhaps it was forbidden only to children. But Anna Kossowski the horse was tied; she could not speak; never would she strike down, with one of her great hoofs, the child who was now climbing about that part of her body she could not see.

Again he braced himself lightly with his left hand; he took a frightened breath and imprisoned it immediately deep in his lungs; then, as serious as he had ever been, despite the winged smile, he restrained the faint dancing motion of his legs and hands, and, standing on his toes, reached upward as far as he could with his free hand and ran the tip of one small brittle finger along the nearly hairless fat neck of the tail where it began. A trembling commenced in the bestial hindquarters. The tail rose. It swung aside. Again the great legs stiffened, increasing the distance they were spread apart; again the muscle that was the neck of the tail exerted itself, as if to assure him that the touch of a child's fingernail could speak to a mountain, and now he saw, up there, socketed in a field of dark velvet, exactly what he had craved to see: the large slightly opened vent he could not have known existed, bearing a few bright oily tears that never fell and that might have come from the great lemon-colored eyes of Anna Kossowski the horse.

Quickly, expelling and catching another breath, and growing suddenly wet inside his baggy clothes, feeling the unexpected return of the need for haste, quickly he strained himself once more and extended the same hand, the same finger, until the very tip of the finger touched for an instant the oily traces of the passionate bestial tears of Anna Kossowski the horse. But no sooner

140

had he done so than he heard an unfamiliar sound at the barn's door and felt in the animal herself an unfamiliar tremor. With both hands he clutched the tail; carefully he leaned to one side and peered around the hindquarters and into the darkness, only to find himself staring into the luminous white and lemon-colored eyes of the horse that had ceased its drinking, lifted its head, and swung around the great neck and head so that now the eyes of the horse were fixed on his own. As small as he was, and as innocent, still through the darkness he recognized the expression in her watchful eyes: reproach. Anna Kossowski the horse was looking at him with reproach in her eyes. She had not understood; she had not intended him to see what he craved. It was forbidden.

"So," cried Anna Kossowski the woman from midway up the corridor of stone, the tunnel of darkness. "So, little Konrad Vost, you have shamed the horse!"

His hands flew out, he toppled from the broken chair, he heard the quick heavy sounds of her wooden shoes on the stones. Then he was on his feet and dancing so extravagantly that he was convinced that he was running in all directions at once, though he was standing still. He had not meant to offend the horse; never before had he offended Anna Kossowski the woman he loved. Yet now she was speaking in anger and making the sounds of anger with her wooden shoes. What could he do if not flutter his hands and flee in all directions at once, going nowhere?

"Stand still," said the woman, "you who have shamed the helpless horse."

She gripped his neck, she kicked aside the chair, from an iron hook on a beam she seized a length of rope which she tied to his neck. Gone was the finger of light, the horse had returned to its drinking, in the darkness and shadows Anna Kossowski the woman loomed as large as Anna Kossowski the horse. Despite his terror, his dancing, his humiliation, still he realized that as the horse had been drinking its water, so had the woman her wine. Its heavy

141

aroma sifted through the smells of dust, straw, leather, wood, cobwebs, mice.

"Please," he whimpered, "please, Anna Kossowski, allow me to go free. I meant no harm. I was only trying to see where Anna Kossowski the horse expels her manure. . . ."

"So," muttered the towering woman, "so you have given my own good name to an aged horse. So much the worse for you, little Konrad Vost."

The rope was burning on his neck. Anna Kossowski was muttering to herself, and now, as she rummaged about in the darkness, tugging occasionally on the length of rope, now in this dark mood she was more frightening than she had been when enraged. She stumbled, he heard her curse, he made out a fragment of her mumbled speech: ". . . Anna Kossowski the horse . . . indeed . . . indeed. . . ." Then at last she found what she was searching for: a long and crudely pointed stick.

"Please," he whimpered, "please, Anna Kossowski, I beg of you. . . ."

She did not answer. She wrapped the end of the rope several turns around her wrist, tugging on it again as she did so. Then she righted the broken chair, positioned it slightly to the rear and to the side of the horse, and seated her mighty and fuming self to wait for as long as she needed to wait in the darkness. Little Konrad Vost, as she called him, did not know what she was awaiting. He knew only that he could not cease his dancing, that he could not escape, that all the mice had fled and that he could hardly see the great shape of the unrelenting woman he loved where she sat in the darkness waiting, jerking the rope, thoughtlessly rubbing her finger against the toadstool that grew on her cheek. The long stick was leaning beside her against the rotted planks of the stall.

Now the interior of the barn was as silent as the dead birds hanging in shreds from the thick white bed of cobwebs growing down from the ceiling; the horse that he loved had lifted its head;

he could hear the drops slowly falling from the still mouth to the surface of the water yet in the pail. Anna Kossowski sighed from the depths of the patience for which she was well known; in another moment surely he himself would drop in the midst of his dancing.

But then Anna Kossowski sat up straight, seized the stick, took a shorter grip on the rope and gave it a sudden furious snap, pulling him abruptly in her direction. She jammed the end of the stick against his side. He thought she meant to pierce him through with the pointed stick. At the same time Anna Kossowski the horse gave an immense lurch, again spread wide the tall hind legs, again swung her head so as to look at the woman and child with baffled and frightened incomprehension. As soon as the urine burst from the great animal with the intensity and heat of compressed steam, Anna Kossowski quickly loosened the rope, holding it like a taut rein, and with the end of the stick began deftly prodding the dancing child. He attempted to spring away; he was held by the rope. He attempted to fling himself toward the woman's knees; he was propelled backward by the thrusting stick. In this way, pulling the rope and pushing him off with the jabs of the terrible stick, Anna Kossowski guided him cruelly and expertly between the spread legs of the horse and directly into the fall of the urine. He gagged, he choked, he danced up and down as he had never danced in his life, all the while held hopping and turning in place by the stick and rope. He heard the urine crashing about him into the matted straw, in an instant his fine-spun hair and his skin and his clothing were as sopping wet as the straw and the great spattered hocks of the horse itself. He thought that he had drowned in the downpour of sour waste; he floundered as if in a tin tub containing all the transformed water that he had fed in buckets to Anna Kossowski the horse for the past three days. He could not even shout for mercy, so fierce was the flow.

Then it stopped. In one moment or several it came to him in dim consciousness that it had stopped, that the horse was empty at last. Beneath her belly he hung limp on his feet. He was no longer dancing. His skin burned. His eyes, nose, wide mouth, pointed ears: all were burning. His baggy shirt and trousers clung to his bones. It was as if he had lived the worst possible dream of the incontinent child. Now, all around him, he heard the intolerable slow dripping of himself and the horse. Then through the dripping silence he heard a different sound: that of the laughing woman who, though she did not know it, was now happily possessed by a fresh thirst for her wine.

She stood up. She flung aside the stick. Without looking she pulled him from beneath the horse and, not so much as once peering over her shoulder, dragged him blind and stumbling down the stone corridor to the high wooden sagging doors and beyond to the sunlight, to the high-banked snow, to the well where he himself had smashed the ice only a short while before. She tied her end of the rope to a rusted iron stanchion of the well; she drew a bucket of water glittering with chips of ice and, hardly bothering to glance at her target, flung the water at the child, who was still squeezing shut his eyes. He fell at once to his hands and knees. He cried out. The large and no longer patient Anna Kossowski then further deluged her charge with bucket after swiftly drawn bucket of icy water.

Then she carried him rope and all toward the farmhouse and the roaring stove.

The silver hand of the little trumpeter became the offending hand of the abandoned child and, in turn, at the end of his days, the silver hand of the uncomprehending Konrad Vost. Only at the last moment did the fierce spirit invested in all forms of female life relent.

Innocence leads inevitably to ice and iron: to bones that become iron, to skin that freezes gradually into a blue and glittering transparency, and then cracks and refreezes until the entire surface of the body is encased and encrusted in scales and broken mirrors of ice, frozen in place.

This is the man who is always cold. He shall be colder.

"Come, little Konrad Vost, the woman is preferable to the horse."

Thus one day in the fourth season, when the snow was gone, Anna Kossowski spoke to him again, and with kindness. Throughout the third season he had lain by the stove, shivering, refusing to move, refusing to speak, unable to rid himself of the yellow stench of urine, like a dog that has managed to soak its own leg.

The well water had done no good; he continued to smell on himself the horse's urine that he thought was his. The snow had diminished then disappeared, the expressionless eyes of the children had reflected the green of the trees, all about the stove the stone floor had become tracked with the black wet mud for which they had yearned: but he had not moved, curled as close as he could be to the hot stove, the elfin child who no longer danced up and down as if over a lighted candle.

Then at last Anna Kossowski spoke to him again: ". . . The woman is preferable to the horse," she said, and reaching down seized his arm and drew him, with only moderate roughness, to his feet. Outside the children were flapping in the mud or lumbering in the green fields; in the kitchen that was as large as a barn the sunlight was filling one of the stone corners, where there was a wooden bench, a stone trough smelling of sewage, the morning's collection of Anna Kossowski's empty wine bottles, standing or flat on their sides. In this corner the walls were inexplicably covered with green slime where Anna Kossowski had been seated all morning with the mouths of the consecutive wine bottles raised to her lips. Now she again seated herself on the bench, still holding the hand of the child who was disordered and dishonored as well. Across the room, at a long sink made of slate, little Kristel, who had herself been one of the disordered children until she had become Anna Kossowski's friend and assistant, was removing the skins from a sackful of onions and dropping them one by one into the cold greasy water that sloshed about in an iron pot as fat as the stove.

"Kristel," said the seated woman, "are you still pure?"

"Of course I am not pure," came the voice of the girl, who did not bother to turn around from her onions. "At my age, how could anyone be pure? I may look like a child, but I am not."

"You do not look like a child," said the woman. "You look like a nice ripe little bird. A man will yet turn you slowly over a hot fire."

"A pretty thing to say to someone. A pretty remark. You have drunk too much wine. But no one will put Kristel over the fire!"

Anna Kossowski laughed, two fat onions fell into the pot, the sunlight was shining directly on Anna Kossowski's face: on the hairs growing from her chin, on the toadstool growing from the right cheek, on the eyes that were red. Suddenly, feeling himself drawn closer to the woman he had once loved, who was sprawled on the bench with her head leaning back against the slime on the wall, suddenly little Konrad Vost opened his eyes, readied his wide lips to receive the long-lost smile, prepared himself to pull free of the hand on his waist and run, or to submit to the hand and to sink as of old into the warm lap. Was he to be forgiven or punished anew? Could he now love Anna Kossowski as he had before, or must he flee?

"At least you are safe with me, Kristel," said the seated woman, who was lolling her head, closing her eyes, breathing more deeply, holding him at the waist with her heavy hand. "There is nothing to fear from children or village idiots."

"Oh, you needn't worry about Kristel. I am not afraid. . . ."

The girl glanced over her shoulder, the sun was warm, were it not for the movements of Anna Kossowski's hand against his waist he might have thought she was sleeping. But she was not sleeping, though her eyes were closed. Trembling, warmed by the sun, readier than ever to smile, aware that his hands and feet were preparing to flutter in pleasure, not fear, he found himself then held by both of Anna Kossowski's hands instead of one. But what was happening to the woman he was beginning once again to love? What was she doing?

"So you are not afraid," said the woman at length, softly, as if she were talking to herself. "But there is not one of them who does not follow you urgently, trying to find in himself the capacity for normal speech. What is it they are trying to say? What do they want?"

"Kristel is not interested in what they want."

"Kristel is not interested," mocked the woman, "Kristel is not pure. Sooner or later one of them will take down his pants. Then you will see. . . ."

But Anna Kossowski had managed to gather into her lap the tangle of rags that were her skirts, and had stiffened and slightly spread her heavy legs. With her head against the wall, the bottom of her spine on the wooden bench, and the heels of her wooden shoes propped on the stone floor, she was as if simultaneously sitting, lying down and floating rigidly in the warmth and light of the kitchen. She was holding him between her stiff legs and in such a way that her hands were now on his waist, now further down, holding him firmly on the hips or shifting on the circumference of his little body so that one hand was pressed to the seat of his pants while the other turned palm up and cupped the front. Half the smile had returned to his face, the green slime was bright, a large slick naked onion splashed into the pot. Anna Kossowski's great calloused hands were careful, comforting; they felt for his body through the baggy pants as though it were not forbidden, as though she had every right to do so, as though in such unexpected friendliness he had nothing to fear. Even when she unfastened the tin buttons of the ugly garment that was not his own, and thrust her entire hand inside his pants, going so far as to lift him slightly off the floor with that thick hand in his pants, still he was not afraid, but rather surprised, confused, and so elated that the other half of the smile came to his face. Anna Kossowski grunted. She was moving her thumb and first two fingers inside his pants as if rolling between them a wet pebble. Now she was holding his little body so close to hers that, when he glanced down for a moment, he could see nothing except the top of his open pants entangled in the rags that were bunching and shifting in the woman's lap. He knew that where they were both naked and hidden from sight they were pressed one to the other. But down there did Anna Kossowski the woman look like Anna Kossowski the horse? He did not know.

He heard a splash. He heard the light careless voice of Kristel: "You should not do that to the child."

"No? No? And you? You would not do the same if I gave you permission?"

"Kristel is not interested in children or village idiots."

Anna Kossowski laughed through her nose, lolled her head to the side, and imparted a stronger motion to her naked massiveness beneath the rags, all the while watching the girl through half-closed eyes. As for himself, he who was held firmly in place between the great white thighs of the legs that were outstretched,

148

he who was happily baffled to know and not know that in his open pants his own small nakedness was inseparable from the woman's sandy nakedness still hidden from sight, now, suddenly, he was both elated and shamed as Anna Kossowski slowly raised one of her calloused hands and, with a sudden tug on the cloth on her chest, exposed one fat breast as if to give suck to an angry infant. She was smiling, the single breast was parading its nakedness on the field of cloth. As for himself, his mouth was dry, with his two hands he was gripping the forearms of the woman, in the distance he who was no longer a trumpeter heard the shrill heraldic cry of a silver horn.

"So, Kristel," said Anna Kossowski in her firm drowsy voice, "you can watch me over your shoulder and yet pretend that you care about nothing but onions? Even now you can be so bold as to deny that your little locomotive is already oiled? But haven't I taught you always to tell the truth to your mistress?"

"I am telling the truth," came the now sullen voice of the girl at the sink. "I am not aroused. For Kristel there must be more than an old woman and a pathetic child."

"He is almost as large as you," said the woman, who was pushing against him so that with every heave he was forced to hold her forearms with a still tighter grip in order to retain his footing. His fine-spun hair had fallen into his narrow face; he was smiling but he did not know where to place his attention: on the hand that was clutching insistently the seat of his pants, or on the nakedness of himself and the woman wrapped together in cloth, or on the exposed breast that was preening itself beside its shrouded twin. "You are not very large yourself," continued Anna Kossowski, controlling her voice and smiling through the strain on her face. "You, the impure girl, are as small as a child. But of course you are rubbing your thighs together there at the sink. I am not deceived."

"You may play with the child. But you may not play with Kristel! Even in words!"

149

As the young tree remains insensible to the twig that sprouts overnight from the slender trunk, so he himself remained in ignorance of what the secret portion of Anna Kossowski's body was doing in his open pants. His mouth was dry, his forehead was wet, his fingers ached, the offensive baggy pants were sliding down on his bare hips and thighs. Now Anna Kossowski's determined hand was squeezing not the seat of his pants but the flesh inside; as he shook to her efforts he began to wish that his hands were free to pull up his pants, while he hoped that at least the girl behind him at the sink would keep her back turned.

"I play with whom I wish," murmured the woman, smiling and jerking her shoulder so as to impart a similar motion to the naked breast. "Now lift up your skirt so the child may see. That's what he wants."

"But you shall not trick Kristel!" cried the girl, stamping her foot. "It is you who wants to look upon Kristel's nudity, not the child!"

The sun, the sound of the knife falling onto the wet slate, the sight of the great fatty thighs applying their terrible pressure on either side of him, the certainty that behind his back Kristel had abandoned her onions and was now watching how Anna Kossowski was making him dance, which she was doing with her thighs, her hands, and by butting him repeatedly with her sandy flesh inside his open pants: even in this strange condition of turmoil and tranquillity, while he was helpless and incapable of making so much as a sound, nonetheless, and quite suddenly, he wanted to understand the anguish that was pinching him in the front of his pants and wanted only to ask Anna Kossowski to pause for a moment and to speak a few words to him rather than to Kristel, so that he might catch his breath, relieve the anguish, and all the better enjoy what was happening. Desperately he wanted to pull up his pants or be free of them.

In the next instant he thought that Anna Kossowski had heard his unvoiced appeal. She stopped moving. Her hands and hips were still. She continued her deep breathing; she continued to squint in the direction of the watching girl; she continued to hold him in the grip of her two hands. Her face and the naked breast were gleaming. Her hair was loose. The muscles in her throat were tight. She was not smiling.

Then slowly she spread her thighs still farther apart, thus releasing him. In his surprise he tottered and felt her two hands climbing up his body and to the top of his head; he felt his nakedness become unstuck from the still unseen sandy nakedness of the waiting woman; he felt his baggy pants fall to the stones; he felt her two hands exerting a slow and tender pressure on the top of his head. Elated, confused, exhausted, nonetheless he did his best to follow the will of the woman and to understand the message of the hands so strangely placed on the top of his head. He closed his eyes and sank to his knees. Between his thin bare legs his anguish was still unrelieved, as if it were a small stone tied to him by a length of thread.

"Stop!" said Kristel in the silence. "No more! You must not teach the little child wickedness."

In the darkness, in the silence, despite the sensation of Anna Kossowski's hands smothering his large pointed ears, suddenly he realized that Anna Kossowski was going to give him on her own body the sight of what she had so long ago attempted to deny him on the body of the great horse. He opened his eyes: he was overwhelmed with disappointment at the sight of the thick hair; then he was sickened as, behind the hair, he saw not at all what he had seen on the horse but instead the briefest glimpse of what to him was a small face beaten unrecognizable by the blows of a cruel fist. In terror he saw that from this hidden and ruined face between Anna Kossowski's legs there were streaming two long single files of black ants. The large black ants were marching out of the face and down the inner sides of Anna Kossowski's thighs. The ants

151

were glistening. The two thin columns were already proceeding toward the knees.

He screamed, he freed his head from Anna Kossowski's hands, he crawled from her until he was able to gain his feet, pull up his pants, and run out of the room and into the sunlight where the well, which he had not seen for weeks, for months, stood gleaming. He drew a bucket of water. It fell on himself. He drew another. Then hardly conscious of the rest of Anna Kossowski's children grunting in the distant fields, he ran back as best he could with the immense bucket swaying and splashing in his hands. But no sooner had he once more reached the kitchen, in all possible haste, when he heard the sound of Anna Kossowski's voice and, somehow, knew enough to stop where he was and put down the bucket. Anna Kossowski's position was unchanged. He was unable to look.

"Little Konrad Vost," she said, "you are distracting me. You are not for women. Go back to your horse."

He did as he was told.

Cobwebs. Snow. Water. Light. Dry dung.

But how could he so detest the matron of the farm for disordered children while nonetheless loving the notorious Eva Laubenstein? For every child there must be the mother and the anti-mother. In his case both women had been anti-mothers. Why love one and not the other?

His eyes were open. He was awake. His consciousness was firm, clear, intense, expectant, and yet also empty. He did not know when consciousness had returned or when he had awakened, only that empty consciousness and the fact of awakening had coincided, so that now he was alert but unlocated. He might have been in a military barracks, a detention camp, a hospital, a place for the homeless or for the old. What did it matter? But as soon as the question presented itself he knew at once that the distinction between one location and another was essential to the definition of himself as he now was: he was conscious and without feeling. But his eyes were wet: in his sleep he had been crying, like a child. But in his sleep he had also been smiling the detested smile. He recognized the condition of contradictions as specifically his own, but now his contradictory selves were more deeply opposed yet closer to reconciliation than ever.

He had only to alter his angle of sight by a single degree to fix himself once more on the stage, so to speak, that was his own. He moved his head and found himself reading a woman's name once boldly written in a tall clear script on the wall: *Innocenta.* Lying as he was lying, perhaps at dawn, a woman had had the presence of mind to write her name on the wall: *Innocenta.* At that moment he again knew who and where he was, exactly. The bloodstained mattress stuffed with wood shavings, the black trousers, the naked chest and arms, and his naked ankles and feet, the black hand on which his head was resting, the glass chimney in which the flame had burned, the woman who had put her mouth to his, the woman who had revealed his own sickening birth: in this way, suddenly, his consciousness was populated by the past that was gone. It was dawn of his first full day in La Violaine. If he had had a stub of pencil he would have written his name beside the woman's: *Konrad Vost. Prisoner.*

The shutters were wide, as he had left them the night before, and now, behind his back, the sunlight was entering the room. The

153

toilet, also behind his back, was silent, though its smell was thickening from the depths of the prison.

He was without flowers. Without birds. Alone. Consumed with the joy of dread, the dread of joy. An imposter in the black pants of manhood. But he was the only man who would ever read Innocenta's name where she had written it.

He did not know how long he lay facing the wall. The light increased, faded, increased in the room which, if anything, grew colder. He heard someone behind him, in the middle of the wooden floor, squeezing her breasts, pinching her thighs, weeping. Indifferently he watched a few last scraps from the memory he could not recover, a few ragged edges of the story that had been his own: the celluloid collar and blue silk tie of the proud man beside the happy woman holding his arm; the tiny creature running toward him with her arms outstretched and the unnatural spectacles bouncing on her nose; the heavy mild-mannered boy friend seated on the flimsy chair, patiently eating from the box of chocolates which he held on his knees; the golden fleur-de-lis covered with flies; the pages of the open book beating back and forth on the broken pavement; the dangling wires; the logs and plaster, the dust, the purple emptiness of the village church that was gone. He watched indifferently as these memories escaped from beneath the lid of the coffin.

A pair of underpants on the wooden floor. Stains and silence in the toilet. The pure man in the prison for impure women. Slowly he turned, changed his position, sat up at last, placing his bare feet on the cold and splintered wood while carefully avoiding the sight of himself, the skin on his hand, arms, feet, chest, which had by now assumed the texture and bluish color of wet clay. He arose. He moved around the perimeter of the room, searching for the names and messages he wished to read. He deciphered the handwriting, he studied the walls, he retained the names he read in icy consciousness: *Tatiana, Solange, Edwige, Zita, Alida, Vivienne,*

154

Inez, Juliana, Eva, Olympia, Honorine, Erika, Thalia, Ursula, Ariane, Claire. In icy consciousness each name, to which he allowed no personal significance, was a crime that denied his own courage, a woman he could not have known.

As for the messages, most of them left him deeply perplexed or deeply offended. But there he was, undressed except for the golden eyeglasses and the black pants and glove, moving slowly about a prison room in the changing light and stooping or stretching awkwardly, like a man in a library, to read not the titles of books but, rather, the humorous or violent jottings of women whose vulgar cravings were the equal of the vulgar cravings of any man. He read certain messages a single time, in haste, while to others he returned repeatedly so as to suffer the guilt unfelt by their authors, or to savor the curious islands of wisdom on the walls covered with filth. Two inscriptions impressed him for their simplicity and shocking contrast to most of the others. He paused a long while before the first, which had been rendered nearly illegible by a crack that had appeared in the wall long after the time when the words had been written: *In memory of a Sunday in summer.* Was it possible that a woman, especially in this place, had been capable of such generosity? After all, the nostalgia and resignation captured in the expression were as shockingly appropriate to the mind of a man as were the obscenities that made him flush with embarrassment. The second inscription was similar: *Love is not an honest feeling.* Again, who but a man could have written these words? Not even the aphoristic Claire could have approached such perception. Yet the authors of these sayings had in fact been women.

Beyond these two brief testaments, as he now thought of them, there was another, a declaration in a tall bold script, that bridged the distance between surprising dignity on the one hand and surprising shamefulness on the other. He did not return again to the portion of the flaking wall where this declaration appeared,

155

but he stood before it in such rigid contemplation that he did not know how much of the day was passing or that he had raised his artificial hand and living hand and was pressing them against the white plaster so as to frame the rough surface where these words had been once written as if on a blank page of an intimate journal for the world to read: *Between my legs I do not have a bunch of violets.* It was a statement that excluded him forever; it was the clue to the object of his desperate quest; it could not have been written by a man.

Once again stretched flat on the thin mattress, aware of its sharpness and metallic sounds, slowly he turned his head to the wall and stared as he had before at the tall bold name of Innocenta. It was she, he decided, who in her pacing had delivered herself of the remarkable declaration that was an homage to woman. The pleasure of this thought sustained him until the arrival of darkness.

Again the footsteps. Again the key. Again the lamp with its flame burning as in antiquity. The wall to which his open eyes were still turned began to glow. When he allowed himself to look toward the dark ceiling and then to his left, where again Eva Laubenstein was seated with her clasped hands outstretched, and where her companion was already kneeling at his bedside and untying her white apron, only then did he admit to himself the passion with which he had hoped for their arrival, and feel the joy of collapsing with the fact of it.

"So, Hania," came the now familiar voice from the darkness, "so this man is still here. How strong is his likeness to our own terrible Doctor Slovotkin, that disgusting man. Oh yes, he is very like our own Slovotkin. Don't you agree?"

In the darkness of abandoned space, filled only with cold air and the smells of absent women and the deterioration of mortar, plaster, splintered wood, iron pipes, in this darkness Eva Laubenstein was again all but invisible while the lamp, with its tall thin glass chimney like extended fingers, cast an even more essential light

156

on the other woman where she was kneeling at his bedside and where she was once more lowering her face to his naked chest.

"Yes, Eva," she said, briefly raising her face and again speaking in her strong clear voice. "Yes, I agree." Then, like some spiritual lion tenderly devouring its devoted prey, again she returned her warm mouth to the cold chest and, as before, commenced her kissing of the surface that was like white wax. He realized that she had placed one of her large hands directly upon his black pants where the shape of his manhood lay hiding. It was a gesture, he realized, of a significance he could not deny.

"But he is the image of Slovotkin. The image. And what a further irony it is that Slovotkin, doctor to this very prison, doctor to the Prefecture of Police, vile and unscrupulous in every way, was nonetheless obsessed by a single question: the difference, if any, between the man and woman. Do you remember? Oh yes, Slovotkin was so obsessed by his question—in the souls of their bones is there a profound difference between the man and woman?—that he was determined to acquire intimate knowledge of every woman in La Violaine. Three of us each night, that brutal man. He never tired of taking his victims or stating his theories. Oh yes, Slovotkin proposed, first, that the person is essentially a barren island and that for each of us life's only pleasure is the exploration of other barren islands: in this way to be a man or woman merely enhances the interesting differences of people who are in fact the same. He proposed, secondly, that in the souls of their bones the man and woman are opposites: as extreme as that. Finally he proposed that the man and woman are both the same and opposite. He was not entirely stupid, our ruthless Slovotkin. Not entirely stupid."

Darkness, coldness. The reciting voice, the cheerful tones. The lips, the tongue, the woman's own breath that came and went on his skin, on his neck, in the hollows created by the collarbone. For the first time in his life he found himself wondering what the woman—this woman—was feeling. At that same moment he realized that the woman had long since taken his gloved hand in her living hand and had placed it in the center of his waxen abdomen. Now her mouth was firmly pressed to the back of the black-gloved hand; now her mouth had once more come to his own. He both smelled and tasted lavender.

"But, Hania," came the clear voice that would never change, "the greatest irony of all was Slovotkin's experiment. To think that such a disgusting man could appropriate such a serious subject! Fifty imprisoned women, Hania. Fifty men selected from the ranks of the Prefecture of Police. And how did our clever Slovotkin conduct his experiment? He ordered the shaving of the hundred heads; he ordered that the hundred naked heads be photographed on their naked necks; he ordered that the photographs be arranged in fifty sets, each containing the head of a man and the head of a woman paired according to similarity in size. So much shaving, photographing, pasting! What a clever fiend! At last, during one of the city-wide periods of inoculation which he himself directed, he ordered that a mixed and randomly chosen group of more than five hundred men and women be exposed to the fifty pairs of photographs and required to indicate which were the images of men and which of women, and to offer brief descriptions of each. The results? Conclusive beyond a doubt: fifty men identified as such, the same with the women. As for the descriptions, they too were conclusive. The dominant opinion was that the men were not sane but that the women were not human. Think of it! What elation for our Slovotkin, with his short stature and bushy beard. How proud he was to have discovered as fact that in the souls of their bones the man and woman are opposites. What an injurious brute was our Slovotkin. . . ."

It was then that Eva Laubenstein enjoyed for a moment her own childish laughter in the dark, while her large and handsome companion drew the lamp and table still closer to the small round

158

space of her concentration. Once again she had kissed his brow; again her palm and fingers covered the front of his pants as the sculpted leaf covers the front of the naked statue; again he felt himself grazed once, twice, by the smoothness of the bared breasts. But now as if to canonize his outstretched and helpless form, carefully she rested both hands side by side on the front of the black pants and then, employing both hands, carefully opened the front of his pants. Again with both hands she gently, firmly loosened his flesh and drew it forth, exposing it for the first time to the natural light of the flame in its glass. With a shock he realized that it was no longer possible to conceal from the intelligence of this determined woman the physical evidence of his own latent cravings. He wanted to look upon what he had always attempted to disown; he wanted to cover himself quickly with his good hand and bad. It was then that he knew suddenly that though the tall woman was not at all repelled by what she was watching so intently with her dark eyes, nonetheless her hands were occupied by that single part of himself that was artful but without feeling: the hand in the black glove. Why was she studying what she had removed from his open trousers, yet clasping aloft, above his flat abdomen, his silver hand?

"But, Hania," came the quick feathery voice of the woman he no longer felt compelled to see, "we shall be fair even to Slovotkin who was fair to women only in what he said and never, never in what he did. But we must be fair. Even this man whose dedication to his single question was no more than a ruse to feed his insatiable craving for the bodies of women, even this terrible Slovotkin revealed in all his debasement a certain truth, a certain respect. Mere hours before his death he insisted that though he had no verification, still his first and third theories were correct. He insisted, in tones that could not be doubted, that reproduction aside, the man and woman were in all their capabilities the same. To bring down the tree, to learn the use of words, to foretell the

159

future: in their capabilities to do these things, to do all things, the man and woman are, he said, the same. He claimed that his third theory was also true: the man and woman are the same and opposite. You cannot be the one without knowing what it is to be the other, reproduction aside. Of course he was right. But what the poor Slovotkin knew was nothing. He did not know anything of what Eva knows. . . .

"We shall begin, Hania, with a proverb from the village of my childhood. Oh, it was a prosperous village and not at all like the poor place where I lived in marriage and bore my child. But from my earliest years the proverb of which I am speaking lay bright and golden inside my head. I hear it now: *Devils and angels do the same things; but you always know which one has been at your door.* You, dear Hania, will recognize these words as the words of an old woman. Never could they have been spoken by an old man, though in a sense they bear out Slovotkin. But more important, Hania, these same words gave rise long ago to a truth of my own: *The woman is not naturally a martyr; the man is not naturally a beast.* But oh, my dear Hania, there is cause enough for these superstitions. Cause enough. For the child the first mystery is what cannot be seen. Oh it is true, Hania, true and sad. I know from my earliest childhood. It was then that I suffered my first martyrdom. From what I say it is already clear that after the first hour together a woman knows what another woman will think and is comfortable with this woman's mind; to the contrary, she can never be entirely comfortable with the mind of a man, despite the sameness of their capabilities. And I will say this, Hania: only the woman who does not live with children retains her youth. . . ."

Again the pause, the laugh, the sensations of shock in his chest and arms and legs, and inside his head the mental image of the small face warmly tinted in the darkness with the colors of youth and the authority of old age, and the two small extended hands pressed together in the gesture of the attendant priest or the

160

physician engrossed and yet detached in her diagnosis. But the fear that had come upon him only moments before was now so strong that it was a dark and dangerous equivalent of his mother's wisdom.

But the hand. The artificial hand. What purpose could the kneeling woman possibly have in clasping and holding aloft in her own two hands the black-gloved palm and fingers? Then in a few distinct and calculating gestures, the woman's own two hands provided the simple answer to his question: he had only to·raise his head and to glance downward with his eyes to see that the woman had already begun the careful process of removing the black glove. He had known from her first touch that the woman and Eva Laubenstein had intended his total disrobement. But never could he have known that the nakedness they had intended for him had also included the removal of his shiny glove. His mother as well as her companion would look upon his unadorned hand. In the darkness Eva Laubenstein chose precisely this moment to continue speaking.

"Oh yes, Hania, in my earliest childhood I too was subjected to martyrdom. A mere child. A very small girl. What could be worse? You must know, Hania, that I was an only child except for an older brother. Since I was a girl and also so unusually small and also born so late in their lives, I had always received the special love of my large and comforting mother and of my father, who knew all there was to know about the earth. My brother was old enough to be my father, a gigantic figure who could break boulders and throw bulls to the ground. But, Hania, perhaps another listener would have even now concluded the simple story of my martyrdom. There are those who would think that the incestuous ravishing of a child is wicked but not unheard of. But you at least will not be deceived, Hania. My story is simple but not transparent, as you surely know. . . .

"It occurred one Sunday morning in the summer. The sun was

161

strong. My mother and father had decided to drive the gray horse instead of the black to the village church. I was left in the care of my much older brother, who was a master of animals but afraid of children. Even now I recall the details only with shame. But I must tell you, Hania, that I have never been able to remember that deplorable episode in its entirety. For instance, I remember my brother's great size; I remember the enormous horseshoe nail which he himself had bent into the shape of a ring and which he never removed from the middle finger of his right hand; I remember the doll that was my first, a creature made of golden straw and dressed in a robe of fur. But to this day I am unable to recall whatever it was I did to provoke my brother. Suffice it to say that I angered him, he who could have held me in the palm of his hand. Suffice it to say that suddenly, in the sunlight, he dropped his trousers, sat down on the warm bench and, snatching me up, flung me head down and feet down across his great knees that were like the broad white backs of animals. He bared my buttocks that were smaller than the palms of his hands. I was clutching my doll and continued to do so throughout the entirety of that episode. I recall my surprise, my confusion, the blood filling my head. When he began to beat me with the flat of his great hand which he was forever smacking playfully against the flanks of horses, never in that sunlit episode did the great pain of his beating exceed the intensity of my first confusion and my terror at being held in such unfamiliar awkwardness and helplessness, with my head and arms hanging down on his one side and my legs and feet on the other. He beat the flesh of his hand against the flesh of my buttocks; I made no sound; in the grip of my small hands my straw doll leapt up and down to the force of his blows. I made no sound and experienced the sudden great pain as nothing more than the pain that rightly defines incomprehension. Now, despite my shame to this day, I cannot recall that other day without admitting that the ironies of that episode exceed its pain. For instance, my brother used me so viciously that he bloodied the terrible sharp iron of his massive ring. But even more important, Hania, at the time of that episode there was no one I loved as intensely as I did my brother. The final irony, my dear Hania, is that every summer in the years to come, long after I had given birth to my child, my brother, by then an old man, never failed to send me a message. He sent it in the form of a poor farmer who, driving a gray horse harnessed to a wooden cart, would appear inevitably at our door one morning in summer and shout to me through his cupped hands: "Love from your brother!" Just once would he shout those words to me, and then drive away. Naturally I always knew that those sentiments which he carried each summer from the village of my birth to the village of my marriage were quite true. But despite my sensible nature, Hania, I was never able to overcome my fear that my martyrdom as a child was somehow responsible for the terrible birth of the child whose life I alone was able to save. . . ."

When at last he realized that he did not know how long he had been listening to the silence that followed the cessation of his mother's voice, Konrad Vost, wishing only to gather in the darkness fold on fold so that the days to come would all be nights, found, without surprise, that the black glove had disappeared from his hand, that the uncovered hand was not silver, and that his mother's companion was now clasping to her naked breasts his own ordinary hand that had been restored. But he was in fact surprised when once again, briefly, out of the darkness, his mother spoke to her kneeling friend.

"Now, Hania, I must tell you that in the village of my childhood there was one proverb that meant more to me than any other: *For the woman who dies unloved there is no repose.* For you, Hania, and for me, there shall be repose."

163

Devils and angels. Shame and grief.

A cesspool of clear water is nonetheless a cesspool.

Pull down the stars.

"Come with Kristel," whispered the voice in the night. "Come with Kristel quickly. . . ."

All around him the disordered children lay sleeping in the farmhouse filled with moonlight. Yet now Kristel was whispering not to one of the others but to himself, she who had paid not the slightest attention to him in the past, and now was searching for him urgently in the pile of rags where he slept.

"Quickly," she whispered. "Kristel will teach you what it is to be a little man. . . ."

In the moonlight he felt her small hand seizing his wrist, felt the successive impatient tugs on his arm, felt himself being drawn forth from the rags. The stone was cold, the moonlit room was warm, the room was silent except for the bubbling sounds produced in dreams, the whispering of the small eager girl, the faint pure song of a distant nightingale. For a moment the girl clung to him, moistened his dry lips with her lips that were wet, and then led him quickly from the farmhouse into the warm night that was like day. Behind them the other children were grunting and crying in their dreams while Anna Kossowski snored in the depths of her stupor induced by wine.

The fields and hillside were warm in the green and silver light, from below them came the thudding sounds of the great beasts secreted in the long low barn of wood and stone. Kristel led him quickly up the path hand in hand, her bare feet marking the way for his own, and even in his haste, confusion and anticipation he saw that though she was a girl and he a mere child, still her body was as small as his. All around them the ravens were nesting in the sweet leaves of the branches while in the distance, small and invisible but nonetheless announcing the progress of girl and child, the small bird continued its melodic singing to the dry hay, to the brook in its bed, to the worms that were slowly moving like a blind carpet toward the young tree where the bird was perched.

"Quickly," the girl whispered over her shoulder with an eagerness he had never until this moment heard. "Quickly. Kristel is aroused. . . ."

He stumbled, he clung to her hand, on a grassy incline they came to a clump of hedge shaped like a horseshoe and smelling of lavender and the light of the moon. The space contained by the hedge was large enough for their bodies.

"Quickly," whispered the girl, drawing him into the protection of the low dense hedge. "Here we are safe. . . ."

Kristel crawled before him, moving and using her free hand in such a way as to raise the skirt of the short loose dress that was appropriate to an orphaned child but now, for an instant, revealed the partial nakedness of a girl who, except for her small size, had already matured into a woman, young as she was. On his knees, drawn forward by her tight grasp and whispering voice, now he knew the happiness of total ignorance, total helplessness, total trust, though he could not have said so. The hedge was dense; he sat cross-legged inside their nest, on three sides the empty hill sloped away so that no one could approach unseen; they were safe. His hands in the grass told him that Kristel had already rid their nest of thorns; when he saw the girl bringing forth from its hiding place inside the hedge

165

the stolen dusty bottle of wine, he knew without words how clever she was and how willful, and what risks she was ready to undertake for his well-being.

Kristel knelt beside him, gathering her orphan's dress above her bare waist, and tilted her head to the side, laughed like a child, drank from the mouth of the bottle and watched as he raised the bottle and brought its now wet mouth to his own. From the bottle came the moonlight, the song of the distant bird, the taste of the wine.

"Now hold Kristel," she whispered. "Kristel is aroused. . . ."

She put his face against her face, she licked his lips, she played with his ears, he felt her small quick hands inside his shirt, beneath his arms, down his spine, on his stomach, inside the front of his thick baggy trousers. He felt the rapid motion of her fingers and the touch of the night air. The moon was climbing higher above their heads. The wine tasted of the empty fields, of the dark and protective hedge.

"Kristel is not an old and selfish woman," she whispered, stroking his hair, licking her fingers, rolling the pebble that was hidden between his legs. "Kristel is an attractive girl. She is aroused. . . ."

She lay back in the soft and flowering grass and lifted her skirt still higher so that the little silver belly sat proudly in the moonlight as if to lure to itself the distant bird.

"You may look at Kristel all you wish," she whispered, spreading her knees and offering herself in small tempting thrusts. "Between the legs Kristel is an attractive girl. . . ."

He smiled. He crept closer. He could see nothing. But he loved Kristel as he had never loved Anna Kossowski, and now he was so absorbed in Kristel that on his knees he was dancing in his need to discover how exactly to do what she wished him to do. The bottle was rolling beside the girl. The moon was high. The bird was singing his faint but unbroken song.

"Come to Kristel," she whispered, reaching for him with both her hands. "Your little twig is ready. . . ."

Dancing on his bare knees between the girl's waiting legs, his hands on arms stretched out to the sides of his body, knowing that his eyes were large and that his smile now bisected his thin face, in the midst of this expectation he heard the words of the girl and so glanced down at himself and with his own eyes discovered that what she had said was true: from the place where his body ended between his legs a small silver twig had sprouted. It too was dancing up and down. What was he now if not the very tree that he himself was shaking for the sake of his fruit?

Then came the sound. He heard it, before he could stop his dancing and fluttering; he saw the fear sitting on Kristel's face; only after he raised his head and eyes and looked directly into the large round white face which, like the moon, was staring down at them from over the top of the hedge, only then did he stop his little dance of expectation and grow rigid with his arms still extended, his silver twig still extended, and his head drawn back as if an invisible hand had taken a tight grip on a fistful of his fine-spun hair.

The large white face was trembling. The sound that had given him warning was a soft but now uncontrollable sound of grunting. The great white hairless head, the urgency of the wordless sounds, the eyes that were both fevered and liquid in their concentration, the ears that were larger even than his own: in all this he recognized the features of one of the disordered children from the farm. So he and Kristel had been followed despite the empty countryside and light of the moon. So all this time they had been spied upon in their flowering nest. Now in the violent helpless face he saw that the pleasure he himself had been feeling was in fact a desperate pain. The pain of his own happy longing for Kristel had become a terrible wet hopeless groan from the slack mouth of the enormous face.

167

He screamed at the very moment the face disappeared. He was on his feet and attempting to flee even as the sounds of grunting and running told him that the poor brutal creature was no less frightened than himself and was already fleeing in the opposite direction. But he could not stop. He was hobbled by his fallen trousers, the girl on her back was crying out to him, the creature who had spied on them was already gone. Yet he could not stop.

He had taken only a few awkward steps into the high grass, and was still so close to Kristel that he might have plainly seen the surprise and disappointment on her face had he but turned and looked, when he stepped on something which, in the light of the moon, appeared to be a large and ancient urn fashioned of clay. He felt it crack open beneath his foot. He stood patiently as the dreaded wasps swarmed upward and about him in the moonlit night. He was unable to move, to fight them off, to cry out, to flee. For a moment the awakened wasps did nothing but wrap him in the smoke of their angry flight, coursing between his legs, up and down his spindly thighs, and into his face, his hair, his inviting ears, his buttocks. Now, without moving, he awaited the pain that the flying wasps would inflict upon him, in the next instant, for betraying Anna Kossowski with Kristel.

"Come back," called the girl from her silvery nest. "Come back to Kristel. . . ."

With the first dreaded sting he began once again to dance. He turned, he gyrated, his hands flew, he hopped and leapt from bare foot to foot, crushing the urn. But he danced in silence. Each of the circling or attacking wasps was an ominous winged sac swollen with the poisoned light of the moon. From every direction they came to him, rising and falling, inflicting upon him singly or in packed formations the pain he could not bear, pumping into him the poisoned light, while the girl called to him, now in alarm, and far in the distance the bird sang.

When the brave Kristel snatched him at last from the fury of the winged demons swarming upon him in the summer night, and carried him back to the farmhouse in her own two arms, he was no longer conscious of anything except his pain, which he wore like a skintight suit of fiery light.

"So, little Konrad Vost, you have been outside in the night with Kristel. . . ."

If he had so recently been plunged into the scalding water it had been but for an instant. Now in the warmth of the morning sun the poison still in his blood caused him to feel only drugged rather than pained, so that had it not been for the strength of Anna Kossowski's grip on his upper arm, and the angry tones of her voice, and the sullen expression on Kristel's sleepy face, he might have enjoyed the diminishing of the pain and the relief he was feeling in the warmth of the dawn. But the tight fingers, the angry and helpless silence of Kristel who was not yet awake and whose childish wrist was firmly held in Anna Kossowski's other hand: now his relief was fading swiftly in the face of shame. Why else had Anna Kossowski brought them here, Kristel and himself, to the great stone room that was Anna Kossowski's own, unless in a drunken dream she had seen the moonlit vision of her betrayal? Already he was beginning to fear that Anna Kossowski's accusations might prove more painful than the stings of the wasps.

"And look what you have done to poor Kristel! Look there!"

The woman, who would never again allow him her kindness and forgiveness, reached down suddenly and with the hand that had been holding the wrist of the girl, seized the bottom of Kristel's skirt and yanked it high, exposing the little naked haunch that was the color of sunlit flesh instead of the green and silver color of the moon in the night. The woman, who had released his arm, was scowling and pointing toward Kristel's thigh. Through the slits of his eyes he saw for an instant the muscles which, from top to bottom of the bare leg, were catching the light and absorbing it into the small perfect shape of the leg. Quickly he turned away. Again the hand gripped his upper arm and pulled him close.

"Look well, little Konrad Vost. Look well. She has been stung by a wasp!"

Though his hands and feet were once again beginning to flutter in four different directions, and though his eyes were swollen all but shut, still he submitted to the horned hand that was gripping not his arm but his neck, and leaned forward to inspect the bare thigh as he had been bidden: the bruise on the glistening skin made him think, for an instant, of angry fingers or even of angry teeth. But then Anna Kossowski shook him again by the neck, his sight grew clear, he saw that the welt inside the bruise had indeed been raised by one of the winged demons of the night before.

"It is your fault, little Konrad Vost. . . ."

He had no need to be told. He saw the mark of the venom, he knew that Kristel had suffered the wasp for his own sake, everywhere on his person he felt what Kristel had felt when the wasp had struck. The welts on his thin legs were like masses of hives, his thin lips had become as large as his ears, his belly was puffed out in a thick red pattern that might have been imprinted upon him by a grille held in the fire. He knew exactly what Kristel had felt. The vividness of the blemish high on her leg made his remaining sight grow dim. He was hardly able to hear the sullen and irritable voice of the girl who had carried him beyond the reach of the wasps.

"Leave him alone," she said. "It is too early for your wicked games."

The sun that was coming through the dusty glass was heavy and warm; like a tide it rose on Anna Kossowski's great wooden bed which, having collapsed years before under the fury of the woman's drunken weight, rested directly without legs on the

170

stone floor, a crippled monstrous piece of furniture heaped with skins and furs, even in the heat of the fourth season, and smelling of the sourness of Anna Kossowski's loveless sleep. The sun that had come through the blue sky, the dry leaves, the dusty glass, was filling and warming the bed that was like a wooden pen for the animals that were the old woman's dreams. This was the room forbidden to the disordered children, including himself, and which he had never seen except through the cracks in the thick and lopsided wooden door. Now he and Kristel were alone with the mistress of this room. The lopsided door was bolted closed. He was aware of the bed, the sun, the garlic hanging from a nail in the sloping stone wall; he knew that the bed still contained the smells and shadows of Anna Kossowski's anger, though he was whimpering and twitching beneath the hand on his neck.

"You dare to speak to me of games? You who attempted to satisfy your cravings with this child?"

"Kristel is not pure but she is innocent."

"The mouth that is wet in the night is as dry as potatoes in the morning. So much for your innocence."

"Kristel does not wish to talk."

"If you open your mouth his little twig will pop out. I understand."

"Kristel will not exchange vulgarities."

"I gave you no permission to do what you did! No permission to share with him the wetness of your little onion! No permission to take down his pants! There must be no wetness, no whispering, no nakedness without my permission."

"Kristel is her own woman! She is not yours!"

"You are too small for such a temper. Besides, I will give you permission. Here, now, in the warmth of the sun instead of the dark night. In the comfort of a bed instead of the fields. You have my permission. You have only to undress yourself. . . ."

The voice stopped. But what had they been saying? Why was

171

Anna Kossowski angry not with himself but with his friend? Why had the voices sounded moist in the morning's warmth? Why were the two women, the one who was large and old, the one who was small and young, talking together as if he were not there but also as if Kristel once again might put her mouth to his, but in this room where there could be no threat of wasps rather than in the silvery fields where his trousers had been left behind with the remnants of the ancient urn? In the instant of silence he wanted to hear the voices, though they made him afraid; he felt drugged and yet alert; he felt that, as their poison was drifting through his veins, so too the silvery bodies of the sleeping wasps were traveling through his bloodstream with their eyes shut, their wings folded, the barbed and curving tips of their bodies filled with a strange light. He was drugged, and yet he would have been smiling were it not for the swelling that paralyzed his lips. Perhaps if he put his swollen lips to the blemish on Kristel's thigh it would disappear. Her raised skirt was still bunched in the old woman's fist; her dark eyes were bright with her pride; on her oval face there were the signs of sleep. As for himself, he was looking at Kristel through his narrow eyes, he did not care that he was dressed in nothing but his ill-fitting shirt that fell only a short distance below his loins.

"Kristel," said the girl, tossing her head, twitching her bare leg, "Kristel will not be your whore to the child."

"Very well," said the woman. "Just as you say. But now you must see that there, beneath the edge of his shirt, the stinging of the wasps has made his little twig pop up. Who shall be responsible for his little twig? Anna Kossowski or Kristel? You may have your choice."

The voices stopped. The sunlight was the warm thick color of a bright orange flame reflected from a field of white enamel. Anna Kossowski was smiling. She allowed Kristel's skirt to fall but retained her grip on his own thin neck. She was no longer interested in her betrayal. On the great bed the pelts and furs were sweating.

172

Kristel scowled, her nostrils flared, gradually her small oval face became impassive. Then in a single gesture, swiftly, she pulled the gray dress over her head and tossed it aside. For a moment she stood there waiting, allowing him to see through his tears and his swollen lids her chest, her knees, the little belly that was the same shape as her face. Then she lay down on the bed and held out her arms.

"Come to Kristel," she said. "Forget the old woman."

He nodded. Anna Kossowski gave him a push and drew a wooden chair close to the bed. He stumbled, he fell forward, in the last of his diminishing sight he saw the beckoning Kristel as he would never see her again except in year after year of dreams he would not recall: she lay in the sunlight and among the black and orange hides of the great bed instead of in the moonlit nest of grass; she was nude instead of partially clothed; her body was the color of butter and almonds lightly turned on the fire instead of the tight silver color of the moon; she was smiling not in anguish but in reassurance; her mouth was small and golden; her hair had fallen away from her face, which it framed, and lay in dark strands on her shoulders; her knees were raised and spread, as they had been the night before, but the hands that were also raised made him think of trust and comfort instead of eagerness and haste. His vision lasted long enough for him to see that Kristel was cocking her head and smiling, that she had rolled herself slightly in his direction, that her mouth was wet and that inside her thighs there were no trailing columns of black ants. But he saw no more. Anna Kossowski's shove had coincided with the sound of Kristel's childish voice and the sudden loss of his sight; the eyelids that had been puffing shut for hours had become finally sealed when Anna Kossowski's hand had sent him stumbling toward the waiting girl.

He fell. He heard behind him the old woman's laughter, the sounds of her chair drawn to the edge of the bed, the sounds of the old woman's heavy breath. But he was as indifferent to Anna

173

Kossowski as he was to the fact that he could not see. After all, the vision of what he had already seen was still in his mind. He knew that Kristel was holding him in her small bare arms and that wherever her bare flesh touched his own it cooled, as by handfuls of pure water, all the burning sensations of the livid welts that covered his chest, his legs, his arms, his buttocks. He was as indifferent to his pain as he was to his blindness and to Anna Kossowski, who was feeling for the battered face between her thighs while gripping with her other hand the nearest of Kristel's ankles where it hung in the air.

He laughed through the lips that could not smile, in his blindness he saw the girl's head happily turning from side to side on the skin of a fox, he knew that she had unbuttoned his shirt and that the narrow reddened cage of his chest was pressing lightly against the swellings he had seen only moments before on the chest of the girl. Her fingers were gathering in his hair, in his armpits, between his legs, between his buttocks from which, the night before, she had extracted several of the small dead silvery bodies of the winged demons.

"You see," came the breath of the bright voice in his swollen ear, "little Konrad now belongs to little Kristel. . . ."

Her hair smelled of fresh lemons and dust in the sun. The hands that cradled his blind face smelled of wet onions glistening, dripping. Her tight and darkening skin was smooth and hard. Flat on her back she was clasping him and in her happy movements was imitating his dancing of the night before. He was certain that she was pressing him, where his body ended, at the white fork of his legs, to the very mouth through which she spoke to him, whispered to him, sang to him.

"Off!" cried the terrible voice behind his back. "Off!" cried the enraged voice that he had forgotten and that he had thought never again to hear. "Off, off!" it cried, as he felt the great hands crushing his hipbones that protruded in the manner of his swollen ears, as he felt himself torn from the girl and held aloft in the air,

174

as he felt himself carried blindly above the bed, above the floor, as he heard the crashing of the chair and the banging of the bolt and felt himself being flung from the room.

Behind him the door crashed shut; the bolt again banged into place; above the muffled grunting sounds of Anna Kossowski, Kristel began to scream. His sight returned.

Again he was running in four directions at once, with his feet in the air, his arms outstretched, the open shirt flapping around his nakedness, careening now against the cold stove, now against the sink, against a wall, against the bench, against a solid beam of sunlight, until at last he discovered the open door and fled from the farmhouse, which he would not see again, and fled down the dirt road that was a ribbon of deep dust between the stunted trees and low hills bare except for the piles of stones and the slow dark shadows of distant clouds in the sky.

The weaker the child, the more fanatical the man. And where is the woman who does not love a fanatical man?

But impostor and tyrant are indistinguishable. They are not for women.

The sum of his secrets. The lessons of devastation.

He awoke. He was a man left for dead in the cinders. But he was not dead. The face so unshaven that it had become a mask of bristles and flaking scales, the body so cold that it had changed color, the nails on the toes and fingers so long and yellow that they might have served as decorations on the sides of a black lacquered box: in all this he was only a cadaver abandoned to its decomposition in the cinders.

Except for the eyes. Though he was unable to move and unable to see himself, nonetheless he knew that the eyes in his skull were unblinking. He knew that his open eyes were staring at the wall, which the sun had already discovered, with a gaze as strong as that of the most intense scrutiny. Only in his violent eyes was he still alive. As if to reassure himself, suddenly he turned his eyes, to the left, to the right, sharply, like a man seeing demons over his shoulder, and then stared again at the wall. But he was no longer interested in what had been written on the damp plaster; he was looking at nothing. With his blind sight he was in fact thinking rather than seeing, though thought and interior vision were indistinguishable.

A horse, an old woman, a girl in the grass, a few hours in the dark with Claire. The sum of his secrets.

At dusk he knew with certainty what he had known at noon and dawn: that now he was fit to live only in the darkness, and that the darkness within himself was always expanding, always contracting, never the same, always the same. Once he smiled to think that as a child he had been made to pose with the walking stick he had never owned as a man. In either case he had been not a victim but a culprit.

Thus he passed the fifth day since the revolt of the women, and his second day in La Violaine, lying on his prison bed and giving shape to the invisible while awaiting the night.

In the darkness that finally descended he saw: a dog emerging from an egg, a dancing man with the face of a pig, a solitary pilgrim with the head of a fox, a tall man without arms carrying a tall man without legs. In the darkness he heard himself groaning for the lamp that was not there and the sounds he had yet to hear beyond the door.

In the darkness he awoke again briefly, only to listen and then to acknowledge to himself that his vigil, like his life, was wasted: they were not coming. But when he awakened for the third time that night and heard the footsteps, he knew immediately that the approaching sounds were those of one person instead of two. But if he was to be visited that night by only one of the two women, which did he hope was now turning the key in the lock? He refused the choice. He denied the question. He waited.

He was not disappointed. The person who had turned the key, unlocked the chain, entered the room and placed the lighted lamp on the table, this person was someone who did not speak and who was standing at his bedside. He saw the purple tint of her shadow looming on the wall. He smelled the scent of lavender. He knew who she was.

At the same time he heard the faint tinny sounds of dance hall music. It did not seem possible, and yet he could not mistake the incongruous sounds and faint rapid tempo of a dance hall orchestra drifting up from an old phonograph that was surely equipped with a spring-driven motor and a loudspeaker in the shape of a fluted shell as large as a child. The tinny music was entering the shadow on the wall and his own cold body through wires as fine as hair; the shadow on the wall was moving; from below in the prison yard came the metallic sounds of a long-dead trumpeter playing his solo for couples who wished to hold each other in their arms and dance.

In a single convulsive movement he rolled over until he was flat on his back with the spectacles crooked on the waxen face and his two hands thrust into the open trousers. He turned his head and looked up at the woman.

"Tonight," she said in her clear alto voice, "tonight the women are dancing. We have learned that in the morning the café across the street will raise its shutter. They are no longer afraid. We shall have no more violence."

She nodded and without haste untied and discarded the white apron. For a moment she allowed her long arms to remain at her sides. Despite its shapelessness, the loose gray sacking of her dress revealed the abdomen that was like an island, the long hips of bone and flesh, even the presence of the hidden thighs that were as large as a man's and yet of the soft line belonging only to a woman. She pressed the cloth to the shape of her lower body and then, with deliberate slowness, lifted the bottom of the dress and gathered it into the narrowness of the naked waist bright and shadowed in the light of the lamp. Even now the belly, flat as it was, was large enough to contain a child. The woman waited, standing as close to his head as she could, and then removed the dress altogether and cast it aside.

Why was it that when a man of his age saw for the first time hair and light glistening between a woman's legs he felt both agitation and absurdity? And yet was he even now beginning to learn that what he had thought of as the lust of his middle age was in fact the clearest reflection of the generosity implicit in the nudity of the tall woman?

The music stopped and, after a moment, wheezed again into faint and lively song. Apparently those who were operating the ancient phonograph possessed only a single record. A reed instrument began to trill. A female voice was singing in the language he had never learned.

The woman loosened her red hair and, turning her back to him, and stooping, removed her shoes. Her buttocks, that were so much more massive than those of the young girl in the shuttered room,

178

still bore the impression of the seat of a crude chair; he stared, thinking that three of Claire's corsets would not be enough to contain this woman's nudity.

Again the woman turned to him and knelt, as she had for the first night and then the second; she put her mouth to his; she covered his chest and abdomen with the flat touch of her hands. With both hands she removed his black trousers and disposed of the severe and modest underpants which the girl in the shuttered room had ignored.

The notes and chords of the music rising thinly from the yard below were like the jerkily moving figures in a forgotten film. Nearly inaudible, the snare drum was marking the tempo with its scratchy sounds as if a small hand had been rhythmically throwing sand against human skin drawn on a hoop. For the third time the trumpeter was commencing his solo.

How could the tall woman bear the sight of him? How could she bear the sight of the long naked body that consisted of little more than gristle and graying hair? Could he possibly have been correct in deciding that for this woman there could be nothing repugnant, not even himself?

As if to reply to the words he had not spoken, the woman lifted his head, inserting beneath it the black trousers bunched into a pillow, and then again knelt beside the bed, placed one hand on his shoulder and the other on his thigh, and tossed back her massive head of red hair.

"Watch me," she said, in her choirboy's voice, "watch me, look at me. You must see what I am doing in order to feel it. Passionate sensation depends on sight."

He noted that her expression did not falter under his gaze of disbelief and desire. While he watched, the woman turned her head and lowered the long handsome face freed from the hair that was the color of shadows on hot coals, shadows on the flesh of the plum. No sooner had he withdrawn his hands than the woman

179

made a deft movement with her chin and tongue, steadying that part of his anatomy that he could no longer deny, and took it swiftly between her lips and deliberately sealed as much of it as she could inside her mouth. The hollow in the woman's cheek exaggerated the high ivory cheekbone, the strong line of the nose, the high clear brow, the length of the throat. Her eyes were open. Her face was so bright that she appeared to have become the flame in the lamp.

"In no other way," she said at last, "can a woman so reveal her eroticism as by an act of the will." She continued to kneel beside him with her arms stiffly spread and her hands exerting a slight firm pressure on his shoulder and thigh. "As for you," she said, "the force of amorous passion is respect. You are now aware of your own respect and mine."

Slowly she raised her hands and, placing them on either side of her head which she was holding high, just as she was kneeling upright with her thighs and back in a long soft vertical line beside his bed, slowly she thrust her fingers into her dark red hair and lifted it away from her shoulders, her neck, the stately head. She was a courtesan inside a tomb. Or a woman in a morgue. But by the mere use of her hands in her hair she was now causing him to acknowledge again his helpless responsiveness.

When she used her tongue as the young girl in the shuttered room had used her childish finger, he discovered that her hair was so long that she could draw it around both sides of his hips to the front of his body and thus wrap and entangle him in the strands of her hair; when she made of his own thin dry mouth the sumptuous mouth of the octopus and caused him to employ his mouth according to the will of her hands, he discovered that the woman's dilation was such that the exterior of her body could no longer be distinguished from its interior; when she encouraged him to discover for himself that the discolorations of the blown rose are not confined to the hidden flesh of youth, it was then that in the midst

180

of his gasping he realized that the distinction between the girl who is still a child and the woman who is more than mature lies only in the instinct of the one and the depth of consciousness of the other.

He lost consciousness. He regained consciousness. He found her hair in his face. The pressure of her long thighs was turning him at last into a dolphin. He heard the cry of her voice, he heard himself grunting and shouting. Thus in a city without a name, without flowers, without birds, without angels, and in a prison room containing only an iron bedstead and a broken toilet, and with a woman who had never trussed herself in black satin, here the tossing and turning Konrad Vost knew at last the transports of that singular experience which makes every man an artist: the experience, that is, of the willed erotic union. He too was able to lie flat on his bed of stars. He too was able to lie magically on his bed of hot coals.

He was roused again to the dark night by the music of the ensemble which, as someone cranked the phonograph in the courtyard below, once more slowly attained its intended tempo. One of the instrumentalists was tapping his foot. Again the slight woman was singing in an unfamiliar language. But the voice of the woman was only a mechanical rendition of silence; the music itself was only the shape, in sound, of a dark space that had once been a cabaret in the past that was gone.

When he forced himself to move, to roll over, to lift himself on an arm which in a mere night had become as white and soft as the arm of a dying man, and when he managed to sit on the edge of the bed with his feet side by side on the floor, he knew without looking that the tall handsome woman had already clothed herself again in the gray dress and the white apron, and without thinking knew that he did not wish to leave the bed and yet wanted nothing more than to follow his mother's companion down through the darkness and out among the shadows of the women gathered together in the night below.

The black trousers that had been bunched beneath his head were wet when he drew them on. The crookedness of the golden spectacles destroyed the proportions of his face as completely as did the smile. The black shoes, which he did not tie, were as wet as the trousers. The black serge suit coat, which he put on over his naked chest and arms, was as heavy with dampness as the worn-down shoes and crumpled trousers. The turtleneck shirt had disappeared.

The woman held high the failing lamp. Behind them the door hung open on the darkness that was no longer the darkness of love or sleep. As for himself, he could move only with the greatest difficulty. Yet he was well aware of the childish eagerness with which he groped his way after the descending woman.

At ground level she unlocked a narrow door, opened it, and held the oil lamp above her head so that he might see into the blackened room.

"Doctor Slovotkin," she murmured. "The body is never entirely still at the end of its length of rope. It turns gently first in one direction and then the other as if it is inhabited by the motion of a moral lesson."

The body hanging from the stiff rope in the small windowless space was bound about the wrists and ankles. The head was concealed inside a tight black velvet hood, the body still wore its long white coat stained with the fruits of experimentation. It was true that the body was slowly turning like a red dragonfly suspended on the end of a thread.

Outside, in the yard of La Violaine, women were dancing with women in the darkness. Even here the sounds of the old phonograph came as from a great distance between the high flaking walls, the slabs of iron, the bars and wire mesh of the prison. The sounds of the women turning, moving, shifting across the sand and gravel dimmed to a mere whistling the sound of the trumpet and the scratching of the invisible drum. The women were holding each other at arms' length, or in the embrace of lovers, or in the curious position of couples dancing formally about a ballroom. But their movements were unaccompanied by talking or the sounds of laughter. In the darkness the paired shadows were identifiable only by their size, the silhouettes of hair, the scraping sounds made by naked feet in boots that had belonged to men.

The tall woman left her lamp in the open doorway and seized him by the waist and drew him with short awkward dancing steps among the shadows. He put his stiff hands on her shoulders and attempted to follow her movements to the left, to the right, backward and forward. He who had been both husband and father had never allowed himself to learn even the simplest dance; now he was dancing at the end of a long night in a place that did not allow for pleasure.

The music stopped and started. He was not disappointed to find himself passed from woman to woman and held by each, as if he had not attacked each of his partners in this same open space only days before. It was growing light.

No one was talking, whispering, laughing. Yet he was not surprised when a younger woman interrupted another to become his partner and, placing her hands gently on his damp shoulders, and moving her feet so as to avoid his clumsy steps, spoke to him while looking directly into his pleased expression. "I have a message for you: *Mirabelle is living with the boy friend.* She says you will understand. She wants you to know."

But then the woman was gone, once more he found himself in the arms of the tall handsome woman who had loved him and seduced him as well. For a moment he saw, among the remaining dancers, his two tormentors of the night in the barn now locked together like two wooden figures on an empty stage.

It was dawn and suddenly he was alone in front of the high partially opened gates of La Violaine. The dusty green vine was climbing the iron mesh. Beyond him the street was empty except for the familiar blue van. He heard the rattling of the steel shutter beginning to rise in the café across the street. He thought of a small dark cup of coffee and stepped through the gate.

"It is you who will die!" cried Gagnon as he braced himself against the wall of the prison, raised in trembling arms the weapon he had discovered in the blue van, and fired.

Through the smoke he saw that Gagnon's face and hands were covered with soot and that from his eyes, ears, mouth, nostrils, were streaming spurts and sudden clouds of feathers shining with all the colors of water thrown into the sun. Through the noise and smoke of the explosion he knew, as he fell, that the hole torn in his abdomen by Gagnon's shot was precisely the same as would have been opened in his flesh by the dog in the marsh.

"Poor Gagnon," he said from where he lay clutching his wound with one hand and the edge of the gate with the other, and looking up at his friend. "Poor Gagnon. . . . They may destroy me, they may devour me. But I am who I am."

With this remark Konrad Vost achieved his final irony, for as he spoke he was already smiling and rolling over to discover for himself what it was to be nothing.

For some months following the death of the fanatical but chastened Konrad Vost, rumors persisted that from the east there had been dispatched a military convoy intended to subdue once and for all the inmates of La Violaine. But gradually these rumors

184

faded and then disappeared altogether. In the words of the noble person who led the revolt and attempted to attain the liberation of her only son, La Violaine is no longer a prison, and yet remains, as it should, under the sway of women.

JOHN HAWKES (1925–1998) was one of the most innovative and widely regarded English-language novelists of the twentieth century. Praised by Leslie Fiedler, Flannery O'Connor, and William H. Gass, who wrote, "when it comes to the engravement of the sentence . . . no one can match him," Hawkes was the author of numerous acclaimed novels, including *The Lime Twig, Second Skin,* and *Adventures in the Alaskan Skin Trade.*

PETROS ABATZOGLOU, *What Does Mrs. Freeman Want?*
MICHAL AJVAZ, *The Golden Age.*
The Other City.
PIERRE ALBERT-BIROT, *Grabinoulor.*
YUZ ALESHKOVSKY, *Kangaroo.*
FELIPE ALFAU, *Chromos.*
Locos.
IVAN ÂNGELO, *The Celebration.*
The Tower of Glass.
DAVID ANTIN, *Talking.*
ANTÓNIO LOBO ANTUNES, *Knowledge of Hell.*
ALAIN ARIAS-MISSON, *Theatre of Incest.*
JOHN ASHBERY AND JAMES SCHUYLER, *A Nest of Ninnies.*
HEIMRAD BÄCKER, *transcript.*
DJUNA BARNES, *Ladies Almanack.*
Ryder.
JOHN BARTH, *LETTERS.*
Sabbatical.
DONALD BARTHELME, *The King.*
Paradise.
SVETISLAV BASARA, *Chinese Letter.*
MARK BINELLI, *Sacco and Vanzetti Must Die!*
ANDREI BITOV, *Pushkin House.*
LOUIS PAUL BOON, *Chapel Road.*
My Little War.
Summer in Termuren.
ROGER BOYLAN, *Killoyle.*
IGNÁCIO DE LOYOLA BRANDÃO, *Anonymous Celebrity.*
Teeth under the Sun.
Zero.
BONNIE BREMSER, *Troia: Mexican Memoirs.*
CHRISTINE BROOKE-ROSE, *Amalgamemnon.*
BRIGID BROPHY, *In Transit.*
MEREDITH BROSNAN, *Mr. Dynamite.*
GERALD L. BRUNS, *Modern Poetry and the Idea of Language.*
EVGENY BUNIMOVICH AND J. KATES, EDS., *Contemporary Russian Poetry: An Anthology.*
GABRIELLE BURTON, *Heartbreak Hotel.*
MICHEL BUTOR, *Degrees.*
Mobile.
Portrait of the Artist as a Young Ape.
G. CABRERA INFANTE, *Infante's Inferno.*
Three Trapped Tigers.
JULIETA CAMPOS, *The Fear of Losing Eurydice.*
ANNE CARSON, *Eros the Bittersweet.*
CAMILO JOSÉ CELA, *Christ versus Arizona.*
The Family of Pascual Duarte.
The Hive.
LOUIS-FERDINAND CÉLINE, *Castle to Castle.*
Conversations with Professor Y.
London Bridge.
Normance.
North.
Rigadoon.
HUGO CHARTERIS, *The Tide Is Right.*
JEROME CHARYN, *The Tar Baby.*
MARC CHOLODENKO, *Mordechai Schamz.*

JOSHUA COHEN, *Witz.*
EMILY HOLMES COLEMAN, *The Shutter of Snow.*
ROBERT COOVER, *A Night at the Movies.*
STANLEY CRAWFORD, *Log of the S.S. The Mrs Unguentine.*
Some Instructions to My Wife.
ROBERT CREELEY, *Collected Prose.*
RENÉ CREVEL, *Putting My Foot in It.*
RALPH CUSACK, *Cadenza.*
SUSAN DAITCH, *L.C.*
Storytown.
NICHOLAS DELBANCO, *The Count of Concord.*
NIGEL DENNIS, *Cards of Identity.*
PETER DIMOCK, *A Short Rhetoric for Leaving the Family.*
ARIEL DORFMAN, *Konfidenz.*
COLEMAN DOWELL, *The Houses of Children.*
Island People.
Too Much Flesh and Jabez.
ARKADII DRAGOMOSHCHENKO, *Dust.*
RIKKI DUCORNET, *The Complete Butcher's Tales.*
The Fountains of Neptune.
The Jade Cabinet.
The One Marvelous Thing.
Phosphor in Dreamland.
The Stain.
The Word "Desire."
WILLIAM EASTLAKE, *The Bamboo Bed.*
Castle Keep.
Lyric of the Circle Heart.
JEAN ECHENOZ, *Chopin's Move.*
STANLEY ELKIN, *A Bad Man.*
Boswell: A Modern Comedy.
Criers and Kibitzers, Kibitzers and Criers.
The Dick Gibson Show.
The Franchiser.
George Mills.
The Living End.
The MacGuffin.
The Magic Kingdom.
Mrs. Ted Bliss.
The Rabbi of Lud.
Van Gogh's Room at Arles.
ANNIE ERNAUX, *Cleaned Out.*
LAUREN FAIRBANKS, *Muzzle Thyself.*
Sister Carrie.
LESLIE A. FIEDLER, *Love and Death in the American Novel.*
JUAN FILLOY, *Op Oloop.*
GUSTAVE FLAUBERT, *Bouvard and Pécuchet.*
KASS FLEISHER, *Talking out of School.*
FORD MADOX FORD, *The March of Literature.*
JON FOSSE, *Melancholy.*
MAX FRISCH, *I'm Not Stiller.*
Man in the Holocene.
CARLOS FUENTES, *Christopher Unborn.*
Distant Relations.
Terra Nostra.
Where the Air Is Clear.

JANICE GALLOWAY, *Foreign Parts.*
   The Trick Is to Keep Breathing.
WILLIAM H. GASS, *Cartesian Sonata*
   and Other Novellas.
   Finding a Form.
   A Temple of Texts.
   The Tunnel.
   Willie Masters' Lonesome Wife.
GÉRARD GAVARRY, *Hoppla! 1 2 3.*
ETIENNE GILSON,
   The Arts of the Beautiful.
   Forms and Substances in the Arts.
C. S. GISCOMBE, *Giscome Road.*
   Here.
   Prairie Style.
DOUGLAS GLOVER, *Bad News of the Heart.*
   The Enamoured Knight.
WITOLD GOMBROWICZ,
   A Kind of Testament.
KAREN ELIZABETH GORDON, *The Red Shoes.*
GEORGI GOSPODINOV, *Natural Novel.*
JUAN GOYTISOLO, *Count Julian.*
   Juan the Landless.
   Makbara.
   Marks of Identity.
PATRICK GRAINVILLE, *The Cave of Heaven.*
HENRY GREEN, *Back.*
   Blindness.
   Concluding.
   Doting.
   Nothing.
JIŘÍ GRUŠA, *The Questionnaire.*
GABRIEL GUDDING,
   Rhode Island Notebook.
MELA HARTWIG, *Am I a Redundant*
   Human Being?
JOHN HAWKES, *The Passion Artist.*
   Whistlejacket.
ALEKSANDAR HEMON, ED.,
   Best European Fiction 2010.
AIDAN HIGGINS, *A Bestiary.*
   Balcony of Europe.
   Bornholm Night-Ferry.
   Darkling Plain: Texts for the Air.
   Flotsam and Jetsam.
   Langrishe, Go Down.
   Scenes from a Receding Past.
   Windy Arbours.
ALDOUS HUXLEY, *Antic Hay.*
   Crome Yellow.
   Point Counter Point.
   Those Barren Leaves.
   Time Must Have a Stop.
MIKHAIL IOSSEL AND JEFF PARKER, EDS.,
   Amerika: Russian Writers View the
   United States.
GERT JONKE, *The Distant Sound.*
   Geometric Regional Novel.
   Homage to Czerny.
   The System of Vienna.
JACQUES JOUET, *Mountain R.*
   Savage.
CHARLES JULIET, *Conversations with*
   Samuel Beckett and Bram van
   Velde.
MIEKO KANAI, *The Word Book.*

HUGH KENNER, *The Counterfeiters.*
   Flaubert, Joyce and Beckett:
   The Stoic Comedians.
   Joyce's Voices.
DANILO KIŠ, *Garden, Ashes.*
   A Tomb for Boris Davidovich.
ANITA KONKKA, *A Fool's Paradise.*
GEORGE KONRÁD, *The City Builder.*
TADEUSZ KONWICKI, *A Minor Apocalypse.*
   The Polish Complex.
MENIS KOUMANDAREAS, *Koula.*
ELAINE KRAF, *The Princess of 72nd Street.*
JIM KRUSOE, *Iceland.*
EWA KURYLUK, *Century 21.*
ERIC LAURRENT, *Do Not Touch.*
VIOLETTE LEDUC, *La Bâtarde.*
SUZANNE JILL LEVINE, *The Subversive*
   Scribe: Translating Latin
   American Fiction.
DEBORAH LEVY, *Billy and Girl.*
   Pillow Talk in Europe and Other
   Places.
JOSÉ LEZAMA LIMA, *Paradiso.*
ROSA LIKSOM, *Dark Paradise.*
OSMAN LINS, *Avalovara.*
   The Queen of the Prisons of Greece.
ALF MAC LOCHLAINN,
   The Corpus in the Library.
   Out of Focus.
RON LOEWINSOHN, *Magnetic Field(s).*
BRIAN LYNCH, *The Winner of Sorrow.*
D. KEITH MANO, *Take Five.*
MICHELINE AHARONIAN MARCOM,
   The Mirror in the Well.
BEN MARCUS,
   The Age of Wire and String.
WALLACE MARKFIELD,
   Teitlebaum's Window.
   To an Early Grave.
DAVID MARKSON, *Reader's Block.*
   Springer's Progress.
   Wittgenstein's Mistress.
CAROLE MASO, *AVA.*
LADISLAV MATEJKA AND KRYSTYNA
   POMORSKA, EDS.,
   Readings in Russian Poetics:
   Formalist and Structuralist Views.
HARRY MATHEWS,
   The Case of the Persevering Maltese:
   Collected Essays.
   Cigarettes.
   The Conversions.
   The Human Country: New and
   Collected Stories.
   The Journalist.
   My Life in CIA.
   Singular Pleasures.
   The Sinking of the Odradek
   Stadium.
   Tlooth.
   20 Lines a Day.
ROBERT L. MCLAUGHLIN, ED.,
   Innovations: An Anthology of
   Modern & Contemporary Fiction.
HERMAN MELVILLE, *The Confidence-Man.*
AMANDA MICHALOPOULOU, *I'd Like.*

STEVEN MILLHAUSER,
  The Barnum Museum.
  In the Penny Arcade.
RALPH J. MILLS, JR.,
  Essays on Poetry.
MOMUS, *The Book of Jokes.*
CHRISTINE MONTALBETTI, *Western.*
OLIVE MOORE, *Spleen.*
NICHOLAS MOSLEY, *Accident.*
  Assassins.
  Catastrophe Practice.
  Children of Darkness and Light.
  Experience and Religion.
  God's Hazard.
  The Hesperides Tree.
  Hopeful Monsters.
  Imago Bird.
  Impossible Object.
  Inventing God.
  Judith.
  Look at the Dark.
  Natalie Natalia.
  Paradoxes of Peace.
  Serpent.
  Time at War.
  The Uses of Slime Mould:
    Essays of Four Decades.
WARREN MOTTE,
  Fables of the Novel: French Fiction
    since 1990.
  Fiction Now: The French Novel in
    the 21st Century.
  Oulipo: A Primer of Potential
    Literature.
YVES NAVARRE, *Our Share of Time.*
  Sweet Tooth.
DOROTHY NELSON, *In Night's City.*
  Tar and Feathers.
ESHKOL NEVO, *Homesick.*
WILFRIDO D. NOLLEDO,
  But for the Lovers.
FLANN O'BRIEN,
  At Swim-Two-Birds.
  At War.
  The Best of Myles.
  The Dalkey Archive.
  Further Cuttings.
  The Hard Life.
  The Poor Mouth.
  The Third Policeman.
CLAUDE OLLIER, *The Mise-en-Scène.*
PATRIK OUŘEDNÍK, *Europeana.*
FERNANDO DEL PASO,
  News from the Empire.
  Palinuro of Mexico.
ROBERT PINGET, *The Inquisitory.*
  Mahu or The Material.
  Trio.
MANUEL PUIG,
  Betrayed by Rita Hayworth.
  The Buenos Aires Affair.
  Heartbreak Tango.
RAYMOND QUENEAU, *The Last Days.*
  Odile.
  Pierrot Mon Ami.
  Saint Glinglin.

ANN QUIN, *Berg.*
  Passages.
  Three.
  Tripticks.
ISHMAEL REED,
  The Free-Lance Pallbearers.
  The Last Days of Louisiana Red.
  Ishmael Reed: The Plays.
  Reckless Eyeballing.
  The Terrible Threes.
  The Terrible Twos.
  Yellow Back Radio Broke-Down.
JEAN RICARDOU, *Place Names.*
RAINER MARIA RILKE,
  The Notebooks of Malte Laurids
    Brigge.
JULIÁN RÍOS, *Larva: A Midsummer*
    Night's Babel.
  Poundemonium.
AUGUSTO ROA BASTOS, *I the Supreme.*
OLIVIER ROLIN, *Hotel Crystal.*
ALIX CLEO ROUBAUD, *Alix's Journal.*
JACQUES ROUBAUD, *The Form of a*
    City Changes Faster, Alas, Than
    the Human Heart.
  The Great Fire of London.
  Hortense in Exile.
  Hortense Is Abducted.
  The Loop.
  The Plurality of Worlds of Lewis.
  The Princess Hoppy.
  Some Thing Black.
LEON S. ROUDIEZ,
  French Fiction Revisited.
VEDRANA RUDAN, *Night.*
STIG SÆTERBAKKEN, *Siamese.*
LYDIE SALVAYRE, *The Company of Ghosts.*
  Everyday Life.
  The Lecture.
  Portrait of the Writer as a
    Domesticated Animal.
  The Power of Flies.
LUIS RAFAEL SÁNCHEZ,
  Macho Camacho's Beat.
SEVERO SARDUY, *Cobra* & *Maitreya.*
NATHALIE SARRAUTE,
  Do You Hear Them?
  Martereau.
  The Planetarium.
ARNO SCHMIDT, *Collected Stories.*
  Nobodaddy's Children.
CHRISTINE SCHUTT, *Nightwork.*
GAIL SCOTT, *My Paris.*
DAMION SEARLS, *What We Were Doing*
    and Where We Were Going.
JUNE AKERS SEESE,
  Is This What Other Women Feel Too?
  What Waiting Really Means.
BERNARD SHARE, *Inish.*
  Transit.
AURELIE SHEEHAN,
  Jack Kerouac Is Pregnant.
VIKTOR SHKLOVSKY, *Knight's Move.*
  A Sentimental Journey:
    Memoirs 1917–1922.
  Energy of Delusion: A Book on Plot.